The Cardinal's Sword

Simon Fairfax

Other books by Simon Fairfax

The Deal Series

A Deadly Deal

A Deal too far

A Deal with the Devil

A Deal on Ice

A Knight and a Spy: Road to Agincourt Series

A Knight and a Spy 1410

A Knight and a Spy 1411

A Knight and a Spy 1412

A Knight and a Spy 1413

A Knight and a Spy 1414

A Knight and a Spy 1415

The Plainsman Series

Law of the Gun

Making of a Lawman

Comanche Moon

Troubled Border

Published by Corinium Associates Ltd.

A CIP catalogue of this book is available from the British Library

ISBN: 978-1-7391470-9-9

simonfairfaxauthor@gmail.com

www.simonfairfax.com

Map of Corneto

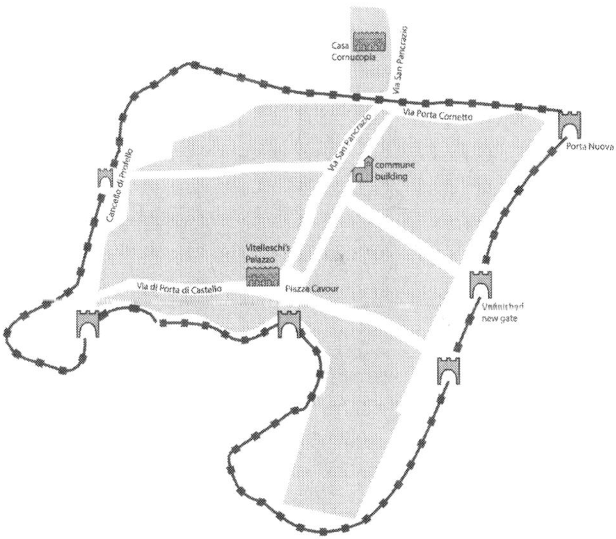

Map of Viterbo

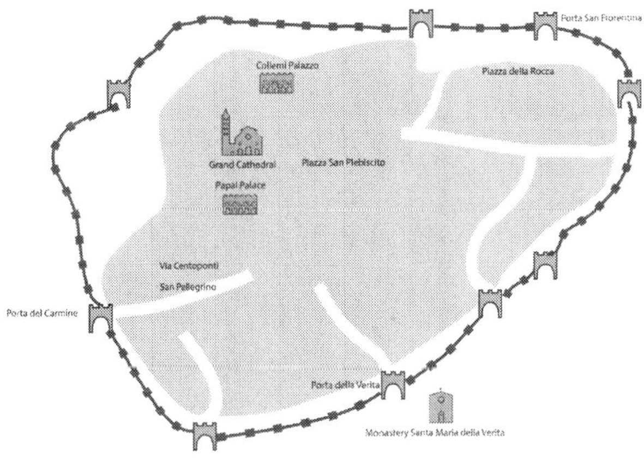

Part One

Authors Note: Street Names. The street names used in Corneto (modern town of Tarquinia), include some modern names such as Piazza Cavour & Strada Emanuele. I understand that these would have different names back in the 14thC, however despite, speaking with historical societies, historic guides, and searching the records of the Commune, I sadly could find no reference to the old names. So please forgive this error, pointed out by an eagle eyed reviewer, yet I have no choice but to use the modern references and hope that it does not detract from your enjoyment as a reader.

Simon.

Corneto, Lazio

Chapter One

The Marta River, Lazio

The dark skiff flowed well with the current leading her down to the sea less than two leagues distant, its single sail barely filled with wind, pulled more by draw of the sea. High up on the cliffs to the south, set upon a natural escarpment, the tall walls of Corneto could be seen, bright in their natural limestone tufa, striking even in the poor, virtually moonless light. Vague shadows played gently across the valley bottom edged and girded by mature fig trees, the riparian shore hidden by sweeping swathes of bamboo that grew like brown topped spears standing in abundance like sentinels along the water line.

The gentle breeze brought with it the sweet but slightly acrid scent of fennel that perfumed the air, mixing with the powerful aroma of the jasmine hedges that were just now coming to full bloom in the balmy *prima verde* air.

Flowing gently upwards from the river, acres and acres of

still unripe wheat waved in an ebb and flow of dark green and silver, rustling this way and that, whispering a language of its own in the night.

The boat bore no lights and a single figure, dark in shadow, stood at the prow, his face covered with a cowl, as were those of his shipmates, each knowing that a glimpse of skin, pale against the sky, would give away their position. The man gave silent hand signals to the crew behind. He was the pilot of the vessel and the leader of the men on board. The man at the rudder followed his every move, his senses alert to any grinding of the keel as the craft hugged the bank as closely as it dared without going aground. They were now halfway past the lines of the town above them, a home to many of them, where they would rest once their cargo was delivered to the harbour in the estuary downriver.

The first warning they had that all was not well was the sound of crossbow bolts thrumming through the air, hitting the bulwarks of the large skiff with resounding thuds, sinking deeply into the wood. Small rowing boats pushed out from the banks on the northern side of the river where the skiff was much closer, even as more bolts flew from the southern side to cries for the crew to surrender. A thick cable sprang up, reeled in from the south bank, made taut by a pulley and tackle hauled by a thick bodied cob horse out of sight in the undergrowth. As the skiff fouled the hemp line the craft rotated slightly, pivoting on its trapped prow.

Seeing his vessel now aligned across the stream, the pilot knew that the bolts were the danger. They were indiscriminate and would easily bring down any of his men at the close range of less than forty yards. "We surrender, no more bolts," he shouted in response to the demands from the southern bank.

The twang of cords ceased as he quietly muttered to his men: "Be ready as they close, and take them as they board!" He hissed. Each of his eight crewmen was armed with the long knives of sailors or horn baselards, and each had a buckler secreted inside the planked sides of the skiff. They were all well tutored in its use with a blade.

The attackers were closing, clad in gambesons covering surcoats bearing the arms of Corneto, the eponymous flowering cherry tree front and centre. They were helmeted with open faced Italian barbutes, leaving the eyes and nose free. Each man carried either a spear or crossbow, their captains shouting for the skiff's crew to lay down any arms and surrender, the penalty for disobedience being death.

The pilot looked behind him, seemingly nervous, judging time and distance as the boats from the southern bank made their laborious way across stream, fighting the current so as not to be swept away. Men grabbed the cable to secure a straighter passage to the larger vessel. They would be a few minutes behind the boarders from the northern bank.

Slowly they came on, grunting with the effort of each oar stroke, fighting the current to stay straight on their course for the skiff. They raised spears in readiness as they neared the side, and one of them threw a grappling hook the short distance between the vessels, its sharp tines biting into the hard wood of the skiff, hands pulling the two boats to lock together as the two rowing boats caught up. The men balanced themselves, unused to the rise and fall of the water, forced to swing first one leg then the other over the higher side of the skiff, hampered by mail and armour, covered warily by their spear wielding companions in arms.

"Help them, *amici*," came the order from the pilot.

Hands were raised to pull the soldiers aboard, despite the enmity between the two parties. But each side expected treachery from the other, and as the first soldiers to set foot aboard turned to aid their companions, the pilot shouted: "*Adesso!*"

The action was sudden and spectacular. The sailors heaved and pushed, throwing soldiers into the water or back onto the decks of their rowing boats in chaos, binging their bucklers up from the bulwarks, weapons glinting in the shadowy night. To the fore, the pilot reached down for a broad axe that was ever to hand and swung it down hard upon the trapped hempen cable. The rope was creaking already under the strain of holding the weight of the laden skiff against the pull of the current, and on the third slash of the axe it parted with a crack like a mighty canon in the night. With the sudden release of tension, the ends snapped upwards in a dangerous whiplash, narrowly missing the pilot who ducked down low, saved only by the protection of the raised prow. Behind him he heard the sound of steel on steel as his crew clashed with the soldiers who were still trying to gain the upper hand and board. Spears were raised on the unsteady platform of the rowing boats, jabbing as they tried to find targets in the skiff's men. Despite the advantage of length, it was an uneven contest and soon dark stains pooled in the fast-flowing river and the familiar metallic coppery smell of fresh blood filled the air as the soldiers were pushed or toppled overboard into the waters of the Marta.

The pilot turned as sounds of chaos filled the night. The two rowing boats that had set off from the southern bank were now adrift, pushed off course by the severing of the cable, and were now ahead of the skiff, drifting and floundering as the current took them in its embrace. The boats' crews took to the oars, seeking the security of the bank instead of conflict, any thoughts of retaliation forgotten until a stable fighting platform could be gained from which to launch a further assault with their crossbows. The skiff, now released from the cable, flowed quickly away downstream out of range of the bolts, leaving the rowing boats in its wake to jeers of the crew who mocked their assailants.

"We gave them short shrift, my lord."

"*Si,* that we did," the pilot replied. "Now let us hasten to the sea, unload and away, for the tide will pull us northwards and up in the rips. The carts will be waiting, and the cargo needs must be moved swiftly. The civic guard will be upon us once more ere we know it.

The skiff sped onwards, and as the approaching bridge came dimly into view in the lee of the rocks below Corneto's mighty walls, the pilot gave the order: "Make ready to drop the mast upon my command, the bridge is upon us."

The crew scrambled in readiness at the second command, bringing down the mast, hinged as it was with two massive locking pins securing it that once withdrawn allowed the entire structure to arc backwards upon the steel hinge, and they passed cleanly under the last bridge before the sea and the estuary of the river. Gliding under the wooden structure, the mast was raised once more to take what small benefit it could from the southeasterly breeze.

The final twists and turns of the river gave way to a wider estuary and the open sea beyond, the sand black in the night, merging closely with the rippling water and the small waves that broke upon the pebbled shoreline.

"Strike north now, not down to the *saline* and the harbour," the pilot called. "For that is where they will expect us."

The skiff, now given her head with a full breeze to fill the sail, followed the rips of the dangerous current upon the Tyrrhenian sea and pulled northwards to a shallow sand bank. There, hidden amongst the dunes, was a barely noticeable wooden jetty standing just above the water line. The waves smacked gently against its pillars with each roll of the water.

Figures emerged from the gloom, barely discernible, clad in featureless, black clothes like wraiths in the night come to steal souls not goods, and as the skiff was pulled up and secured against the wooden rails they began taking the cargo ashore, padding softly over the black sand of the beach to waiting carts.

One man, cloaked and cowled, seemingly older than the rest called softly to the pilot. "What do you have, Flavio?"

"Spices from the east, incense and in especial sacks of saffron, well secured against the damp."

The older man chuckled and rubbed his hands together. Saffron, as he knew, was more valuable than gold and would fetch huge, inflated prices at the markets in Rome to the south. Though the merchants of Corneto ever decried the smugglers who procured such goods, the wealthy hypocrites would be keen enough to avail themselves of the delicacy on the black market.

Once loaded, the carts were pulled away by mules that laboured hard in the sand before reaching the white stone track that led inland, passing under the road through a little known tunnel that came up into the gardens of a palazzo, emerging into dense trees in a far corner next to a narrow pathway that led to the cellars beneath.

The pilot, Flavio, followed on horseback, disappearing into the stables where he left a groom to take the horse, entering the elegant building through a door that led to a small rear staircase. He moved freely once inside, pouring himself a glass of wine and admiring the Sangiovese that he held upon his palate before swallowing, twirling the dark ruby liquid in the Venetian goblet, watching the depth of colour in the lamplight of his bedchamber. He pushed open the double doors to step out onto the terrace two floors up from the scented garden below. The doors were glazed to let the sunlight stream into the room, but opening them let in a fresh spring breeze on which the smell of jasmine and stocks competed with each other.

He looked up at the imposing walls just across the river where they had been waylaid what seemed like only minutes ago, debating in his mind as to what the consequences of those actions might be. There was a knock at the door to his rooms: "Enter." he responded.

A servant stood at open doorway. "Signor, there are men at the gates to the estate, demanding in the name of the commune to be permitted to enter."

"Double the guard, Beppo, and forbid them entry. Tell

them to return at dawn if they wish to gain an audience with me."

As you wish, Signor Sabatini," the servant replied, closing the door behind him.

Flavio Sabatini returned to the terrace. His men would know what measures to take, which would include releasing oil from the machicolations above the gatehouse. It would not be boiling, but it would be hot enough to dissuade the guards from their purpose if they continued banging at his gates. He cared not, for nothing could be proved of his involvement in the smuggling.

Flavio sipped his wine and stepped back into his bedchamber, pausing in front of the looking glass to see if any signs remained of his earlier adventure.

He saw reflected there a figure of medium height, a bush of wavy hair rising up from his scalp, shorter at the sides and cut long almost to the shoulders at the back. The dark hair framed a long face that bore a slanting scar running from cheek to chin, raised white against the darkly tanned skin before disappearing into his neatly trimmed beard. It was the eyes that people noticed after the scar. They gave him a faintly piratical air and offered a window to his soul, or what any could perceive of it. They were dark, and glittered in the subdued light. Those eyes had seen much and held within them a deep darkness that none could fathom, speaking danger to any who may cross him.

It was not a pretty or a handsome face, but it carried the confidence of one who knew his worth with the ladies, who found him frightening and fascinating in equal measure. His shoulders sloped in the lopsided manner of one trained in arms, broad muscles tapering to a tight waist and the thick legs of a horseman. He would do, he decided, running his free hand through his thick hair. He turned away, banishing all thoughts from his mind, knowing the demons would come unbidden, invading his dreams as they did every night to revisit upon him the horrors of his past.

Chapter Two

The following morning, Flavio Sabatini dressed in a fine brocade doublet of embroidered silk, cut short in the latest fashion above woollen hose of contrasting colours. He slipped his feet into supple, tanned leather riding boots that now bore spurs. Around his waist was a bejewelled belt of ornate links clasped with a sapphire buckle holding a rondel dagger in a sheath at his right hip. He knew that this morning would bring a summons from the master of arms to attend upon *il Podesta* in the central *comune*, where he would be interrogated upon last night's activities – probably by the mayor himself.

In the early morning, as the bells of Corneto's many churches rang the hour of Prime, hammering was once again heard upon the outer gates. Flavio's face was impassive as he considered what he had been told. It was as he expected, they could prove nothing: the skiff's name had been covered and it bore no recognisable markings. His crew had been cowled and the boat would by now be safely harboured down the headland at Graviscae harbour, empty and innocent of any wrongdoing. Yet it begged the question in his mind: how had they known? For they had laid in wait for him, setting a perfect ambush. Was there a spy at the port in Lake Bolsena, or was it one of his own men? The second alternative worried and angered him. With so much at stake, someone would pay, his whole livelihood and everything he had fought for was invested in this venture.

Flavio ordered his groom to saddle his horse and smiled as it appeared. Carbone was a handsome Maremma stallion with a black coat of rippling silk that rolled and creased with each flowing movement of its lithe body. The mane, as was the custom, was not pulled, and flowed in long rivulets of crinkled jet, falling well below the crest to reach the top of the shoulder line. The horse's eyes were dark and well set in its huge handsome head.

He went to the stallion's side, checked the girth and took the reins. Accepting a friendly nuzzle, he stroked the soft nose, then with kind words lifted a booted foot and swung into the saddle, landing gently as he knew the stallion would sidle and skitter. He beckoned his groom to follow him: "Come, Pietro, let us attend upon *il sindaco* and see what he has to lay before us."

The tone was light, but all within hearing knew what force that voice could bring to bear. The two men rode out through the gates, crossed the river using the same bridge the skiff had passed under the night before with its mast lowered, and took the winding road up to the northern gates of *Porta di Castello.* Although the road was carved in a series of switchbacks to alleviate the steepness of the climb, the horses were still blowing at the fast trot up to the gates. The walls before them swept upwards some thirty feet and though the mighty gates were open, the spikes of the portcullis peeked menacingly down in their running guides, greased and slick. The groom shuddered, "it always makes my skin crawl when we pass under the *saracinesca,"* he muttered, giving the portcullis its true Italian name. He looked further up at the imposing church of Santa Maria di Castello on his right, crossing himself as they rode by.

"*Ma di,* Pietro," Flavio chided. "It is only there to skewer Saracens or Frenchmen, not good Cornetani like you and me," He assured his servant with a grin.

They passed through the archway into a narrow cobbled street, high walls either side confining any who entered the castle walls before riding under another arch with its own *saracinesca.* The guards above on the ramparts looking down at them as they passed into a dogleg or *rivelino* that was narrower still, each end guarded by turrets and fitted with murder holes. It was a formidable defensive system, Flavio thought, and not for the first he considered it as good as any he had seen in his travels, which had been varied and wide. It was now his turn to shudder, thinking back to the day he had nearly died in such a trap on the outskirts of Siena. The memory caused him to reach up to the scar on his cheek.

As they passed through the second arch they saw the twelfth century castle perched high overlooking the flat plain to the sea a league or so distant, shimmering in the sun. The stone of the walls and turrets were faded to a mild yellowish grey by two hundred years of harsh sunlight, and the main doors stood open to a small courtyard within. The castle was unusual in that it did not house the administrative centre of the town, nor even the largest part of the garrison. Yet the constable still governed and maintained all the town's bastions and administered everything to do with its defence from it.

Passing into the town itself, they rode south along Via di Porta Castello towards the Piazza Cavour, up the shiny cobbles of Via Corsa Vittorio Emanuele to the main piazza and the *comune* building. As they went, the townsmen and women they passed nodded or offered brief greetings. They all knew Flavio Sabatini, and many contracted illicit trade with him. Equally, they all knew that if he was abroad and heading for the *comune* higher up the steeply sloping street, trouble was in store, and they had all heard about the fight on the water the previous evening. Despite its population of some thirty thousand souls, Corneto was more of a small village than that a bustling market town in its mentality, full of prosperous merchants and business owners only forty six leagues north of Rome.

Shops were already open, and the smell of fresh bread pervaded the street, with hoardings open and owners shouting for custom. The spice shops showed the rich reds, greens and yellows of ground spices in tall glass jars, with fennel bulbs layering the air with a deeper and more acrid scent. It had become all so familiar to Flavio, and he remembered the desire for peace that had caused him to return and settle here. Two butchers' shops came into view to the left down a side street, flies already buzzing at the fresh meat as swathes of moving sheets swished back and forth in an effort to dissuade them.

Reaching the top of the steep street, they dismounted and tied their horses to the rail in front of the grand building. The front column of rusticated stone faced an arch to the street from which a large flight of wide steps led upwards to a covered loggia at the top guarded by two soldiers, halberds at half port. They immediately recognised Flavio and allowed him to pass, leaving Pietro with the horses.

Ascending the long flight of stone steps he arrived at the covered stone loggia, where another guard stood ready who again nodded him through with a brief exchange of words, as the two men knew each other. This confirmed that he was expected, and as Flavio passed the guard he caught the whispered, "You are not to leave this day. A warning."

He barely heard it, but it was enough to send the hairs upon Flavio's neck rising, and he wondered if he should turn and run now. No, it would be better to face whatever lay in store for him. He could always escape. He had done so before – from worse gaols than he would face here – and he had friends upon the outside, unless he had been betrayed once more.

A servant of the *comune* came forward, nodding in recognition, and asked Flavio to follow him. Flavio removed his fur felt hat, smoothed the sides of his tunic and strode forward with confidence, marvelling at the beautiful frescoes upon the walls and ceiling that would have done credit to a high church in Rome or Florence, let alone a provincial town hall. The blues, reds and yellows vivid upon the walls depicted scenes from Rome and the celebration of battles, with papal emissaries marching forth. The vestibule smelled of new plaster and paint, reassuring in its way, as new to the building as the recently elected mayor of Corneto, Signor Manrico Bastari.

The servant knocked and opened the polished wooden door to the office within. Seated at a large rosewood desk was a man of about forty years, his jowls sagging prematurely, a beard streaked with grey running along his jaw. Full lips pushed forward beneath a wide nose, and the man's hair receded in a widow's peak above cruel and deep set eyes. His pudgy hands were flat upon the desk as though he had just slapped them down to emphasise a demand or make a point.

"*Salve, il Sindaco.*" Flavio gave the time honoured Roman greeting, neither formal nor informal and certainly not showing any particular respect to the mayor's rank.

"*Buongiorno,* Signor Sabatini. The hour I assume suits you, or do your nocturnal activities preclude such an early rise?" The cruel eyes crinkled in what passed for merriment.

Flavio did not rise to the bait, but shrugged blandly, feigning ignorance. "I know not what you mean, I am always happy to attend upon your excellency," he flattered.

"Not so yesterday evening, when my men called upon your gates demanding your presence and that you accompany them. The captain of my guard was threatened with boiling oil, so he tells me. Where then was your unswerving devotion to my needs?"

"Ah my lord, I feel that there must have been some misunderstanding. My servants failed to wake me from a deep slumber, tired as I was after my day's ride from the north."

"Signor Sabatini, you toy with me. I know full well that you were not riding from anywhere. You were smuggling goods down the River Marta, as ever you do. Half the town is in your thrall, willing to pay for your contraband. You, sir, are a *vagabondo* and shall pay the price, and there will be no more smuggling goods abroad."

"I beg to differ my lord, for I am innocent of such charges and would bring witnesses to prove that I was at home asleep." Fabio spread his hands wide in a manner of one who has been much maligned.

"Bah, I care not for your protestations of innocence. You shall await the federal *podesta* where you will be tried for charges of smuggling and murder. Two of my men died last night upon the river and you were responsible, and so it will be found. Bind him and take him away, secure him in gaol with no visitors." Bastari gestured to two guards standing either side of his desk.

The shock of the words caused Fabio to pause as the guards moved forward. Behind him the door flew open, and two more soldiers entered on the command of a guard captain. His hand went to the hilt of his sword, but steel flashed, glinting in the light through the open shutters as the points of two halberds flew down to breast height and he felt the prick of a sword point in the small of his back. No man could face such odds sword undrawn and live. The mayor smiled, almost seeming to will Flavio to resist and draw his sword.

"Ah, so even the great Flavio Sabatini cannot face my men. So be it. Take him away," he ordered with a wave of a hand.

The captain behind gave a sharp command and Flavio's hands were drawn fast and hard behind his back where they were bound with rope, the bonds cutting into his wrists. He spat at the mayor in frustration. It was a futile act that increased his punishment still further.

"Manacle him once inside and give him only water for two days!" Bastari bellowed, wiping the spittle from his face. He did not come around the large desk as Sabatini had hoped, where he could have kicked him and vented his spleen. A large, gloved hand punched him hard in the jaw and the hilt of a sword was rammed into his kidneys. He doubled over, retching at the pain and gasping for air like a beached fish. Finally, reason overcame his hot Latin temper, and he straightened, forcing himself upright to look the mayor in the face. No words came but his eyes, dark and evil in their intent, spoke volumes as the mayor blanched.

The guards unclasped his sword belt and he was dragged from the office, his heels scuffing on the marble tiles of the floor. With two more blows from the hafts of the halberds he was manhandled to the rear stairs at the back of the *comune* building. It was here that a narrow lesser staircase led down to the cells beneath. Twice on the way down Flavio fell and was only saved from serious injury by a last minute grab at his tunic as he was wrenched upright before falling headlong down the stone steps with his hands tied behind him. At the lower levels the air became much cooler and turned damp as the gaol had been excavated into the depths of the limestone beneath the town. The only ventilation was a tiny, barred slit about six inches wide by eighteen inches long at the bottom of a shaft that led to the street level above. It also provided the only form of light to illuminate the dingy stone cell, which stank of excrement, urine and the stale smell of fetid human existence as though all the woes of humanity had been gathered here in one sorrowful place.

Water trickled in rivulets down the walls, leaving a green slime to grow in its wake. Flavio shuddered. If he was kept here for long he would die of gaol fever, as he knew many did. Pushed against the far side of the cell, he was made to sit on the hard wooden bed as a shackle chained to the wall was secured and locked upon his wrist.

The guards laughed. "Escape from that, Signor Sabatini!" the captain sneered. "No more river trips for you or fine ways in your palazzo. We hear that the *podesta* is expected to be engaged for a long while and your case may not be heard for many months."

The heavy wooden door slammed shut, condemning Flavio to his fate. The peek hole slid across, leaving him in semi darkness to contemplate his future. An extended period would kill him or damage his spirit and his physical well-being beyond repair as he rotted away in this dingy cell with little food and scant protection from the damp and cold. He raised his manacled wrist in despair, watching the metal encircling his arm glint dully in the poor light. He thought back to the terrible times as a *condottieri*, knowing that the nightmares would be worse here, parading in front of his closed eyes as the ghosts from his past reached out to him in anger or pleaded for pity.

Chapter Three

Flavio languished in his cell for two weeks, becoming more desperate and weakened in both mind and body as each day passed. He was given rancid water and stale bread with a layer of mould growing on it, the gaolers laughing and taunting him when they pushed the meals, such as they were, through the hatch under his door. Then it seemed that fate took a hand; the head gaoler fell mysteriously ill with some unknown malady and could not be roused from his bed. A new man was brought from Viterbo, the state capital some twenty-two leagues to the north east.

The new man was portly, with the happy round face of one who overindulged constantly and cared not one iota. He was dressed more expensively than one would imagine for a man in his position, yet despite the clothes he had a scruffy appearance that no amount of grooming would cure. The sergeant at arms in charge of the gaol gave him a guided tour, coming lastly to Flavio's cell in the lower level.

"This one," the guard said, sneering, "he will stay here a

long time, so you will get to know him well. He is to be specially treated upon *il podesta's* orders. He killed two guards while smuggling and will come before the *podesta* later this year," the guard shrugged, "if he does not die first. No visitors and nothing but bread and water. One of my friends died that night trying to apprehend him and his pirates."

"*Va bene*, I shall make him my personal charge," the new man assured him.

They left to a clang of the peek hole being shut, and after the brief point of human contact Flavio's spirts dropped once more. He coughed for the first time as the damp seeped into his bones. He knew the signs, for many of his comrades in arms had died of gaol fever. As the footsteps echoed away, he fell back once more and reclined, using one arm awkwardly as a pillow. His other wrist was still manacled to the wall, and the steel had gouged wounds in his wrist that bled occasionally and woke him when he moved the manacle as he slept. He wondered for the thousandth time who could have betrayed him and what they stood to gain.

He was surprised when he heard soft footsteps some indefinable time later moving quietly along the stone subterranean corridor to stop outside his cell. He wondered what fresh tortures were about to be visited upon him. The peek hole slid open and an unknown face appeared, the glow of a lighted brand beside it throwing it into shadow. The hole was closed, then Flavio heard the bolts being drawn back from the door. It was the first time since his incarceration that the door had been opened, and he blinked at the light thrown from the lighted brand. The new chief gaoler appeared, raising a cowl to his face and nearly retching at the stench inside the dingy cell. "*Porca miseria*!" he swore, "you are being harshly dealt with, yet I can aid you, for I come on a mission from your friends."

He put the brand into a hole hollowed out of the soft limestone rock for that purpose. Shadows flickered ghoulishly upon the walls as unnamed creatures scurried away squeaking, looking for shelter from the light.

For the first time hope began to grow within Flavio as the gaoler returned from outside the cell, bringing a pail of water, coarse soap and a towel, and a wicker basket. "Wash," he ordered. "for you stink. You are a man, not an animal."

He unshackled Flavio's wrist, and Flavio moved his arm at the elbow and shoulder, gaining relief from the slow movements, almost unsure what to do with the arm now that it had been released. He rubbed the raw sores upon his wrist, wincing as the open flesh stung. Tentatively he eased his arms into the clean water, relishing the small pleasure it gave him and splashing his face, lathering the soap that was olive oil based and fragrant with lemon and sandalwood. He breathed deeply, inhaling the scents of freedom, sighing softly even though the soap made his wrist sting.

"I have a salve once you're clean, and I will leave the manacle off. It will help you to heal and give you freedom to move. If any approach bar me you must relock the clasp or we will be found out. I can do nothing for your clothes, and you will have to suffer the indignity for now. Yet here is a blanket and some food." Flavio took the two bundles, one smelling of freshly laundered wool and the other of fresh bread and cooked meat. He felt himself salivating like a rabid dog. "Hide them well under the wooden bed when you hear any approach or all will be lost," the gaoler finished.

Flavio had almost lost the use of his voice, and after sipping the fresh watered down wine, he rasped, "Who are you? And how do you come to be here as my guardian angel?"

"Slowly with that!" the gaoler admonished, still whispering to him before answering his questions. "You will be ill with bad humours and your stomach will revolt. Now eat your food slowly, and I will answer your questions.

"The corridor here and the rock amplifies everything, and voices carry, so we must whisper and not be heard." Flavio nodded, ripping off a hunk of fresh bread and putting a piece into his mouth, chewing slowly and heeding the warning.

"You have many friends in the town, none of whom like the new *sindaco* or those who back his power to rule. When the chief of guards took ill I was brought in from Viterbo as one who seemed to have no involvement or friendship with you or others, yet I am a friend to those who would aid you, and so here I am," he shrugged. "Gianpaolo Agneli at your service.

"Now, there are plots being hatched in which even you are but a pawn, but we have no time to give discourse to such matters now. Know that I am your friend and will aid you however I may. Now take the blanket, pillow and food, for I cannot linger for fear of raising the suspicions of others. From now on you will receive one good meal a day and will not immediately starve.

Flavio, desperate for answers and company, asked: "What is to be done?"

"Fear not. We make plans as your friends and allies. Now I needs must depart."

With that, Gianpaolo retrieved the now empty basket and filled the wooden beaker with watered wine before putting a finger to his lips, closing the door and leaving Flavio once more in near darkness.

A small glimmer of hope entered his mind. His friends had not forgotten him. He also realised that this was not just the power play of a new mayor, and that greater and more malignant forces were behind his incarceration.

For another week he was held, and each day Gianpaolo Agneli managed to smuggle food in to him and give him light and hope for a few brief minutes. His clothes were soiled and filthy and his beard and hair were matted, but the food and wine made life bearable until the day he could be free and exact his revenge.

A week later there was more noise than usual in the corridor outside his cell and the sound of footsteps upon the stone floor. He heard two voices arguing as they stopped outside the door. Flavio quickly pushed together the manacle bracelet, hearing the lock click shut as it secured his wrist once more just as the bolts were drawn back with a screech of steel on rusty steel.

Two guards entered, one of whom pushed the lighted brand into the hollowed stone placement. The two men coughed at the stench within the cell, and Flavio looked back at them with hollowed, deep sunk eyes, blinking in the unfamiliar light.

"By God's grace you stink, Sabatini. Stand up!" one commanded.

Flavio stood on unsteady legs as his manacle was unlocked and he was ordered to walk out of the cell on shuffling feet, unused to the movement.

"Let us get out of here quickly. Who knows what foul miasma lingers to haunt us here," one of the guards urged. With the brand lighting the way the three men made for the steep stone steps rising one flight to the ground floor at the rear of the building. Here he was halted and his wrists were bound with rope, then he was pushed forward into the enclosed street behind the *comune* building. It was early morning, and the heat of the day had not yet risen to its summer levels of intensity, but the change in air temperature hit Flavio like a warm blanket and he made a vow then and there that he would not go back to that cell, that somehow he would grasp a dagger and sell his life dearly perishing on a guard's blade, at least taking them with him. He mustered himself for a final flight or fight, pleased that the additional food given by Gianpaolo had allowed him to husband some of his former strength, yet his hopes were dashed.

Six more guardsmen were summoned and he was hurried down the back streets running parallel to Corso Vittorio Manuele, ending up in the small Piazza Soderini at the rear of the grand palazzo that faced onto Piazza Cavour. Despite his quiet release into the backstreets of the town, a small crowd of townspeople – including some of his own servants – began to follow them, shouting and calling for his freedom. Despite their extra numbers, the guards became wary, gripping their halberds tighter as four of their number turned to face the crowd, shields and weapons raised. Someone had tipped off the crowd in advance of his movement, Flavio realised, and they were ready. He prepared himself to spring away at the first opportunity.

They reached a small door, its existence unknown to Flavio even in a town he knew like the back of his own hand. It was discreetly enclosed by cornicing and approached at an oblique angle, shrouded in a walled porchway. The leading guard banged heavily upon it, demanding that it be opened in the name of the mayor as they had a prisoner to hand over. Even in the midst of the turmoil, Flavio was puzzled. *Why was he being taken to the cardinal's palazzo?* There was no judiciary court that sat here. Was this yet another twist in the strange events since his incarceration?

The door was opened cautiously, and a few quick words spoken. Flavio saw a brief glimpse of the ecclesiastical purple of the palazzo guards before he was shoved forward, received by grasping hands and arms. The small door was slammed shut and bolted behind him. He heard raised voices and shouts on the other side, but they were to no avail. He was trapped once more – in a gilded cage this time, rather than a filthy gaol cell.

The guards were gentler than those of the mayor, cutting his bonds and allowing him to move freely for all their drawn swords. "By the good Lord, you do stink," one of the guards said. "Follow us, for you cannot meet his eminence in this woeful state."

Again he followed guards, passing through a narrow corridor into a central quadrangle bordered with arched columns and fine marble flooring, open to the sunlight above that glistened in a fine elegance of light, reflecting off the marble so brightly that Flavio had to shut his eyes against the glare. It was the first time he had been within the papal precincts, and he marvelled at the elegance of it all as he saw it displayed before him once his watering eyes had half adjusted.

He was taken to a garderobe, ordered to strip and bath in a wooden tub that had been prepared for such a purpose, lined with linen with steam from the hot vapour rising from it. Flavio needed no second bidding. He stripped off his wretched clothes that were taken away to be burned. His boots were removed to be cleaned by the women of the household, who looked upon his lean naked frame, blushing and amused at his embarrassment. His skin bore the marks of a long serving soldier, criss-crossed with scars, evidence of wounds of honour from past battles.

He slid into the hot tub, and as he did so another woman came behind to wash his hair with little gentleness, scouring his skin with rough, work-hardened fingers. Finally, he was scrubbed, de-loused and dressed in a poor shirt and hose with his boots now burnished. He was bidden to follow the cardinal's men, the swish of their purple silk drawing him onwards through the corridor into the courtyard and up two flights of stairs that offered stunning views across to the sea with each window they passed.

The guards knocked, and a strong voice from within bade them enter. The hallowed chamber of the cardinal was an assault upon Flavio's senses after the deprivations of the gaol cell. The chamber was cool and fragrant with the scents of jasmine and sandalwood pervading the air. Deep pile rugs adorned the wooden floor and richly coloured arrases hung upon the walls of the opulent room. A servant moved swiftly to his side and the guards remained standing behind him, alert to his every movement. He was presented with a silver platter bearing a goblet of wine frosted with condensation from the ice cool liquid within. Flavio took it gratefully and sipped. He recognised the fragrant white wine as a local Trebbiano Giallo and Procanico mix. It was delicious, and he felt it slide down his throat, cooling him as it went. He would have to be careful, he thought, for it would affect him very quickly with the lack of food, unused as he was to undiluted wine.

Now aware of his surroundings, he gave pause to study the man who had thus far engineered his release. The man stood to one side of his desk dictating a note to a clerk as the scribe scratched away on the vellum before him. He did not look up, but continued his dictation until the end of the missive. Flavio inspected his potential saviour, seeing a man of about the same height as himself, broad of shoulder and with the musculature of a soldier, or at least one trained in arms. He wore a purple gown of light silk that displayed his ecclesiastical status, and around his neck a thick gold chain supported an elegant jewel-encrusted cross. To Flavio's eyes he was a wolf in sheep's clothing, for he was used to sizing up such men. His hair was dark, yet hidden under the traditional *zucchetto* that was perched upon his head.

The round face when he looked up was plain, almost ugly, with a typically long straight nose so characteristic of Cornetani, showing the lineage of his Etruscan forbears. The two lines that led from his nose to his full lips were deeply etched and his high forehead bespoke intelligence. Yet it was as ever the eyes that showed the soul, and in them any benign presence or godly exterior was extinguished, for they were dark and cunning, those of one who had seen all man's vices and embraced many of them. A person to be neither trusted or befriended, far worse and infinitely more powerful than any upstart mayor. Here was a man not to be underestimated at any cost. He waved away the guards, who closed the door behind them.

"*Piacere,* Signor Sabatini, or should that be Vicomte Sabatini da Montalto di Castro?" The voice when he spoke was deep and rounded. He held his ringed finger forward for Flavio to kiss, which he did, bending over it and giving himself more time to consider the words and the fact that the knowledge of his title was known.

"Your eminence, I am merely Flavio Sabatini, all else has been lost with the passage of time and circumstance," he answered deftly. He had met such men as this before and he knew that the man before him was truly dangerous, more so than any knight armed and bristling with weapons. This could be such a man in another guise, yet he could also retreat into his ecclesiastical position to feign piety and peace. A master puppeteer pulling the strings of others to his will, a raptor set upon the world to harvest others.

"As you wish, yet I have seen you upon the field of battle and you are anything but insignificant. You were there at the sack of Cesana at the mighty Hawkwood's side – God rest his soul. You were a captain in his feared White Company, defeating all before you."

"You were there at Cesana?" Flavio cast his mind back to

a young knight seemingly bound by the cross, yet as aggressive and warlike as any, fighting with another captain, Conrad Landau, an Englishman known for his brutality in victory with no quarter given. Flavio shuddered inwardly, thinking back to those days and the horrors of war in which he had participated.

"Forgive my manners. I am Cardinal Giovanni Vitelleschi, and I have the honour to be appointed protonotary apostolic by His Holiness Pope Boniface in Roma. I prithee, be at your ease. Enjoy the wine. It is, as you probably discern, of the region, from a local estate grown and produced just north of the town at Forca di Palama," he offered.

At once it became clear. Flavio had heard of the legendary cleric, who was cutting swathes through the church and the politics of Rome. He was said to be the pope's right hand man and commander of all the papal armies. His star was rising, and rumour had it that he did not care upon whom he trod to make himself ever more powerful.

"Your eminence, I am honoured to make your acquaintance," he responded, asking no questions and allowing the prelate to speak, nodding appreciatively at the wine.

"You must be wondering why I have had you brought here and released you from your incarceration, albeit temporarily." Flavio nodded, giving nothing away. "Allow me to illuminate you as to my intentions. I was born here in Corneto, yet I come from the noble Vitelli family hailing from Citta di Castello. So much for my family, they will be of little consequence," the cardinal waved a dismissive hand.

"What is of far greater import is that I control all the armies and means of the church in his Holy Father's name. As such I control Roma, and I seek to fight the anti-pope of Avignon. My influence covers the states of Napoli, Romagna and Toscana. His Holiness wishes to unite all the Papal States within Italy, including those currently under the malign influence of the other anti-pope in Pisa."

Here the cardinal paused, allowing his vision and its meaning to seep in, his face unreadable and as casual as if he had been discussing the weather.

"So in what manner, you will be asking, does this concern me? Allow me to enlighten you. I needs must concentrate my governance upon Roma, where the Colonna family are in revolt and must be contained and controlled in the far flung states. I know all that occurs in many states and towns, for my spies are many and rest within the church itself. Yet for all that, I need a strong right arm, one who can move freely amongst all men, one who is connected with *i vagabondi*. Pray do not deny it, for your reputation proceeds you, and you are such a man. You are well thought of by the merchants you supply and the smugglers who in turn supply you. You are a man who is able to move between towns with no suspicion other than the smuggling of which all know you are guilty. You are fighter who if called upon could raise a group of men and raid or take a town from within or without.

"You are someone who moves within the criminal fraternity, secure and above their suspicion. Such a man will need certain qualities to cope with the vicissitudes of conflict upon the open road, in towns and between the warring states of Firenze, Pisa and Siena. And the influence of such states must be profound if we are to maintain control of all, including the malignant forces in Milano and their growing power. Added to all is the growing force mounted upon our borders as France seeks to raid and plunder our western flank under Count Gerard du Puy. In short, we lack strong leadership from men who know of war and how to win it, men with a soldier's courage and a routier's spirit. And are you not such a man?" he finished with an arched eyebrow and a piercing stare, the raptor once more appearing from beneath hooded lids.

Flavio sipped his wine again, considering all: "I know not of what you speak, and my past is behind me – though you have the right of it, for I did fight at Hawkwood's side."

Vitelleschi cut him short: "Aye, and with the famous Galeazzo da Mantova, where you trained together under the maestro Fiori dei Liberi, whose skill in arms is already legendary."

Here Flavio was taken aback. How had this man come to know so much about him? He had deliberately left his past behind, and only a handful of loyal servants who had accompanied him through the terrible years of destruction had any knowledge of his previous life, or indeed his training under the master at arms, Fiori.

"Do not dissemble here, Signor Sabatini. I know who and what you are, and I say to you are you with me or against me? For in Italy there is no other course to take. I am the law." He spoke the words quietly, yet there was more menace in his voice than if another had shouted the question.

"If I refuse?"

"Then you will not live to see the outside world again. I shall ensure that you are returned to your cell, there to rot until you die where no one will hear of you again."

I shall kill this man one day, Flavio pledged to himself, man of God or no – that is if someone does not beat me to the task.

Chapter Four

The Maremma, north of Corneto

The wild lands of northern Lazio held some of the roughest country in the Papal States. The hard scrub and stunted wild oaks sprawled inland away from the sea to Mount Amiata and then north up into Tuscany. Here the towns were tucked away, hidden by forest, with few roads leading directly north, where the lawless routiers ruled. At the northern eastern tip lay the small hamlet and the castle of Porrona, stronghold of Salimbeni family.

Agnolino Salimbeni was holding forth in the presence of other members of his family and his captains of war. "We hear reports that Flavio Sabatini has been held for good, and that he will never see the light of day again. Manrico Bastari will ensure that his case is never heard before the *podesta*; he will be hidden deep beneath the *comune* until he rots to death.

"And with him held we have control of all the trade routes – including the Maremma. There is nothing on this side of Lazio that we do not oversee. Once Viterbo is ours we shall have a stranglehold across all routes down to Roma. Firenze and Siena will be isolated and shall be ours for the taking."

Agnolino's dark and swarthy good looks spoke of a well to do family that due to the fortunes of war was now one of the richest within the area.

"We have spies in Firenze, and we shall destroy it from within now that Hawkwood is gone."

"What of Luigi da Capua? He still fights for what remains of the White Company and is employed by Firenze to defend it," asked one of his captains, Remigio Lanfredini, a vicious and amoral soldier of fortune who controlled the roads through the forest of the Maremma, and to whom all paid tolls. His name alone invoked fear in any who travelled north and south between the two states who did not have at least a hundred men as their guard. Tales of torture and rape abounded, and he was said to be happier if his captives resisted, as it invited greater acts of violence against them. His thickset frame, edging towards corpulence, was encased in a greasy leather brigandine reinforced with strips of studded iron. His round, evil face was framed by lank oiled hair and eyes that had no trace of human goodness within them.

"Luigi is a true *condottieri*, and will be persuaded by the largest purse. His true colours are gold and silver."

"And Cardinal Vitelleschi?" one of Lanfredini's lower ranking officers asked. "For he commands the papal armies and seeks – so we hear from our spies in Roma and the church in Firenze – to unite Italy under the Papal States. Will he not aid them?"

Salimbeni smiled unpleasantly: "He has his own adversaries in the Colonna family, with whom we have a pact. He disturbs their influence and power in Roma, and they have no love for him. I perceive that he will encounter many problems there, and the last thing he will do is turn his attention to matters north of Roma – in particular the warring states of Toscana, where even now Visconti marches on Firenze as our friend," he opined.

"So where do we strike next?" asked Lanfredini.

"Viterbo. We must secure that town before we head north and bring our conquest there, offering a pact with Visconti. Corneto is under the control of the new *sindaco* and with him lies our power. The merchants there will be brought to heel, and we have others within the town on our side. The grain harvest is important, as it controls the wheat throughout the whole of Italia. And with such governance we have a bargaining chip to force all to bow before us if we withhold the largest wheat harvest from Roma. When Viterbo is ours, we will control the whole of the Marta valley east to the sea.

"We continue to tax the Maremma roads, then once we have control of Lazio, Firenze and Siena will turn to our cause, and the Papal See will beg us to open the trade routes once more. There is, I hear, even less *simpatico* between the Holy Father and his chief cardinal and that weakness is ours to exploit." Salimbeni finished.

* * *

Flavio's palazzo, Corneto

The day after he was released from gaol and from the more salubrious custody of the cardinal's palace, Flavio reflected on all that had occurred as he sat upon the loggia looking out towards the sea, sipping a fine Grillo that he had imported from Sicily. The straw coloured wine, at once both fruity and flinty, slipped down easily and he vowed never to be taken in again by anyone, even at the cost of his life. He had explained all to his meiny, whose members had gathered much of what had occurred from outside the prison, for Flavio was popular within Corneto and many had rallied quietly to his cause, persuading the head gaoler to feign illness and substituting Gianpaolo Agneli. Officials had been bribed and palms greased without the new mayor becoming aware of anything untoward.

Flavio gazed at the clouds floating above the distant sea and wondered for the hundredth time who was behind his incarceration and how he had been betrayed. None of the answers that sprang to mind made him comfortable, yet with a full stomach and finally scrubbed clean and dressed in fine clothes once more, he had decided to sample the delights of the town that evening and celebrate his freedom. Flavio strapped on his sword belt that had been returned to him with a short missive from Cardinal Vitelleschi saying: *A present, in good faith, to seal our agreement.* He had crumpled the vellum in anger and thrown it to the floor, hating that he was in any man's debt. Tossing back the last of his wine, he called for his horse and this time took with him his groom, Pietro and Maurizio Stoica, his chief man-at-arms. Ensuring that both men were armed with swords, daggers and bucklers attached to the horse's saddles and that they wore padded aketon's despite the heat, albeit unfrogged and open, they rode forth through the palazzo gates.

Maurizio, who originated from Milan, had served under Flavio in the White Company, and had followed him home to Lazio and the end of his wars as a *condottieri*. He was wicked in a fight, and what he lacked in formal finessed training with an arming sword he more than made up for in lethal aggression and use of arms with a bull like strength and speed of movement, that was completely unattached to any sense of the sanctity of human life. They rode up to the gate of Santa Maria on the north side of the town just as the sun was starting to dip low in the sky, and looking back on one of the two switchbacks in the road, Flavio saw the sea cast in a shimmering haze of coral and burnt ochre. There was little breeze to give any form of relief from the midsummer heat, and the sultry air carried the gently wafting fragrance of a jasmine hedge as they passed through the first gate as the bells of Santa Maria in Castello rang out Compline, signalling that the massive *Saracinesca* would soon be lowered for the night. The guards gave them close scrutiny as they passed though at this late hour before nodding in recognition.

They rode into the town along the familiar route, passing the piazza where even now some of the bars and trattorias were opened out onto the street, where gatherings of townsfolk out on an evening *passeggiata* concluded their evening stroll. The noise from the crowds was loud and festive, a mass of people celebrating the fact that life was good on a balmy summer's evening. Nods and smiles were offered by some, along with the odd word of encouragement, for all had heard of Flavio's incarceration and rumours now sprang forth as to how he had managed to escape the clutches of both the mayor and the cardinal.

The three men rode up through the two main piazzas crossing the via Porta Corneto, a new street that led to the recently constructed city walls to the south that had nearly doubled the size of the *civitas.* The massive walls were still yellow, as yet unbleached by the sun, and some of the ramparts were still unfinished.

They rode on upwards, turning left where the cobbles were shined to a dark blue grey haze, polished by thousands of feet, then sharply right into the dark, cool street of Via San Pancrazio. High walls drew upwards on either side, then the street opened out to show a pair of large iron gates and on the wall the name, Palazzo Cornucopia. All who knew of it smiled at its aptness, for within one could find a wide range of pleasures to answer most tastes.

At the gate a liveried gateman admitted them immediately, recognising Flavio and offering words of conciliation for his recent incarceration. With the gates open they rode into the elegant courtyard, the sound of the horses' hooves echoing back from the walls. Vast terracotta pots lined a flagged driveway where private carriages awaited the return of their owners. Horses were tethered elsewhere, and the perpetual atmosphere of a *festa* prevailed as always at Casa Cornucopia. Lamps flickered brightly in the growing dusk, and ribbons and chimes festooned the trees. It was a magical display designed to sway the senses, and it worked well, Flavio considered as he dismounted, leaving his horse with

Pietro. Two more livered men, their silk pourpoints embroidered with a large white cornucopia shell in the Etruscan style, stood by the door, round-hilted rondel daggers at their belts. They also bade Flavio good evening, and in the time honoured fashion asked that he take off his sword belt, for no weapons were allowed within the walls of the palazzo.

The doors were opened to admit him alone, and there before him was a spectacle of light, pleasure and decadence, where a man could lose himself and all his troubles for a few hedonistic hours. Different perfumes mixed, heady in the air, swamping the senses as much as the colourful scene before him. Candles flickered from sconces, carefully arrayed throughout the large salon, offering flattering light to all. Arrases were draped around pillars in a faux Roman fashion, and gambling tables were laid out at which men played dice or gambled with the hand painted cards to the new game of *Ronfa*, the chink of coins changing hands cheered by the gleeful raised voices of victors and the solemn grunts of losers.

About the tables Flavio saw many men he knew, including two priests, well respected merchants and guildsmen, away this night from their wives to seek the company of the elegant and beautiful women who lured the customers to the gaming tables and encouraged them to spend more on wine. Windows were open and from a terrace outside an unseen group of musicians played delicate music.

To one side was a bar and elegant place settings where diners enjoyed fine food and wines. Men travelled far and wide to the Casa Cornucopia, which was legendary throughout Lazio. He wondered if any of these men – most of whom he knew – could be the one that had not only betrayed him but set about plotting with the mayor to have him incarcerated. But as he stood there, pausing for a moment at the top of the three steps that led down into the room, Flavio felt the cares of the last few weeks drop from him. This night was for pleasure and to celebrate his freedom, and to banish those darker thoughts from his mind. Stepping down, he stopped to pause and talk to the occupants of some of the tables, watching as he went for any eye that showed a flash of guilt or a glint of ill will concealed behind a vulpine smile. He would drink a little wine and maybe gamble at cards. He saw that some of his usual friends had gathered to join them in a few hands of *ronfa*, and he felt reckless and carefree, ready to sample all life's pleasures. And on that thought the answer to his unspoken prayers appeared – Federica Serafini.

No one knew much about her; she was as much an enigma as Flavio himself. Flavio knew the story – or the legend she saw nothing to dispel. She had arrived one day out of the blue as a teenager, cast adrift on life's currents, coming down the river on a skiff similar to Flavio's own. She stayed in the town and worked hard, first as a maid then within a merchant's house, where she married the man, who died shortly thereafter of a spasm. It was said that he had been poisoned, but it was also said that he had treated his young wife cruelly and beat her often, and that he deserved his fate. Few mourned his passing, least of all Federica, who inherited the business. With no interest in the mercantile world, she sold it to the highest bidder – and her late husband had many competitors vying for his influence – taking the money to buy first one, then two houses within the town, from which she ran gambling and pleasure houses similar to the Casa Cornucopia, which she now owned. She had consolidated her position, selling both houses and buying the run down palazzo where she now lived, refurbishing it to her own design. She was despised and admired in equal parts, usually according to sex. Yet those who had tried to have her removed or shut down had achieved little, and now, six years later, she was mistress of the most successful pleasure house in the area, with her own stable of beautiful girls and gambling tables.

Flavio took in her beguiling beauty, which was unusual in itself. Her dark red hair spoke of the northern areas of the Italian lands, and it fell in curled tresses, bound only by a jewelled band. Her curls were in stark contrast to her almost opaque green eyes with unusual dark circled irises, and yet despite this colouring her skin tanned easily, and she sported a band of summer freckles across her nose. She had an oval face and the broader nose of the north, and from her delicate ears hung dropped pearls. She was clothed in an elegant silk gown taken in just below her breasts to fall decorously to the floor, etched with beading and fluted sarsenet sleeves of a contrasting ruby red against the gold of the bodice. Her voice when she spoke had a deep husky edge to it that put a spell upon every male that she charmed. She was reviled by the women of the town as a money hungry harlot with the morals of an alley cat, yet they were happy enough to have their men give them respite from their duties as they flitted off for an evening of company and cards.

"*Buona sera, caro mio,*" she greeted Flavio with a

beguiling smile, her arms wide for an embrace. As Flavio came forward he caught the deep scents of bergamot and jasmine at once so elusive and yet so familiar, beguiling upon her warm olive skin.

"*Dio mio*, *cara*, you get more lovely each time I witness your beauty, and you were all I dreamed of in that hole from Hades where I languished for too long."

"Fie upon you! You favel me, upon my soul. Yet it is meet that you do so, for I sorely missed your looks and charm during those dark days of your absence. You must tell me more as a salve to your hurts – yet not here, later!" she finished in a lowered voice, whisking her fan to her cheek so only he could hear her the last words. Flavio was one of the cherished few within her inner circle, and he enjoyed more than mere friendship in that regard. They were lovers who kept each other at a certain remove, demanding nothing of permanence, yet Flavio for once in his life wished for something that he could not have. He knew not whether, in the manner of so many men once the chase was over, he would lose interest, yet he was always entranced and left wanting more when he left her bed and her embrace. For she provided him with more than physical love through the deep salve of her presence. Flavio often wondered if they were two scarred, damaged beings who sought salvation in each other's company, although despite this *simpatico*, he felt that he had never quite managed to breach the inner sanctum of her soul.

They sallied forth onto the floor, with Federica flirting outrageously with all she passed, each time keeping a handy eye upon her girls to see that they were attentive and free of undesired attentions. Above the courtyard were a variety of rooms that catered for more intimate liaisons as the mood took the customers, and these were always in great demand. Federica put no pressure upon her girls and contented herself with taking a percentage for every indulgence, as she called it. It was an amicable arrangement that pleased the clients and the girls themselves.

With their arms linked, they walked to a table on the raised level, Federica's hips swaying with every movement of her long legs beneath her gown, drawing all eyes across the salon to her.

Hours later they lay in a sprawled embrace, from which Flavio woke with a start as the nightmares came upon him once more, this time with images of the gaol cell walls closing in as the green slime sprang from the walls and came to take him, spurred on by one of the nameless victims of the field of battle. He cried out, suddenly wide awake, and sat bolt upright. Federica murmured soft words of comfort, bringing a cool hand to his brow as she too sat upright, the covers falling from her heavy breasts.

"Ssh *caro, tranquillo, non ti preoccupi,*" she cooed.

Flavio took the cool hand in his own, removing it from his sweating forehead as he assured her that he was all right now he had woken.

"What dark angels attack you in your dreams? Was it the wars again, or the gaol?" she asked.

"Ah my love, you know me well. It matters not, for they are all the same but in different guises, and now in these early hours I will no longer be able to slumber in peace. I needs must walk off the dark humours." He reached for her mouth and kissed her long and deeply, tasting the last of the sweet wine upon her breath. He rose and dressed slowly, in no hurry to leave her chamber, yet knowing that he must for any peace to be had.

"Where will you tread?"

"I shall seek the new walls and see how they fare in the moonlight."

"Would you like company?"

"No, my love. I am better equipped to be alone in moods such as these." He smiled wanly, then raised her hand and kissed it.

"*Va bene.*" Federica replied. "Yet there is something you should know that we did not discuss yester eve. I brought about your release and got word to the cardinal. I also arranged for certain guild members to aid with the bribery of the old gaoler and the hiring of Gianpaolo from Viterbo." A silence reigned between them as Flavio's mind turned over what she had just said.

"You are acquainted with Cardinal Vitelleschi?" he asked, suspicion in his voice, for he knew of the cardinal's lax morals. He was like most of the supposed celibate members of the Catholic church, which was said to have more whores than Babel.

For once she could not meet his eyes. "We have been acquainted for some time..." she trailed off, and Flavio knew better than to push the point. He just shook his head, knowing that the world was full of secrets and mistrust. "Yet you must know that you were betrayed by one of your own the night on the river, and others higher in might than those of the town are involved," she continued. "Men from the north. I know not their names, but I will find out."

"North? La Maremma?"

"I know not, but trust me, I will find out and aid you as I may." Her eyes rose defiantly to meet his, and he knew not to push for more information or to make judgements, for he knew that he too was no angel.

Chapter Five

Flavio left via small doorway that led directly to the walls with steps up to the ramparts of the town. The night was warm, and he had his silk doublet unfrogged, his left hand resting upon the hilt of his sword as he walked slowly along the ramparts towards the newly constructed *porta nuova*. At this point the city walls came nearly to street level on the town side, offering a fabulous sweeping vista over the Marta valley across the waving wheat fields now ripened, showing a gently swaying forest of greyed cream sentinels that rustled in the soft air.

He passed the time away as his dream faded, exchanging a few words with the guards, who were used to people wandering at night in the stifling heat, unable to sleep and staying out of reach of the annoying predations of the Watch, who were ever vigilant, knowing every back lane and cobbled alley in such a small town. Crossing through the arched walkway over the tower gates and now lowered portcullis, Flavio continued his perambulations, looking out over the Marta valley as the river wended its way west and north, a twisting line of quicksilver under the half-moon. He caught a quiet conversation between Pietro and Maurizio, who trailed in his wake along the ramparts leaving him to his own designs, alone with his thoughts. He followed the walls round to the south, the new stone brighter in the moonlight, skirting the Piazza Daga with the beautiful church of St Francesco, eventually look fully south at the new and as yet unnamed lesser gateway off the Via Porta Corneto. This entrance was much smaller, with two lower towers on either side that protruded forward from the gatehouse, offering crossbowmen the opportunity to lean over and catch any attackers in a cross fire from either buttress. In places the walls had not yet been constructed to their full height, and there Flavio found two guards standing only half awake, leaning against the crenulations that were already in place, spears resting on their shoulders, talking about some woman they had both been chasing, barely bothering to nod as Flavio approached. The other two lazy oafs must be within the gatehouse, he mused, and despite having no jurisdiction he shouted:

"Why do you not seek foes beyond the walls? Are our enemies here within, that your gaze is so distracted?" He was angry. As a man of arms, he had seen a lack of diligence result in tragedy so often, as men taken unawares were late to react. Indeed he had himself played upon such laxness. But this was his town, and he felt responsible. The one talking glared at him, pushing himself upright from the wall with his shoulders. Whatever he was going to say was cut short as he plunged forward, an arrow protruding from between his shoulder blades, driven in hard almost to the fletching. The other guard at his side had no time to react, and did not even register why his comrade-in-arms was falling forward. He then sprang upright, chest pushed forward arms back like a strung bow. A short rasping breath of pain expelled from his lungs before he too collapsed onto the ramparts.

Flavio reacted quickly, stooping to shield himself behind the stone and peering carefully around one of the crenulations. He saw shapes, darker than the background shadows, seemingly rising up out of the ground like wraiths in the night. This time he caught the faint twang of a bowstring and the whistle of an arrow in flight, as a shaft sped through the gap in the crenel where his face had been a split second before. *By Hades, they are good!* "Down, Pietro. Maurizio, raise the Watch, raise the hue and cry, for we are under attack from *Saraceni*!"

It had to be Saracens, for only they used the short recurve composite bows that launched arrows with deadly speed and accuracy. No longer than three feet, he had seen the nature of their construction at close quarters on a pilgrimage to the Holy Land – a mix of wood glue, sinew and bone. They were fast and easily manoeuvrable, more so than the long war bows used by the English bowmen in the White Company that had worked to such good effect.

Flavio heard voices and muffled shouts from within the guard tower as his two men banged upon the door, having dropped to the lower level, where even now the battering of steel against wood was heard as the tower vibrated to the concussion upon the outer doors. A battering ram thumped home, building to a steady rhythm.

Then came the most dreaded sound to all defenders: the clack of wood against stone as siege ladders were braced against the walls, slamming home. Flavio drew his sword and dagger, aware that they would soon be overrun. He would sell his life dearly rather than be taken by the heathens.

A dark face appeared, one hand on the ladder pole, the other wielding a curved scimitar that flashed dully in the pale moonlight. There was no time for the finer points of swordplay, and Flavio saw that the head was helmeted in the conical Saracen style, rising to a point topped by a small crescent with a broad nasal guard running down the face. Fierce eyes stared out and the attacker's mouth was open wide, yelling a war cry in the ugly guttural Saracen tongue. Flavio, with his long experience of siege warfare, did not hesitate. He sliced down at the hand holding the ladder, severing thumb and fingers in one stroke, the Milanese steel biting home and cleaving all before it like butter. Dark blood flowed forth and the final little finger had no hold. The man's war cry turned into a scream of pain as he tried to halt his downward slash and grab the ladder with his right hand. He failed and fell back into the night catching the man beneath him, who also dropped with a cry of fear to the unyielding cobbles below. Flavio pushed hard and the ladder toppled, balancing precariously for a few seconds before it fell backwards, taking ten men with it as it arced beyond the cobbles to the rocky dry moat below.

To his left another ladder was raised and an invader nimbly vaulted the wall's defences, his small shield up and a curved scimitar in his hand. He gave a war cry and charged at Flavio, the domed brass shield thrust forward to deflect any blow. Flavio knew the danger, as the shield was slightly larger and deeper than the western buckler and could be as much used as a weapon as a defence.

Extending his arm and thrusting forward, the Saracen lunged, twisting his wrist to cut with a side slash at the last minute, lashing forward to cleave Flavio's torso in half. Flavio moved with the habit of long experience, allowing the blade to scythe in, holding his sword at an angled vertical guard, taking the lighter weapon's energy upwards to his hilt, where it locked. He twisted, bringing the sword across, making it difficult for the Saracen to us the shield as a buffer. Going with the action, he slid in the rondel dagger up under the armpit, driving for nerves and lungs. As the blade grated on bone, he twisted and withdrew it to a sucking sound and a spray of dark blood. The Saracen dropped, writhing in agony, and he kicked him aside to trip the next man over the walls, who had to jumped nimbly into the air from the crenel. Flavio squatted slightly, slashing sideways to catch the legs beneath the shield, and the man screamed as he landed on the stumps where his feet had been.

Flavio skirted past the fallen man and went to the top of the ladder, pushing it sideways this time, watching it skitter in an arc into the moat below. He blew hard, his chest rasping. He was out of practice as his time in the gaol had hurt his stamina and strength. Yet there was no time for reprieve. The top of another ladder appeared and a face rose above the walls. He drove the balanced blade of his arming sword into the uncovered eyes as he sent the man backwards, screaming. More ladders were raised, and men came over the ramparts in numbers now, turning the struggle into a desperate melee of slashing steel and the rasp of blade on blade, the rampart slippery with blood and gore as the guards came for the *porta nuova* to aid him. Brands were lit and men ran from houses into the streets, raising the alarm. The barracks lay at the bottom of the town near the Piazza Cavour, and it would be some time before reinforcements arrived, and the soldiers may come too late and find this part of the town overrun. The new southern walls were the lowest and most vulnerable part of the town's defences, with level land running from the old Etruscan tombs of their ancestors, giving a sweeping run down the main road to the dry moat and the walls above.

Flavio's arm was tired, his tunic was gashed, and blood flowed down his arm as he wiped away more blood from his eyes. He was just in time to catch a scimitar on his dagger before thrusting forward at the throat of his assailant, and still the heathens came on, ladders propped up as soon as they were pushed away, a hoard of chanting voices below calling in their foreign tongue. Then soldiers arrived on horses that were unsaddled and hastily bridled. The riders slipped from the backs of their mounts and ran up the stone steps to the ramparts. Men with spears and kite shields bearing the white cherry tree of Corneto appeared, a blessed relief after the ugly designs of the orient. More came now with crossbows, picking their targets below as oil was poured over and brands thrown to ignite it. The flaming oil puddled, flared and spread, and men ran screaming like flaming devils, human torches, surreal and macabre in the drama that unfolded before Flavio's eyes.

"Hurry! Hold them! For they swarm the walls like flies on a dog's turd." Flavio shouted as the newly arrived soldiers ran up the steps, falling immediately under his command as a leader of men, none thinking to question his order.

With a clatter of arms, the twenty or so members of the Corneto garrison, the first soldiers to arrive, ran to his aid, better protected in a full mail, with helms, shields and spears offering protection to the crossbowmen who sought targets in the flaming light below. Even now one fell back, struck by an arrow from a Saracen bow, screaming as he toppled backwards to hit the street below with a thud that silenced his cry. Another soldier dropped his spear and shield to take his place, retrieving his comrade's crossbow from the rampart, spanning the weapon and inserting another quarrel into the tiller. He leaned out carefully from the protection of the merlon just as another ladder clattered against the wall and dark figures began to scurry upwards. He shot downwards, taking the first man to tumble others below him, before a shield-bearing brother-in-arms pushed the ladder sideways as another arrow flew, ricocheting harmlessly off the kite shield that was strapped to his arm.

Flavio edged back, panting hard with exertion as he sought to regain his strength, his sword arm weary from fighting and slashing at the seemingly endless horde. He looked around him, seeking any attacker that may have slipped through the surge of reinforcements. He was thirsty and his mouth was dry, his nose filled with the coppery stench of blood and voided bowels. He threw a wounded Scarcen from the ramparts, hearing the man cry in fear as he fell until he landed on the cobbles with a sickening crunch. He heard the scrape of another ladder above the cries of battle, and a voice began to imprecate the Saracen god and shout for his blessing. Flavio launched himself forward, driving the point of his sword straight at the face, aiming for an uncovered eye. The point skewered home meeting little resistance, and the attacker cried in pain before dying on the point of the sword. Flavio once more pushed the ladder off sideways, sending more tumbling to their deaths.

He stood back behind the merlon, his hands on his knees, shaking with fatigue and looking down to his left in a brief respite from the battle. There he saw a terrible sight. The ramparts on the other side of the gatehouse were the site of a fierce fight for supremacy as the Saracens had managed to take hold and secure a bridgehead. He saw a spirited resistance led by Pietro and Maurizio as more of the guard came to their aid. Yet even as he watched with horror, he saw Pietro fall, stabbed by a spear thrust that was barely deflected by his buckler, turning it slightly aside to pierce through the gambeson on his right side. The Saracens stepped over him as they pushed to gain their advantage, growing in numbers now. He saw their intent, for the battering had continued below upon the gate, the ram protected by a rough cover of dried cow hides over a wooden frame. They had secured access to the stone steps down to the street below. If they reached the gate from the inside and raised the *saracinesca*, all would be lost, for they could lift the bar to the gates beyond and Corneto would be theirs.

Even now he saw a war party break off, running down the steps two at a time and swarming back to the gate, just as reinforcements came up on horseback from the garrison barracks to the west of the town. Crossbow bolts flew, crossing with arrows from the Saracens, men fell and then the Cornetani *conroi* charged forward, shields raised and spears levelled to the enclave. Those who were still mounted slashed down at the hated heathens within the walls of their city. Yet more poured down from the ramparts, forming a two pronged attack against the relief force who began to fight for their lives. As Flavio watched impotently from the ramparts above, he saw three Saracens break away to the rear, running back to the *saracinesca*, which they raised using the large, spoked drums around which the chains were attached. The portcullis rose steadily to a clank of chains and then locked in place. The invaders focused upon the barred gates and began to lift the large oaken bressummer out of its metal holders.

"No!" he cried, picking up a kite shield from a fallen guard and running to the small door, which he hoped against hope was unbolted from within the tower. It should have been bolted, and only upon the password being given would anyone be allowed to enter. It was unlatched – the guards had been slack in the heat of battle. Flavio squeezed through the small opening to a set of stone steps leading downwards. These he descended two at a time, hearing the scrape of another ladder above hitting the tower itself. It was too late to worry, he needed to stave off the imminent opening of the gates.

He pulled open the wooden door by two inches and saw the three Saracens through the crack, heaving the first wooden bar out of the holders. If they did the same for the second they could open the gates, which were the only impediment to the city being overrun.

The battering of the ram continued, accompanied by

cheers of glee from outside as the attackers saw the gates move, held by only one bar now. Flavio was unnoticed, and as the three men bent to their labours again with the second bar, he pulled back the door and ran forward three paces silently, making no war cry as he rammed the point of his sword into the back of the first man, driving through the thin steel links of his mail hauberk with the force of the thrust. The man's back arched in pain and he collapsed, but Flavio had no time to confirm his kill as the next Saracen span around, reaching for the hilt of his scimitar. As the blade was withdrawn Flavio slashed across, severing the wrist. Hand and blade fell to the cobbles, hazed with a bloody spray of crimson and the coppery tang of blood. The man screamed, yet he was not done, and launched himself at Flavio, clasping him in a bloody embrace, trying to claw at his eyes, his right knee pumping upwards.

Flavio drove the edge of the shield into his face, smashing through the nasal guard of his helmet, driving metal and bone back into the brain and killing him instantly. He pushed the man off, covered now in his blood, but the third man had had time to prepare and was ready with a scimitar in his hand, taking an odd guard, left hand forward as though to deflect. The pose was a feint, and the Saracen rotated the scimitar from the wrist, thrusting forward point first under the guard of Flavio's shield, left arm looking to grapple with Flavio's sword arm.

Flavio had just enough time to drop the shield and step back, driving the quillon forward and punching hard at the open face, cracking bone and rupturing an eyeball. He smashed, once, twice with his shield, buffeting the body and offering the Saracen no opportunity to bring his blade to bear. At close quarters now, Flavio thrust a leg behind his opponent, sweeping his leg away in a wrestling move that sent him tumbling to the cobbles. Now with space created, he thrust down with his sword, aiming for the neck where the mail ended and the face was exposed, finding his target with deadly effect.

His chest heaving with exertion, he looked up to see that other members of the heathen hordes were now aware of his presence, as two left their comrades to rush him simultaneously.

Chapter Six

Flavio gripped the shield tighter and prepared to sell his life dearly as two more Saracens joined their comrades-in-arms to kill him and lift the final bar of the gate. Shouting their war cry, the first two rushed him, their domed shields to the fore, scimitars raised at half guard, twisting and whirling in their manner to confuse and disguise the angle of attack with their light, razor-sharp weapons. They saw his lack of mail or armour and attacked accordingly to pincer him between them, the right hand opponent twisting the sword from the wrist, first right then upwards, crossing the centre line as he stepped to his left, slashing down at an angle towards Flavio's waist, the buckler coming up through the arc to give himself a rear defence. His comrade thrust forward, the scimitar hissing in the air and moving like a butterfly's wings, the way an English soldier would use a battleaxe.

Flavio stepped right as fast as he could, using the kite shield to deflect the left hand blade, his sword arm bringing his heavier weapon to meet the diagonal slash from the right.

Instead of deflecting it, he flexed inwards, driving the blade back while blocking the next attack from his left. He did not disengage, but swept with his right foot as he had before, bringing the man down as he took his feet from under him. He raked across as he moved back again, blinding his opponent with a cut above the eyes. It had no depth of penetration but flooded the man's eyes with blood. The first attacker, now in range again, brought his weapon down hard, the razor sharp blade biting into the wood and steel of Flavio's kite shield, cutting a wedge in the steel binding as it sawed free.

Now three came at him, and Flavio knew that without armour he was in trouble as the two newcomers had short spears with wicked cross hilts at the base of the tip that could hook and pull down a shield, exposing the man behind it to a thrust from another spear. They began the deadly dance of Saracen fighters, back and forth, jabbing with spears and staying out of range of Flavio's arming sword. The third man jumped in, scimitar whirring, knowing it would just be a matter of time before one of the spearmen found their mark. Flavio stepped back and took a high guard, blade raised backwards and shield up to guard his left, leaving the centre open. The middle spearman, seeing the opening, took the opportunity, lunging forward and thrusting the spear at Flavio's stomach. Flavio barely had time to sway back, but that was the move he had expected, and he grabbed the haft with his hand inside the shield grip. He jerked on the spear and the Saracen came forward as he brought down his blade, cleaving the Saracen's neck through the mail links of his hauberk. The dead man's impetus blocked the other spearman for an instant, giving Flavio a short reprieve. Yet the man to his left was not idle and span the blade at the wrist, crashing it to Flavio's back. He bent forward, fearing the sharp weapon, taking some of the force from the blow as it collided with the edge of his shield first, then cut at the rear of his ribs through the padding of his silk doublet. He fell to the street, rolling in an effort to evade the next strike, knowing it was futile as one of the two men would stab him now.

Flavio tried to twist and bring the shield to bear as the scimitar twirled again, the agile wrist wielding the weapon with skill. His back was agony as he fought valiantly to get his own blade in a cross to defend himself. He barely managed as the rictus smile of the Saracen swordsman sneered down at him, ready for the death blow. The wrist twirled again, the blade arcing in a flash against the light of the brands. Then the man's eyes widened in pain and surprise, his back arching forward like a drawn bow. Blood appeared at his mouth as he staggered forward, all thoughts of the attack forgotten. An arrow protruded from his back – a Saracen arrow, Flavio saw, as puzzled as the soldier who had been skewered by it. He had no time to consider the riddle as the remaining spearman, seeing his supine figure, raised his pointed haft to drive down into him. Flavio pulled the kite shield to protect his body as the sharp tip skidded off and slashed around with his sword, cutting into his opponent's booted legs where there was no armour or mail.

The brilliant blade cut through to the bone and beyond, taking a foot off above the ankle. Flavio rolled with the cut, coming to his knees in the expectation of another attack, yet none came, and as he looked up to rise he saw two more

Saracens lying dead, pierced seemingly by arrows from their own side. He turned now, looking back at the gatehouse, and there stood a man of dark hued skin showing only his exposed face beneath a Saracen helmet. Flavio watched the man nock another arrow, raise his arm and draw the powerful recurved bow to send an arrow plunging into the Saracen captain on the steps, who a moment before had been exhorting his men to greater efforts.

In that moment the attack faltered, as happens so often in the heat of battle as events turn and courage flies away. The men of the Cornetani garrison redoubled their efforts, seeing their enemies waver, and pushed through to the gate. The heathens divided and fled left and right along side streets to join comrades that had scaled the walls in other places.

The captain of the garrison ran forward, a broad blade in his hand, ready to attack the tall mysterious Saracen bowman who had saved Flavio's life.

"Hold!" Flavio called. "Hold, for he saved my life, and I wouldst know his reason. There is a riddle here, and I would hear it. I pledge my honour that he will be my responsibility, but hold him securely, captain, until my return."

"*Si, Signor Sabatini*," the captain muttered reluctantly, as dealings with any who wore the Saracen armour were usually merciless. Two men moved forward as the tall Saracen surrendered, dropping to his knees, arms outstretched in supplication, bowing his head.

Flavio had no time to ponder the identity of his saviour, but ran off across the street heading north and then right up the via Alberata Dante Alighieri. His head pounded and his bleeding back ached. He was desperately thirsty, yet he feared for the *porta nuova* and more particularly the Casa Cornucopia as here the walls were low to the ground inside, and if the new gate or the walls either side had been breached all hell would be let loose upon the town. Groups of citizens stood on street corners, mixed in their armament, with servants in gambesons, wielding swords and with a few bloodied bodies at their feet.

The Saracens had breached the walls!

He arrived at the small Piazza Belvedere, where a group of citizens had joined soldiers of the guard and were making a valiant defence against those Saracens that had either jumped the walls or run from his own battle below at the second gate. The combatants swayed, hacked and struck at each other as the Saracens started to press forward. Flavio shouted a war cry of his own and slashed at their backs, cutting through the mail of two even before they realised they were under attack from that quarter. A third he nearly decapitated with a single stroke as the fine mail of the man's aventail did little to protect him beneath his rounded helm, his head lolling forward in a spray of red mist. Flavio battered his shield into a fourth, and with this attack the pressure on the Cornetani was relieved, allowing them to regroup and take the upper hand. Then he was through, his chest heaving, his body battered and tired. He reached the three short steps of the low rampart, where seemingly an age before he had wandered at his leisure, lost in thought.

* * *

Federica walked along the ramparts, having left her courtyard via the same door Flavio had used only minutes earlier. She was on the rampart taking the night air, unable to sleep now that Flavio had left her bed. She heard the hue and cry raised to the south of the town and saw fire take to some of the tinder dry buildings. The hooves of horses rattled and echoed against the cobbles and the shouts of war were abroad upon the night. Fear prickled upon her skin at the sights and sounds.

"Signorina, what is happening?" cried her maid, a few steps behind her on the rampart.

"Go, Maria, raise the household, have guards posted at the gates fully armed. We are under attack, for I believe that the Saraceni come. Go!" She urged.

"Signorina, look!" Maria cried, raising a hand to her mouth, pointing behind Federica, who turned that instant to see two dark figures padding along the rampart. They were armed and holding swords in the reflected light of brands and fires now taking hold.

"Go, Maria, run!" Federica shouted, turning to face the oncoming Saracens. The maid seemed petrified, until the spell was finally broken by a cry from the invaders and she turned, raising her skirts, and ran back along the rampart to the door and safety crying in alarm.

Federica stood passively, facing the two oncoming heathen soldiers, and sank to her knees seemingly in supplication with an outward appearance of calm resignation to the fate that undoubtedly awaited her. The pose took the aggression away from her oppressors, who smiled lasciviously, sheathing their weapons and muttering to each other in their own language. "Go after the other Christian whore, I will take this one," the foremost soldier ordered.

"Take me but do not kill me," Federica imprecated, pleading for her life, as one of the men ran past her to chase after Maria. As she spoke she pulled down the top of her gown, exposing her breasts to the Saracen, whose thoughts aligned in a single accord. As he came on he raised his mail above his waist and began to fumble with his braies, standing directly before Federica, a look of panic now upon her face, her mouth open in fear. Her hands met from being crossed beneath her breast and now rose up. Too late the Saracen saw the glint of steel as a stiletto flashed in the light of the flames, driving straight up at his exposed groin. He screamed in white hot agony, blood spraying between his legs as Federica twisted the weapon, withdrew and stabbed again, this time at the femoral artery on the inside of the thigh.

"Die, you heathen pig," Federica muttered, her right hand now drenched in blood, spitting down upon his face as she rose. She heard a cry of alarm from behind as Maria reached the wooden wicket gate, slipped inside and flung the bolt across just in time, screaming all the while as if to wake the dead. The dying soldier's comrade-in-arms was running back now towards her, angry at the deception played upon them. A voice at Federica's back steadied her.

"Let me pass, Feddy, for he is mine." Flavio eased past her, determined to save her from a fate worse than death.

"Come and meet your God, heathen!" he shouted, and raised the war cry of the condottieri: *"Hawkwood and St George!"* His battered shield raised and his arming sword at half guard he strode forward, aware of the deadly speed of the scimitar, knowing he was tired, wounded and weak from loss of blood.

The Saracen unsheathed the scimitar, whirling it in his wrist as he pulled a curved dagger from his waist belt. With his own cry of war he raced forward, a dervish of hate and deadly speed. The arcing blade came up and around from Flavio's left hand side, then flicked up to come crashing down to split his head open.

Flavio dropped, and upon seeing the move he reacted just in time, bringing his shield up to take the blow, tucking his head beneath it. He hated going low as it reduced the options for further defence and attack, yet he knew instinctively that this was the way to win. With one knee bent he pushed forwards, driving the tip of his sword at his attacker's exposed groin, ramming the blade home and rising as he did so with such force that the Saracen was lifted off his feet, taking the blade trapped in his groin with him, pulling from Flavio's weakened grip to roll around on the floor in his dying agony, eviscerated by the blade. Flavio, now standing, watched as the man begged for mercy where he would have given none, every movement causing white hot agony within him until he passed out from the pain to lie twitching on the floor.

Flavio turned to face Federica, his head light and seeing stars in his weakness. "Are you alright, *amore*?" he asked tenderly.

"Yes, yes. Oh Flavio, it was horrible, yet I would not let them take me." She said, safe at last within the circle of his arms.

"Sssh, *con calma*. You were brave and all is well. See, your men appear, go to them and I will return," he gestured as some of her servants armed and ready with swords and bucklers ran towards them to escort their mistress back to the safety of the *casa*.

"Where do you go? You are wounded, Flav," she said, her voice filled with concern.

"I will be well, fear not, but I must see to the *civitas*, for all may still be lost if they gain entry to the town. They seek not to conquer and hold, but to rape, pillage and sack for their own evil ends. Go now. All will be well."

He kissed her lightly on the cheek, pulling her gown up for the sake of decorum and left her there sobbing with relief as he padded back down towards where the rampart dropped to a lowest street level, seeing flames catching buildings as dark acrid smoke filled the air.

He ran down to the Piazza Trento a Triste opposite the main *comune* building where he had been held so recently Before him was a newly constructed grand palazzo where fighting was still in full force between the invaders and the garrison as citizens joined in to help, crying and screaming at the invaders in fright and anger. The palazzo was the official residence of the mayor, and there before him he saw that the doors had been broken in, one hanging from its hinges. He strode over, killing a Saracen in his way as he stood over a fallen member of the garrison, poised to skewer him with his sword. Smoke was coming now from the curtains at the upper windows, raided and sacked by those within, and he heard the scream of women from inside. He rushed in, seeing a heathen rip a nightgown from a serving girl, readying her for rape. He gave the man no quarter, thrusting his sword into his back before helping the girl up. He bowed to her, averting his eyes from her nakedness, then ran as quickly as he was able up the marble staircase, pain jabbing through his back with every step.

The screams were coming from two rooms on the first floor, and there was blood on the marble tiles trailing from one bedchamber to the other. In the first one he entered he saw two figures lying prostrate on the bed. One was a woman of middle years, her mouth slack and open, covered in blood, no life in her glazed eyes. The other was the *sindaco*, wounded but alive, rolled in a bedsheet, his grotesque bloated belly heaving with each breath, his good arm flapping like a fish out of water.

"Sabatini, 'tis you. Save me and my daughters next door. You are a good man. Save us, for the love of God," he rasped, his voice hoarse and his eyes pleading.

Flavio looked at him in disgust and hatred: "Save you, Bastari? You who condemned me to starve and die in that stinking hellhole of a gaol, you now ask me for clemency? You, with your trumped up charges at someone else's behest, now ask that I save you? Who set you upon me? Who informed and paid for my incarceration?

"No one, no one. It was just the law, you must understand..."

"So be it, then. I shall leave you to your fate and the rape of your daughters who will be carried off to slavery as whores to the heathens." Flavio made to turn and leave the chamber.

"No, don't leave us. I will tell you everything," Bastari whispered in a dry voice, waving Flavio close to him. He listened as the mayor told him everything he wanted to know, showing no reaction at the names.

"*Grazie*," Flavio said, and with that he thrust his sword straight into the mayor's chest, killing him and leaving him in the room with his dead wife. He curled his lip at Bastari's final expression of surprise, turned with no remorse and walked out onto the landing, striding across to the second chamber, where he could hear cries of anguish and sobbing. He pushed open the double cherry wood doors to see a horrific scene before him. Two Saracens stood half naked and ready, with Manrico Bastari's daughters tied prostrate, naked and crying. Flavio did not hesitate. Two strides and he was upon the heathens, and a second later they were dead, twitching in their own blood.

He sheathed his sword, cutting the girls' bonds with his dagger. Gently he took sheets from the bed to cover them, urging the sobbing pair to come with him from the burning palazzo, where soldiers of the garrison took control of the fray upstairs and in the main grand entrance salon below.

Chapter Seven

Flavio staggered outside, supporting the two sobbing teenage daughters of the dead mayor. He saw that the night sky was now afire, throwing flickering shadows as fires raged in buildings that had been set alight by the heathen hordes who had sought to sack the town.

He gently took the girls to the safety of other women who came forward, easing them gently from his arms. They thanked him between sobs, and he sank to a stone bench that was one of many that circled the piazza, where the fountain still sprang defiantly, giving hope to all within the town that life would spring eternal. He forced himself upright, feeling suddenly tired: tired of fighting, tired of the stench of battle that he thought he had left behind forever and tired of being given no peace, for this night's affair would surely join the others in his dreams to haunt him when the demons came.

He sat upon the marble wall of the fountain and dipped his hands into it to gently wash his face. The water was cool to the touch and refreshing, and he took deep draughts of it to quench his thirst. The water relaxed him, but his hands came away smudged with soot and blood and his back ached and stung with every movement. He rinsed his face once more and looked about him as if for the first time. All was coming under control, with captured Saracens being herded and kept prisoner until they could be hanged in the morning from the walls of the town.

He pushed himself upright and walked wearily up the hill towards the Casa Cornucopia, hoping against hope to find some solace there within its walls. He arrived at the entrance, and upon being recognised in the torchlight he was admitted through a small wicket gate at the side, guarded by heavily armed servants, with two crossbowmen ready in embrasures above to skewer anything untoward that came to the gates. He came at last to the door of the *casa* and was admitted, allowed this time to keep his sword and dagger. A servant – Maria, who had been on the walls with Federica – came down the marble stairs and beckoned him to follow her. They entered Federica's bedchamber, where Flavio saw that she had bathed and cleansed herself from the bloody encounter she had endured earlier. When she saw Flavio she ran forward to embrace him muttering terms of endearment, suddenly apologetic at his wince.

"*Caro*, sorry. Come, let me attend to you, Maria is having hot water brought for a bath and I will see to your wounds better than any surgeon."

She gently began to strip off his doublet, now a torn and bloody ruin, barely in one piece. He cried out as the dried blood stuck to the skin on his back, pulling the cut apart once more. Finally naked, he slipped gently into the bath, breathing in quickly as the heat hit him and sweated the main wound. With careful strokes of a soft cloth, Federica bathed the wound and then poured brandy upon it, together with some powders of her own devising. They said little, each lost in thought and stunned by the barbarism of the night and the ferocious attack upon the *civitas*.

When he was dry she bound the wounds, particularly the one upon his back. "In the morning I will fetch my seamstress," she said. "She will stitch it together, for it is deep and will heal poorly without help. Now come to bed, *amore*." She laid him down on his front, propping pillows in the feather bed, and slid in beside him, pushing her hand through the dark curls on his head.

Flavio woke with a start as slanted slivers of light came through the shutters, his head thick from the brandy that had helped him sleep. He took a moment to realise where he was, and the events of the previous night came flooding back. He groaned when he tried to move, waking Federica, who helped him to dress and drink what felt like a gallon of water to quench his seemingly depthless thirst once more, before he insisted on finding out the circumstances surrounding his saviour from the night before. His torso was still bare when Rossanna arrived. She was a seamstress for the town and who worked principally for Federica. She had many skills, of which one was stitching wounds. They seemed never to suppurate and rot under her care, as she used brandy and poultices that kept them clean. Where she learned her skills no one knew, for she was ageless and of unknown origin, having arrived one day in Corneto many years ago like so many other pieces of driftwood that fell under Federica's spell.

She bade him sit and inspected his back, carefully removing the stained dressing Federica had put in place the previous night. She washed her hands and called for a bowl of brandy, dipping the curiously curved needle and thread into it.

"This will hurt, Signor Sabatini, for the wound is deep and the muscles are torn. Are you ready for some more pain and scars to join those others upon your poor body?" she asked, seeing the criss-cross of previous scar tissue raised and welted, white against the olive of the surrounding skin.

"Go to, *Signora,* go to, for I have endured pain before in such a cause, and before God I fear I shall again," he said, trying to relax as she began, as the wound started to weep and bleed.

Flavio sucked his breath in quickly at the first bite of the point, then it became a string of pricks and tugs as the slash from the scimitar was closed up, washed with more brandy and a poultice applied and held by a bandage securing his bruised ribs.

With her work finished, Flavio thanked her and offered to pay her for the work.

At this her true colours showed, and she scolded him: "*Porca miseria*, how dare you?" she said to him, "I do this as a gift for a man who does much to aid us here in Corneto. Aye, and one who hides behind the mask of a *vagabondo*, for who was it I saw aid the daughters of *il sindaco*, rescuing them from the terrible fate the *Saraceni* dealt to their parents and then helping them to escape the flames? Bah! Keep your coin and do well in God's eyes, for he too must have his dark angels such as you, Flavio Sabatini."

Giving him no chance to reply or argue, she bustled out of the chamber flicking her hand as she did so in dismissal of all, much to the amusement of Federica as she helped Flavio into a clean shirt and new doublet that fitted perfectly across his broad shoulders.

"Fie on you. I declare that she is the only one I know who ever gets the better of you."

Flavio shrugged in his insouciant Italian way and smiled genuinely at her. "Thank you for everything, *cara*. I shall return, but first I must solve a riddle, and one that sorely vexes my thoughts."

She frowned: "Tell me more."

"No, I am not able to do so, nor have I the time, fearing as I do for my saviour's life, yet I will return *presto*." At which he attempted a valiant bow and failed after a sharp stab of pain shot through his back.

He kissed her softly, held her for a moment, then took his sword belt and left the chamber, leaving her puzzled and shaking her head.

Half an hour later, having visited the barracks to seek out the captain from the previous evening, he found that the Saracen captive was still alive and was being held away from the others in a small holding cell in a corner of the stone barracks. He was shown to the lone cell, which he found occupied by a solemn figure who sat upon a bench in the corner. The man had his eyes closed and his hands raised in the Christian manner, and seemed to be praying. At the clanking of the door to the cell he opened his eyes and dropped his hands. His face was more angular and larger than most Saracens Flavio had seen, and one eye was partially shut from a deep bruise that was even now colouring to a deep purple. They had beaten him. Flavio was angry, for this man had saved him from death, and in return he had demanded that he be kept safe.

He bade the guard leave them, but the guard raised a querying eyebrow.

"Leave us, I say!" Flavio repeated. "Do you think that he shall attack me and try to kill me, having saved me yester eve? I believe not."

He turned back to study the man before him. He was more strongly built than a typical Saracen, less wiry, and his skin was lighter and more Mediterranean than Middle Eastern, yet he wore the typical dress and armour of a Saracen warrior.

They studied each other, each sizing the other up as warriors do. Flavio broke the silence, speaking slowly in Italian he asked: "What is your name and from where do you hail?"

The warrior before him answered in Latin, the good, high Latin of a well-educated man: "I know little of your tongue, save that it is close to Latin, a *lingua franca*," he said.

Flavio was shocked, as he had not expected this response. Flavio spoke Latin, French and some English as well as his native Italian, having been tutored by his family when growing up. He continued in Latin, asking once more his name and from where he came.

"I am Yusef..." the man paused, collecting himself "I am Bānīnā Severus of the Copts. I am a Coptic Christian, captured in my homeland of Egypt to my eternal shame and disgrace. My name translated means, *the one of chain*, or if you will a Guardian. For I led the *conroi* assigned to protect our priests when the heathen came. I am of a noble family, yet I was found wanting in our time of need."

Here he dropped his eyes in apparent shame at his inability to protect his family or the priests of his church.

"If you were captured, why were you not killed? How came you to fight alongside the heathen Saracens?"

The man continued, the words torn from him in his shame as he recounted the events that had led to his capture. "Five years ago they caught my family. They slaughtered the menfolk but held my mother and sisters captive. I was given the choice to convert to Islam and fight for them or to lose my tongue and my manhood and become a slave in their court, with my sisters and mother forced to serve all in the slave markets.

"I recently learned that my mother had died, but my sisters were rescued and smuggled away by saviours of our faith who struggle against the oppression of our lands. As they did here, the Saracens raid, sack and leave, holding no place where they can be savaged in return, until the day when they will simply conquer all by attrition."

"Please God I never see that day," Flavio opined, crossing himself.

Bānīnā Severus continued. "When I heard of my family's deliverance I thanked God and made a pledge to him that I would leave the hated forces of evil and repent by doing good in His name. I could not leave at will, for I was still watched carefully and never fully trusted in their eyes. It was merely a matter of choosing the most propitious moment. Yester eve, having watched you fight, I knew that the moment had arrived for me to change sides.

"I slaughtered those in the tower above you, pushed away their ladders, and upon seeing you kill the hordes, I knew you were a man whom I could follow, should I be spared. Thus committed to my course, I sought to aid you as you were about to be overcome."

"For which I must most heartily thank you, for indeed I was in a parlous state and wounded for lack of harness."

"Indeed, and I was glad to come to your aid." The strange Copt stood up from his hard wooden bed and bowed formally to Flavio.

"If you are true to your word, I would have you shriven, for are not your terms of faith similar to ours, if I can remember well the words of your teaching?"

"They are indeed. The Copts are a creed founded by St Mark the Evangelist some thousand years afore, and we adhere to his teachings. I would therefore most heartily welcome the chance to be shriven, for the road has been long and my sins many."

Flavio gave him a hard look and nodded, calling for the guard. He still did not trust that this man was not a Saracen spy sent here to gain trust and open the city to attack – for what better way, he reasoned, than to save one life to take many?

The guard looked askance, but upon the agreement of the captain from the previous evening he relented and allowed the Saracen prisoner to be released into Flavio's care. Severus blinked as he was led outside, Flavio keeping him on his left. They walked across the Piazza Cavour and up to the grand palazzo of Cardinal Vitelleschi. He begged entrance at the gates that were guarded by two of the cardinal's personal troops dressed in his livery of swirling silver and reds, centred with a plumed jousting helm. They were allowed to enter the cool, cloistered courtyard where they were made to wait. A marble fountain splashed in the centre, and the air was fragrant with orange blossom and jasmine. The newcomer looked upwards to the rising levels and marvelled at the magnificence of the building.

"Who resides here, for this is not a church?" he asked.

"His eminence Cardinal Vitelleschi, the highest denomination of the church in the *civitas*. It is he who, if he will see you, shall shrive you and decide upon your fate. Though I shall appeal on your behalf." Flavio was wise in the ways of the world and the actions of men of power. He knew that what he was about to do would absolve him of all responsibility by making the Copt, if that was what he was, known to the cardinal.

A servant appeared, well dressed in the apparel of a clergyman, and beckoned them to follow him. He explained: "His eminence is at his ease and offers you *signori* pre-prandial refreshment before his own luncheon that begins at midday."

"That will suit us well, for I have a boon to beg of him and him alone." Flavio said to the cleric. The man nodded, giving nothing away, and Flavio noted that they were being closely escorted by four armed guards who by their manner seemed cautious and tense. His senses were suddenly alert. Something was not quite right here, but he knew not what.

They were ushered into the main salon of Vitelleschi' s chambers on the first floor. The cardinal wore his usual benign expression that Flavio knew from bitter experience could change to full aggression and menace in the blink of an eye.

"Signor Sabatini, a good day to you. I trust you are coping with your wounds, for I hear that you did good work upon the walls of Corneto yester eve, repelling the hated heathen dogs," he said, with a provocative glance at Severus.

"Your eminence is too kind, yet I would not be standing here before you but for the efforts and offices of this man, a Copt of Egypt who was captured by the heathen and forced to fight for them. He saved my life, and I wouldst repay him in kind."

Vitelleschi looked hard at the man seeming to strip away his soul. "And how are you called?" he asked in Italian.

"He only speaks the Latin tongue, your eminence," Flavio said.

"Does he indeed?" Vitelleschi said, arching an eyebrow, and switching languages he again asked his name and how he came to be here in Corneto fighting for the Saracens. Severus felt the deep dark eyes boring into his soul as he faced interrogation by the ultimate interlocutor who sat before him. Vitelleschi began a conversation that tested the Copt's views and beliefs as they had never been tested before, invoking the scriptures and asking what they meant to him. It was a stringent examination of the man's faith, and Severus proved wise and intelligent in his answers. Flavio was pleased that he had brought him before such an eminent son of the Church.

At length, Vitelleschi nodded and agreed to hear his

confession, and Severus retired with the cardinal's guards to a small chapel where within was a small ornate wooden confessional box. His final glance back at Flavio offered a hint of reluctance, and Flavio guessed that the man's sins had been many and varied.

"Await our return, Signor Sabatini," the cardinal ordered, "for there is much I wouldst discuss with you." He motioned to the servant to fetch wine, and with a nod and flick of his hands the two guards secured the main doors to the chamber. Flavio was trapped, and liked it not, fearing the worst. He cast his mind about to find a reason that would cause such actions by the cardinal.

Chapter Eight

After a seemingly endless wait, the side door from the chapel opened and the two men re-entered the chamber. The expression upon Bānīnā Severus's face could in Flavio's eyes only be described as sublime. The haunted look that had dominated his expression seemed to have left him, as if some Damascene conversion had occurred. It was a look that could not be affected, the relaxed shoulders showed his ease, and the very lines that had been etched into his face appeared to have dissipated.

The cardinal's face, as ever, was impossible to read, yet there was no sign of relenting or pleasure when he returned to the main chamber and Flavio's presence.

"My son, you may return to the outside world. Go with my blessing and serve God," he said piously. Severus nodded, thanked the cardinal with a bow and turned to Flavio. "Signor, will you too leave now?"

"No," Vitelleschi interjected, "I have matters to attend to with Signor Sabatini. Pray leave us now." To Flavio's ears, the cardinal's seemingly innocuous words had the effect of an order that was not to be flouted.

"I shall await you without," Severus said to Flavio as he bowed to the cardinal.

"Then have great care, for there are those amongst us in the *civitas* who would wish you great harm upon seeing you," Flavio warned. Severus nodded and took his position beside a guard who would guide him below. Once he had left the room and the doors had closed, leaving just Flavio and the cardinal together, Vitelleschi began in his usual forth-right manner: "Do you trust the Saracen?"

"No. I have little trust of anyone."

"Then why aid him and seek him out to give him his liberty?"

"He saved my life in last night's melee. There was no mistake; it was a deliberate act to preserve me. And in so doing he prevented the Saracens from opening the gates," Flavio replied.

Vitelleschi probed further. "Yet still you do not trust him?"

"What better way to place a Trojan horse within our ranks than to send one of their own into our midst as a saviour? I have seen similar acts many times under Hawk-wood, who would to pay or bribe an official to open a door or gate. What better stratagem than to have one of your own within a town, allowing not just an attack but a full scale pillage of a *civitas*? For last night they came as they always do, not to conquer and hold but to sack and pillage. Yet if they were to secure command of the whole and full subjugation, they could extend their control along the cost and raid from here to secure our harbours and trade routes. Once held, Corneto is virtually impregnable, set upon the heights and cliffs as it is. The only way to conquer it would be by a long siege, which would always be relieved by Papal armies from Roma or Viterbo. So it is more likely that we should be betrayed from within."

Vitelleschi looked at his agent, knowing that he had chosen the right man, not just for his fighting prowess and ease of command, but for his ability to discern and deceive. "Bravo. So what will you do now?"

"I shall see what he wishes and act accordingly, all the time watching him closely. I shall have someone put upon him to watch his movements. If he is innocent he will wish to return to Egypt and the Copts, or seek out his family wherever they may be. If not..." Flavio shrugged. "If not, then we shall see how he prevails."

The cardinal changed direction so swiftly that Flavio felt he was in a sword fight, parrying a skilled opponent. "Now of other matters. I hear that you rescued the daughters of the *sindaco* yester eve – after killing their father, that is."

All that showed to accompany this accusation was a narrowing of the eyes. Flavio vehemently denied the claim by habit. "That is a lie. I went to his assistance, hearing cries from above and seeing the heathen within and flames threatening to burn the palazzo. I found him dying from his wounds, at which he bade me aid his daughters, whose cries and unimaginable fate was being played out in another chamber. I ran to their aid and now understand that *il sindaco* is dead, either by his wounds – for they were many – or by another's hand. For there were Saracens within the building that were still at liberty. If there are those who wouldst dispute this, have them brought forward and we shall see who has the right of it in God's eyes," he continued defiantly.

Vitelleschi deflected the final barb as though it had not been said, knowing that it would be futile to argue the point, particularly for what he had in mind. "It is of no consequence, and in point of fact it suits my purpose well. For there are those who are suspicious both within the *civitas* and without, seeing your release from gaol untarnished as an indication that you are my man. I have many spies and agents abroad in the papal states, yet you are almost unique. Not only are you an able *insidiore*, but you are able to pass amongst those who deceive the state, and you have the singular benefit of having fought in wars and possess the experience of a tried and battle hardened soldier.

"But all these qualities are of little use to me if you are treated with suspicion as my agent. Therefore, whenever the situation demands I shall have you arrested for interrogation of your potential crimes to alleviate any thoughts that you may be in my service. This is one such situation."

Flavio felt a chill dread come over him, suspecting what was to happen next. "To wit I shall have you incarcerated once more pending an investigation as to the exact circumstances of Manrico Bastari's death. No!" Vitelleschi cried as Flavio made to grasp his sword, which had been taken before he entered the chamber. "It will not be as before. You will be allowed comforts in the upper cells, and I promise it will not be for long. In return, I ask your word that you do not try to escape. Do I have it?"

Flavio's face was a mix of emotions, dominated by his hatred for this man and the coil in which he had trapped him. Yet within the anger and the desire to kill him with his bare hands he saw the futility of such an act, if indeed he could do so in his weakened and wounded state. For Vitelleschi himself had been a soldier. More warrior than priest ever he was, and he had a dagger at his belt, from which his hand rarely strayed.

Flavio forced back his anger, and with eyes glittering with a desire to kill and avenge, he nodded.

"Good," Vitelleschi said. "Even better that I know that there will be outrage from the citizens. 'What?' they shall decry, 'the hero of Corneto imprisoned upon the hour of saving us from the heathen dogs?' And in that outrage I shall have your name cleared and mine besmirched as a man of impartial justice, for would I have an agent of my own arrested?"

With this evil logic, he permitted himself a thin lipped smile and spread his hands wide with a shrug. "Guards!" He called. When they arrived, he gave them instructions to hold Flavio for a few minutes while he scratched a note of direction to the chief goaler, Gianpaolo Agneli. After this, Flavio was taken away via the small rear door through which he entered not many days ago.

Oh I have chosen well with you my son, for you will serve my ends so very well in all matters, Vitelleschi thought with a mirthless smile.

Flavio found himself locked in an airy cell at the back of the building, which meant that it was above ground by two stories due to the change in level between the front and back of the *comune* building.

It was twice the size of the cell he had but lately departed, and had a wooden bed with a mattress, pillows and blankets. He was allowed to use the garderobe, and his immediate cell door was left open. Only the final door out to the chambers was locked, secured by steel bars. A wooden table and chair were inside, with fresh watered wine from a jug. Food was to be brought regularly, he had been told, and more importantly to his mind, he was allowed visitors. Word soon spread of his incarceration, and he was visited first by his majordomo, Maurizio. The faithful servant came bearing news and gifts of wine, cheese and fresh bread. Having explained all to him, Flavio heard the surprising news.

"There is one outside who calls you master and begs to be admitted. He is dressed as a Saracen and speaks little of our tongue, and I needed the apothecary to translate from the Latin," he muttered uncertainly.

Flavio was surprised, having thought that if Severus was not a spy, he would be fearful for his life and long gone from such a potentially hostile environment. Maurizio showed him in under the watchful eye of one of the guards, who left him in Flavio's cell. Severus had cuts upon his face and there was blood on his tunic. It was as Flavio feared; he would not be looked kindly upon within Corneto, particularly in his foreign garb.

"Bānīnā, I had not expected to see you again," Flavio offered with a question in his voice. "How come you here?"

"For you, my lord."

"I am not your lord. I am no one's lord. You saved my

life, for which I am grateful, but you are free to go as you please. I will arrange for some different clothes, for in those garments you will attract attention. 'Tis bad enough that in Corneto everyone knows everyone else, and you will stand out. You will be marked as a *straniero,* at your peril." Flavio warned him.

"You must understand, my lord, that within the calling of our race I am a guardian, as I told you, and upon such precepts hang responsibilities. I have saved your life, but you too have redeemed me and in so doing saved mine. Until I have paid my debt I must protect and serve you."

"No, this cannot be. I am not one to be served blindly out of some misguided honour as you propose, and I hereby release you of any debt by which you think you are shackled."

"You cannot do that, signor, though it is honourable in itself that you should choose such a course. I am tied to you as a sea to the shore, ever to be of service."

Flavio shook his head in dismay, frustrated at this display of bondage.

"Bānīnā, this cannot be. You must leave and find your sisters. Seek them and serve them, protect them if you must. Leave me in peace to fight whom I will." At which point Maurizio returned with clothes for the Copt.

Severus accepted them with good grace and asked where he should await Flavio's release. Flavio sighed with irritation and switched from Latin to Italian. "Maurizio, take him to the palazzo. Give him some work, yet trust him not. I will deal with him upon my release." At which he turned back to

Bānīnā and reverted to Latin, instructing him to follow Maurizio.

Once they had departed, he sat and reflected upon his circumstances. The cardinal was as ruthless as he supposed, yet he could not fault his reasoning. It did not change his feelings, and if he could kill him and get away with the deed, he would surely do so. More than that, he pondered what Vitelleschi would want of him upon his release. What deeds would he require done? To run a papal army? He had after all referred to Flavio's skills as a soldier. Only time would tell. Meanwhile he needed to rest and consider the information the mayor had given him before Flavio had killed him.

He needed to consider the fate of the Salimbeni family.

Chapter Nine

Flavio was held in the cell for three days, during which time he wrote letters to his head of estates giving orders on what was to be done and asking to be informed if they were attacked as some other outlying estates in and around Corneto had been. It seemed that all those estates to the north were spared, and only those to the south and the outlying areas of Civitavecchia had been ravaged by the Saracens. He found to his relief that his estate had been spared, although a series of watch fires had been lit all along the Marta valley alerting everyone to the offensive, and all possible precautions had been taken. His estate was like a small, fortified manor, a castle with half turreted towers giving good lines of sight for crossbows, and he even had a small band of English archers that had returned with him from the north and his days as a *condottieri*. There were many who had left England with Hawkwood to fight for the White Company, and some had married Italian women and were now wealthy in their own right. Their fortunes were far improved over what they could ever hope to be back in England – where even now he heard that the new King Henry was fighting to keep control of a land riven by the tyranny of the previous king.

With such defences it would take a large and well-disciplined army a long time to overrun or besiege Flavio's estate, but all it took was one traitor to leave a gate unlocked or betray his comrades and all would be lost. For now Flavio put himself at his ease and enjoyed receiving visitors. Signora Rossanna came each day to tend his wounds, as did Federica, causing comment and scandal amongst the town merchants' wives. Yet all were of one accord on one account: everyone from the lowliest garrison soldier to the highest merchant praised Flavio's name and protested his incarceration outside the doors of Cardinal Vitelleschi's palazzo, demanding that he should be released and all charges dropped against him in the matter of the death of Manrico Bastari.

Flavio learned that Vitelleschi had interviewed certain witnesses who came forward, but none could prove that he had killed the mayor. Even Bastari's daughters claimed that he had saved them and had tried to protect their father. When he was released the town was happy, but four days later he found himself once more in the cardinal's palazzo for another audience with his eminence.

"The findings of the papal court are that you are innocent of any crimes concerning the death of *il sindaco.* You are therefore released with full honour and the gratitude of the mother church," Vitelleschi said piously.

Flavio said nothing on that account. He raised an

eyebrow and asked with a degree of asperity: "Then I am free to go, your eminence?"

"You are – once I have asked you for one small favour." The cardinal continued, with little regard for Flavio's feelings on the matter. He steepled his fingers on the desk before him, his rings gleaming in the sunlight that entered through the open casements. "Let me explain," he said. "The wars in which you and indeed I fought in the name of freedom are at an end, but so is the political influence of the Papal States. Before, it was *civitas* against *civitas*, but now the states are coming together under new condottieri. You will have heard their names. They are men from your past who seek to conquer and amalgamate the towns to form new states, bending them to their will. Foremost amongst them is the Duke Visconti of Milano, who seeks, I am told, to be called king of Italy upon conquering Firenze."

"This cannot be," Flavio responded. "I have heard of the success of Visconti, and he is a mighty force who fills the void left by Hawkwood, yet these are strong forces that would oppose all and to try to unite Italy? Pah! He will not succeed – in especial within Firenze, who would call such forces to their aid and pay them in coin the like of which no other town could match, with the exception perhaps of Venezia."

"Then you are out of touch, for already Visconti seeks victory and has Firenze in the palm of his hand. He comes from the north and the Gascons of Bertrand de la Salle and Bernardon de Serres hold sway of lands north of Roma. If these forces somehow became united under a single banner whether by force or by means of an allegiance, why then Roma would fall, and with the schism having weakened the church all would be lost. The town of Viterbo is the key, lying as it does in the middle, twixt the two main seats of power. As the state capital, if Viterbo should fall under the influence of Visconti, then he would indeed be king of Italy in all but name – aye and that will soon follow," Vitelleschi grimaced.

"What would you have me do, your eminence?" Flavio said with little enthusiasm, as a part of him knew the answer to that question.

"I would have you do me the service of seeking out what plans are afoot in Viterbo and meeting with one of my agents there to find out what you may and put an end to any plots that may be fomenting."

"Viterbo is one of the most strongly fortified towns in Italy, and if it is well provisioned, an army would take months to lay siege and capture the town," Flavio reasoned carefully.

"I have chosen well with you, my son. Yet consider, if one such as your Saracen were inside, ready to open a gate and allow the enemy to enter, then the city would likely fall. I recall this happening more than once in the company's wars of the *condottieri*, did it not?"

Flavio nodded his agreement, recalling how Hawkwood and others had paid for deception and bribed traitors to betray their own. "I have agents there, my own *insidiores*, and not just priests and papal envoys," Vitelleschi continued. "And there is one, an apothecary by calling, who will direct you and aid you as he may. As you would expect, he is well connected and knows many within the town. He is loyal to me for various reasons, and will be expecting you within the week. When will you next have reason to venture forth?"

The light tone of explanation was now gone and the steel was back in the cardinal's voice, still calm yet somehow menacing to Flavio's ears. The question was a thinly concealed order, he realised.

"I needs must sail back up river to visit Lago di Bolsena in a sennight. I can disembark the boat on the way inland and ride from there. No one will see me go or be any the wiser as to my true destination," he offered.

"'Twill do well for all concerned. The agent's name is Signor Ceasar Dezi. I shall write down the details of where he may be found and how you need to identify yourself – for I warn you, he will be suspicious and guards his position like a jealous lover."

"I look forward to making his acquaintance, yet I shall tread warily," Flavio said, once again with minimal enthusiasm.

"Afore you go, how does your Saracen?" Vitelleschi asked provocatively.

Flavio sighed in irritation. "He is neither mine nor a Saracen. The Copt visited me in gaol and asked to serve me. Though how that is possible and not vice versa I know not, for it was he who saved my life, not the other way around. He seems to labour under a strange bond of obligation, to what end I know not."

"Then have a care, yet watch him and use him to your ends, for mayhap he will have information on the Saracens that will prove useful. Should you find out anything of use, pray do inform me of such intelligence."

"I shall make it a priority, your eminence." Flavio replied with more than a hint of sarcasm, which Vitelleschi deflected with a grin that was entirely devoid of humour. Flavio made a brief genuflection and turned, collecting the vellum message from the cardinal's clerk as he left.

Go with God my son, Vitelleschi thought, *for where you travel I fear you shall need all his protection. Yet in many ways I fear more for those who rise against you, for you are the very Devil when roused, as I myself have witnessed.*

Flavio left the palazzo, cursing to himself at the snare in which he had become trapped. He found the faithful Maurizio waiting for him outside with two horses. He thanked him, taking the reins in his hand and mounting, feeling the stitches pull in his back as he did so, taking care not to rip the wound open again after all Rossanna's hard work.

"I heard that you were to be released. The cardinal seemed to make no secret of the matter, and frankly I rejoice in it, for it was wrong that they should persecute you so." He paused, waiting until they set off away from the guards who gave a brief nod of approval at seeing Flavio released. They rode down the cobbled Via Di Porta Castello and passed under the double turrets of the guard house out, along the *rivelino* and finally through the Porta Di Castello e Torrione gateway to overlook the Marta valley. Once away from the gatehouse Maurizio asked quietly, searching his master's face for an indication. "So did you kill Bastari?"

Flavio laughed out loud at the seriousness of Maurizio's question. "Of course I did," he said. "I swore on the saints I would. The whoreson dog had me falsely imprisoned and consigned to a terrible death by starvation and rot. A few more weeks and I would have been dead or so ill as to never recover. With that act alone he put me in servitude to that devil Vitelleschi, who is as devout as a whorehouse, and has more vices than I can count.

"Yet here I am a free man again – or as free as I can be whilst chained to that cardinal of sin. I chose my time well in the battle, and with the Copt's intervention I was able to lose myself, knowing full well that the Saracens who were sacking the town would choose the wealthiest houses. Yet it was not just on Manrico Bastari's whim that Vitelleschi should persecute me so. We have a traitor in our midst, and there are those within the town who paid him to get rid of me. The power comes from above, from Salimbeni no less, for he seeks full sway over all the lands to the north and the Maremma. He no doubt sought to take my trade upon the rivers and all the profit and power that goes with it. For all is wrapped together in a fight for power.

"And of matters to do with the raid upon the town, how does Pietro, for I saw him fall upon the ramparts?" Flavio asked.

Maurizio shook his head: "He fell at my side and later died of his wounds. There was nothing we could do."

Flavio crossed himself: "May God rest his soul. Then they will pay. For this was no raid of opportunity, and once again someone informed upon us. The Watch was slack and the walls weak and unfinished. We were preyed upon from all sides. And now I learn that Viterbo itself is threatened from within." Flavio shook his head. "And of threats, how does the Copt, Severus? Did he follow my order and seek shelter within the palazzo? And if so, do we have our own wooden horse of Troy within our walls?"

Maurizio shrugged. "I know not. He speaks little Italian and my Latin is poor. Yet he is skilled with a blade, having retrieved his own arms from the sergeant of the garrison, including his recurved bow. Our English archers are suspicious of him, and they are sure he is a Saracen. Yet even they cannot but envy his skill at arms. Though I wouldst not give you two florins for that curved blade against full plate the like of which you wear to war. Full Milanese harness will not be pierced by a weapon of such lightness.

"The bow is of a different matter, though. There is power there that will pierce maille, if not at the distance of our English archers and their war bows. As to his loyalty, I know not." Maurizio finished. After a brief pause he sought to know more of Flavio's words with Vitelleschi and asked when he planned to travel inland.

"I needs must heal more and have Rossanna look once more at my back afore I leave. Yet it itches, and that is a good sign as I know of old. We shall sail up river in a sennight. Grain and more await us at Lago di Bolsena, and I shall leave you to make the trade. If they try to cheat us, tell him I will return with *condottieri* and burn their warehouses to the ground."

"Where do you go?"

"I shall leave the boat near the thermal baths and take a horse from there. I am to meet with an apothecary, an agent in the employ of Vitelleschi. He has news for me of men he suspects are working against us and the Papal States, who would I assume side with both Visconti and Salimbeni against Rome. I do not need to tell you how appalling it would be if Viterbo came once more under the influence of those such as the Di Vico family. Recall how their benign influence and corruption nearly destroyed the city? The papacy must hold sway for the good of us all."

"Yet to go in amongst such a nest of vipers with no one to guard your back does not sit well," Maurizio replied.

"Fear not for me, for I have a friend there in the apothecary, and I can call upon papal guards if needs must," Flavio replied. Yet a deep cold gnawed in his gut at the prospect of digging deeply into Viterbo's nether world, knowing that he could trust no one. He sloughed off this foreboding and pressed on, riding down the steep twisting road towards his home nestling in the valley below.

When he entered he found a display in progress that was turning into more of a competition. On a piece of sward to the side of the palazzo encircled by a low internal wall, a butt had been set up by the English contingent of his archers. To one side of it stood Bānīnā Severus, now dressed in western clothes, a quiver – or what he was to learn was called a bow case by Severus – strapped to his waist and angled so the flights were pointing backwards for ease of withdrawal. But what was stranger to his eyes was that he had three more arrows held comfortably in his draw hand, allowing him to nock, draw, loose and hold more arrows simultaneously between his fingers.

Flavio noticed two other odd things: Bānīnā drew the bowstring using his thumb alone, locked it in place with his index finger with the arrow on the side furthest away from the archer, not on the near side as with western bows. One of the English bowmen, Will Humbert, called out ready and the two men pitted themselves against each other. Bānīnā's arm became a blur as he loosed four arrows in the time it took Will to loose two. They travelled not as far or as accurately in the faster time, but Flavio realised the devastation that would be caused by such an arrow storm if many fired at once into massed ranks of an enemy.

"Flavio, by the good Lord, Bani seems to shoot right fast, tho' he do it right strange. On 'orseback too, mind," Will commented as Flavio approached.

He spoke in the strange coarse tongue of the English, which always sounded harsh to Flavio's ears and had strange rules of grammar. Yet it had oft been used in the ranks of the *condottieri* run by Hawkwood, and it was essential that Flavio learned to communicate with all ranks who often only had a little Norman French. He also noticed how they had shortened Bānīnā's name in the manner of so many English he had encountered. It seemed to suit the Copt, and was easier on the tongue.

"So it seems. How is the draw?" Flavio nodded to the strange little bow.

"Light by our bows, maybe half the draw, yet they get the killin' done at shorter distances, by the Lord Harry so they do. But not through plate, I'll wager. For that you'll need a good war bow of stout yew to see the job done," he finished, nodding down at his own bow.

Flavio nodded and came forward to meet Bānīnā – or Bani as he seemed now to be called. The Copt bowed slightly to Flavio, who gave a nod in acknowledgement. "My lord, I am grateful to you for your aid to my cause and for permitting me to serve you," he said.

Flavio shook his head. He did not like or appreciate this level of humility and dependence. "'Tis of no consequence, and you are free to leave at any time, for I will not have you indebted to me. Remember that it was you who saved my life before I saved yours," he added brusquely.

The others watched this byplay, unable to understand it as it was in Latin, yet the tone spoke volumes.

Part Two

Viterbo

Chapter Ten

Viterbo: A week later

The skiff made good progress up the river Marta, sailing on the inbound tide with its main sail up to catch the following breeze. It was early morning and barely daylight, and the air was still cool before the heat of the day could rob it of all moisture. A heavy dew had gilded the grass, and the wheat had been harvested, leaving fields that had been a sea of green when Flavio had last been here shorn, with only golden stubble and dust to show. The soil itself was laid out in swathes of different clay, and the land changed colour as the miles passed.

Flavio did not fear an attack, as the hold was empty apart from two horses carefully stabled in loose boxes that were easily erected and dismantled yet sufficiently robust to prevent the animals from panicking. Carbone, being from the Marema, was used to boats and fretted not at the motion of the waves or the tang of the sea.

Flavio wanted none to know of his business or his

comings and goings, and with the dawn just lifting, few souls would be about as he heard the church bells ring Lauds to start the day. As the skiff made its slow progress up river in the peace of the morning, he considered again the reputation of the Salimbeni family and the influence that its members wrought, not just throughout the Maremma but elsewhere, affecting Flavio's own life and finances. Yes, all knew of their lust for power, but there were links missing in the chain, both small and large. Who above the Salimbeni pulled the strings of the mawmets, Flavio mused, and just as importantly, who controlled the local towns that would allow them to conquer larger cities like Viterbo – towns that held the key to Italy itself? Maybe these questions would be answered when he met with the apothecary, and that would suit his own ends as much as those of his master, Vitelleschi.

He passed the time teaching Bani Italian. Over the last week or so his companion had improved greatly, finding it in many ways a poor man's version of Latin, with many similar words. The Copt had insisted on accompanying Flavio to Viterbo, and with some reluctance Flavio had agreed. Bani's outward appearance had changed, and he now sported a trimmed beard in the Italian style. His hair had been cut and he wore Italian clothes. Only his armament gave any indication that he was anything other than a typical Italian servant or soldier, for he preferred his scimitar and buckler and had his bow in its bag attached to the saddle of his horse.

They came at length to the small jetty where they could disembark. The horses were easy enough to unload, going straight from the skiff to the jetty that overlapped the side of the skiff slightly at one point, meaning that all they had to do was step up a slight lip and they were effectively on firm footing. They were skittish after their journey on the water, sidling and prancing a little, and even Carbone pretended to be ill at ease until Flavio smoothed his coat and rubbed his muzzle with a gloved hand before blowing gently into the animal's nostrils. Carbone calmed and snorted once more, settled with the familiar scent of his master. Tightening the girths, both men drew down the stirrup irons, slid in a booted foot and mounted easily. Flavio noticed hardly any strain upon his wound now, other than a slight tug as he pulled upwards.

Looking around, he saw two buildings, one a tavern, the other a large warehouse with a tiled roof that sealed it against the elements. Here was a dropping off point, a trading post serving all roads in every direction of the compass. He had struck many a deal here at the inn of Il Grappolo, and would strike many more in the future, he hoped. The owner took a small percentage of each deal and was happy with his lot, as it added to the custom.

He turned to his major domo. "Maurizio, when you return do not tarry here long, save but to trade with Gubbio," he said. "If we are not here, wait not more than a day before returning to the safety of Corneto. The roads will become more dangerous, and I fear spies reporting of where and what we do. They will be constructing a new jetty for me upstream from the palazzo. Look for it, and if has been finished, unload there, for the waggons will be waiting."

Maurizio nodded in agreement, and waved reluctantly as they pushed off upstream, now needing oars to supplement the breeze as the river twisted and turned as they made their way onwards to Lago di Bolsena.

They passed the thermal baths that even now gave off steam into the sunny haze of the morning as the stiff welcoming breeze took the clouds of moisture inland. It was less than twenty leagues to the trading port, and they made good time, setting off on horseback from the lakeside towards the city of Viterbo.

The two men rode easily in the heat, not pushing the horses, yet the animals broke into a sweat before long, the white flecking of foam upon their thick necks as they pulled up the rising road towards the city. Passing beneath a row of lime trees that covered the approach, Flavio paused once more to take stock of the mighty walled fortress that was the principal place of governance and administration for the state of northern Lazio. At one time he knew that it had even surpassed Rome, when the popes had fled to set up their court here in a place of safety against the warring factions to the south.

"There she is, Bani. Beautiful and mighty, is she not?" he said, speaking slowly in Italian so that his companion could gain the meaning of the words.

Bani replied in kind. "Indeed, yet she is well built for defence, and it would needs must take a mighty siege to conquer her."

Flavio nodded in response, eyeing everything with the eye of *condottieri*, wondering not for the first time how he would take the mighty town. The walls of mellow tufa rose to a height of nearly fifty feet, and looked well-nigh impregnable to his eyes. At last they came to the huge gates of the

Porta Fiorentina, with its triple arches covering two smaller entrances that flanked the main arch and gates. They made for the left hand arch, where guards were watching all who entered the city carefully. One recognised Flavio from previous visits, and passed a ribald remark to which he responded in kind. Another nodded to a man loitering by an internal gate, eating an apple as though he had not a care in the world. The man caught the nod, threw the core away, wiped his hands upon his hose and sauntered off easily behind Flavio and Bani, merging with the crowds. Flavio motioned that they follow the Via Cairoli that would take them to the centre and the Piazza San Plebiscito, then on from the direction provided by Vitelleschi's note to the area known as San Pellegrino. And there lay the soul of the city, where all commerce was abroad, away from the papal castle and palace. Here were his people, and it was an area he knew well.

Everywhere they looked there was bustle and endeavour, with the smells of human existence much stronger here than in Corneto, being five times its size. Everything was traded upon its streets, from grain to cloth, and this day there had been a market and the strong smell of sheep still lingered in the air, made more pervasive by the heat that seemed to cloy the nostrils with every breath they took. As the street rose upwards, the shoes of the horses slipped once or twice upon the crushed slimy dung left across the cobbles as they sought better purchase, releasing a sweet, sickly scent of their passing as they rode on.

They came to the Piazza San Plebiscito, and Bani marvelled at the elegance of the arched porticoes and the elegant proportions of the ochre coloured buildings. In the centre stood the beautiful white marble tower of Santa Rosa, spitting forth water from it fountains.

They passed through the busy piazza, brushing through the throngs of crowds and the market stalls, avoiding the hawking vendors. Flavio nodded to this man or that as he was recognised and saw familiar faces in his turn. Passing through to the south side, the crowds parted in front of the large black stallion, who tossed his head in disgust at being held up by them. Allowing no time for them to move, he pushed forward, raising curses from those who were too slow to heed his snorts of irritation.

They made for the San Pellegrino district through the eponymous piazza that was almost intimate in comparison to the larger San Plebiscito. Arches and small balconies surrounded the square, and the smell of wealth and power radiating from the surrounding tall stone towers was as strong as the stench of sewage upon the surrounding streets, defining the moral decay of its occupants. Men looked out from their talk of business and commerce, and despite the smaller dimensions this was the heart of the city, where true power lay.

The stone walls of the houses and shops narrowed in the smaller street, which led onto a side street, the Via Centoponti. Above them, stone bridges crossed, making the way still darker and gloomier, and both men shivered as the stark sunlight was shut out. With Flavio hoping that it was not a portent of doom, he halted, checking once more the number of the house he sought. *Thirty four*, he noted.

"Come, Bani, dismount and I will enquire whether

Signor Dezi is within," he said as the two men slipped off their horses. Leaving Bani holding the reins, he pushed through the door of the shop under the pestle & mortar sign denoting its identity as an apothecary. The door, Flavio noticed, was partially glazed, an extravagance, as glass was expensive and bespoke of the success of its owner. A small bell tinkled as Flavio entered, announcing his presence.

The inside of the shop was small and well kept, its walls lined with wooden shelves. The smell of spices, herbs and potions filled the air. A long, polished wooden counter stood to one side, and Flavio saw a door open behind it to admit a man who was broad of shoulder, still in his prime. His dark skin was swarthy, showing that he had seen some sun rather than being trapped within the confines of the shop. He wore an apron around his waist, covering his doublet and hose. His neat, pointed beard was well groomed and the eyes wary even in repose. The smile he offered Flavio did not quite meet them.

"*Buongiorno, sono* Flavio Sabatini," Flavio began. "I am here to ask for a Signor Ceasar Dezi, are you he?" he asked.

"*Piacere,* I am Ceasar Dezi, how may I be of service to you?" the man responded, his voice gruff and deep, his large hand spread wide to receive him.

"I have come at the request of a mutual acquaintance," Flavio paused, ready to reel off the words he had been taught, claiming a bad headache. "I have a terrible *mal di testa,* and wonder if you could prescribe something for me."

Signor Dezi gave him a searching look as though suddenly realising what was required in response. "Ah, then come this way," he said. "For we shall be more intimate in my chamber within."

Flavio was surprised, yet nodded in acquiescence as Dezi came around the counter with an open arm extended and went to the front door, bolting it. "We do not wish to be disturbed," he explained.

Flavio raised an eyebrow and went forward through the doorway, sensing a quickening of pace from behind as he moved through to the next chamber. He jumped sideways to the left, which was the best move to avoid a right handed assailant. Flavio dropped into the room, extended his hands into a forward roll, following through with the momentum to gain his feet, facing back towards his suspected opponent, his hands raised, holding his rondel dagger, blade extended downwards.

The man came on fast, recovering from his downward dagger strike, his blade now held horizontal and his clenched fist levelled as though to punch, yet the move would be much more deadly. It was, Flavio recognised, the posture of an assassin who was skilled in the art of killing with a stiletto. All artifice of amiability was now lost, and the man's teeth were bared in a merciless grimace as he came forward, balanced perfectly on the balls of his feet, left hand forward for distraction, swinging, jabbing to and fro.

Flavio knew the signs and let him come on, obliquely hooking his foot around a stool which he swept forward, the seat skidding along the floor as his attacker made to slash at him. He stumbled in his haste, unbalanced, and with a sweep of his leg, Flavio turned to the side, driving the point of the dagger into the extended forearm of his attacker, wanting him alive. The man was brave. Dropping his blade from his injured arm, he reached up with his left hand to secure the weapon and drove upwards, seemingly immune to the pain in his right arm. It was a good ploy, and one that almost caught Flavio by surprise as he continued his movement to the side, avoiding the point of the dagger. He jumped back as the deadly blade came for his groin, and with no choice he drove his own dagger down to the exposed shoulder, forcing its point straight into the joining of the neck and trapezius muscle, the long blade piercing deep to the chest and lungs. Bright red blood sprang forth, and Flavio's opponent gulped and doubled up in agony, wheezing as he tried to find his breath. Flavio withdrew his dagger to a sucking sound from the tri-tined blade. His attacker fell back, a hacking cough wracking his body as he tried in vain to speak as the internal bleeding took its toll.

"Drink ... water ..." he pleaded, and Flavio turned to fetch a flagon from the table. As he did so he saw another figure lying trussed and unconscious upon the floor. This one would wait, he decided, and returned to the dying man, offering him water as the cool liquid splashed from the flagon into his mouth.

Flavio put a hand behind the man's next and raised his head. "Who are you and on whose orders do you act?" he demanded.

"Told to ... silence the old man ... Couldn't be allowed to spy ..." he coughed again, bringing up blood.

"Who told you to kill him? Who? Tell me?" he ordered.

"Go to ... the church ... for answers ..." At this the life left his eyes, which stared sightlessly at the ceiling.

Flavio let the man's head fall in disgust, cursing him. He wiped the blade of his dagger on his jupon and rose to cut the bonds of the unconscious bound figure lying under the table. As he released him he gently slapped his face and brought water to his dry lips, noticing a bruise already turning purple on his jaw. The man coughed as consciousness returned, a groan coming from his lips, and as the eyes flicked open showing alarm, he raised his hands in fear.

"*Con calma*, signor," Flavio said. "I wish you no harm. Your attacker lies dead there," he pointed. A series of rapid knocks came from the shop's front door, and Flavio realised it must be Bani trying to come to his aid. He helped the older man up. "Are you Signor Ceasar Dezi?" he asked him.

"I am he, and I thank you for your aid, for I feared that I was dead – or worse, to be imprisoned and tortured for my sins."

"And what sins would they be?" Flavio asked, not wishing to be taken in a second time.

"Those of a certain cardinal. Who are you?"

"I am Flavio Sabatini at your service," he answered with a flourish, "and if I did not have a *mal di testa* before, then I most certainly do now."

Dezi smiled for the first time. "Ah, then I am indeed in your debt as God is my witness, for I thought that I should perish. And I am expecting you."

Before any more could be said the sound of an argument and a struggle came from outside the rear door of the room, which was flung open to show Bani holding a young woman, who was flourishing a dagger trying to stab him as he sought to grab her wrist.

"My daughter Ilaria, leave her be!" Signor Dezi shouted in anguish.

Flavio repeated the words in Latin and Bani stood back quickly, avoiding the blade as he released her wrist and holding both hands before him to parry any further attack from the spirited young woman.

"Let us have some calm, for there is much confusion here and we are all of the same side," Flavio said to her gently. "This man is Bani Severus. He is of my household, and he means you no harm, signorina. Bani, unbolt the front door and see to the horses, for I trust no one and there may be more. Thieves and assassins rarely work by themselves, there is always a lookout." Bani nodded and left the room with a sour look from the Dezi's daughter, who rubbed her wrist and then stooped to help her father rise and then sit in a chair, firing off fast questions at him.

Flavio assessed both figures. Ceasar Dezi was a man of middle years with an intelligent face, well-formed and angular, his dark hair showing flecks of grey, parted in the middle in a widow's peak beneath his felt hat. A pair of pince-nez spectacles that were usually balanced upon the bridge of his long nose were now hanging from a gold chain round his neck. He had a knowing look upon his face, as though he was sharing a secret with himself and smiling at the knowledge.

His frame was well filled, but his body had not yet run to fat, and his shoulders were slightly stooped, Flavio assumed from constantly being hunched over his bench preparing potions and grinding ingredients.

Ilaria was a different matter. She was a young woman in

her late teens or early twenties, Flavio supposed. Her dark hair flowed in curls to below her shoulders, surrounding an oval face that probably favoured her mother rather than her father. She was beautiful, high cheeked and full lipped, standing around five and a half feet, her figure hidden beneath a flowing silk *houppelande* of iridescent turquoise. Her eyes were flaming with outrage and concern for her father, and she looked to blame Flavio until she turned and caught sight of the dead assassin, whereupon her attitude changed.

"*Scusi,* signor, I thought you one of them, and I would thank you for saving my father," she muttered, the words seemingly torn from her.

Chapter Eleven

That evening, Flavio and Bani returned to share supper with the Dezis in their apartment above the shop. They had bespoken rooms at a local *osteria* that Dezi had recommended, *La Locanda delle Capra.*

The older man was now looking much better, despite the swollen jaw where the assassin had struck him. Flavio had helped him load the dead man onto a cart to be tossed unceremoniously over the city walls under cover of darkness, as though this was the most natural thing to do.

"I need to understand more of the situation here in Viterbo," Flavio said. "Cardinal Vitelleschi advised me as well as he was able, yet it is insufficient if I am to root out the elements that may betray the city."

Signor Dezi shrugged, and his daughter looked on with concern in her face. "The city, like many," he began, "is pulled and pushed by money and power as each faction tries to vie for position. Even within the guilds there is often little loyalty. The *Signoria* is governed by people who strive for power, as happens in Firenze and Siena.

"That is the secular struggle, but above that you have the power of the church itself, backed by a papal army that is here ostensibly for the protection of the mother church. Then there are the noble families such as the di Vicos, who even though they were ousted from dominance years ago still wield power and influence – albeit supposedly benign – again through the *Signoria* and the *classe artigenale, classe di cambio and classe nobile.*

"With all these factions vying for position and dominance, one needs to ask only two questions: who stands to gain the most and who stands to lose the most if forces alien to the city were able to enter and gain control?"

"And?" Flavio asked, intrigued at the logic behind Dezi's summation.

"And there are many answers to those two simple questions, and many reasons behind them. But one thing is certain; if the Salimbeni family was successful in taking over the city and commanding in some way or other – even passing that power on to a higher command – then the church itself would be the biggest loser. Of that there is no doubt in my mind."

"So the church loses, and its dominance of the area would be lost along with it, which is as much as Vitelleschi told me," Flavio said. "For then, he said, the path would be open to take Rome itself and maybe join with the Colonna family, creating an unholy alliance against the Holy father and supplanting him with their own man, as was their ambition from the beginning.

"So we have as ever the church on one side, the Salimbeni and Visconti families on the other, along with the Colonna family, and in the middle forces as yet unknown who would sell their soul to obtain command of this city with all that entails. By God's grace it is a coil, and as bad as any of the political machinations and duplicity I encountered in the northern Papal states in my years fighting for first one side then another, according to whim or money," Flavio opined, forgetting himself for a moment.

"You were a *condottieri*?" Ilaria asked, aghast.

"*Si, signorina*, I was. But that was a long time ago, and now I am a peaceful man of trade who merely serves the cardinal where I may," he answered.

"And why would one with such a past choose to do this?"

"To salve my soul and conscience, my lady," Flavio answered suavely.

She arched an eyebrow and looked pointedly at where the assassin had lain. The floor still bore a damp stain.

Flavio ignored the look and asked her father more about who could and could not be trusted. "And if you take such care, who do you think may have ordered this attack upon you? Will you now be safe, or do you need to leave the city?"

"As to the first question, I could think of a few people who may suspect my involvement with the papacy, setting me against their interests," Signor Dezi replied. "As to the future safety of myself and my daughter, I know not. Mayhap now that you are here they will not be so obvious, and bide their time in taking any further steps against us."

Flavio said nothing, but he considered it a strange

response from one who had come so close to death only a few hours ago. He said nothing more on the matter, accepting wine poured for him by Ilaria as both he and Bani tucked into their supper of fine white bread – from the harvests of Corneto, no doubt – and a dish of minced pork in a rich fennel sauce that was so typical of the area. The dish was as good as he had ever tasted, and he complimented Ilaria upon her cooking. He received the first favourable expression from her since making her acquaintance. Flavio quietly noted this with a secret smile. *So, then, not completely immune to my charms,* he thought.

The apothecary cut through his thoughts. "Tomorrow you will go to meet with another of my calling on the other side of the city. I will give you a script bearing a formula, and this shall be your password. If you do not receive the correct ingredients then he shall be false or under pressure from unseen watchers. Be wary, for this city is already under siege."

Flavio nodded. He had been given the same kind of code by Vitelleschi for his first meeting with Signor Dezi, with no response in kind given by the assassin and no chance given to provide the correct answer, warning him that all may not be well. It was a good system, as innocent as it was infallible, because none but those within the calling would know the answer to a seemingly innocuous question.

The following day he set out on foot through the thronging streets of Viterbo, aware that he could be and almost certainly was being followed. Whoever had harmed Signor Dezi would be watching closely when the hired assassin did not return. He strode forward, heading north-west for the Piazza San Lorenzo and the Cathedral of San Lorenzo near the papal palace.

The streets were narrow and shrouded in shadow by the arches and overhanging stone buttresses. They were already filled with the effluence of the night's soil, and he trod carefully, weaving as he went and avoiding the hawkers and the shop's boys seeking trade, the smell of new bread fragrant in one street and in another the clean smell of fresh cloth woven away in Florence, now for sale in the heart of the town. Spices merged for dominance in this feast for the olfactory senses as he turned down on the via Vallecuppa, the street sloping away from him. He called at a small bar offering refreshment, where he ate a sweetmeat and sipped watered wine.

Bani fell in innocuously by his side, placing his own order and whispering: "You are followed."

Flavio nodded almost imperceptibly. He had asked the Copt to follow him at a distance, leaving the *osteria* a minute or so behind him. Bani had thankfully proved competent at such shadowing. Flavio finished his mouthful, called the owner over to pay, pressed two coins more than he needed into his palm and with permission slipped out through the back door into the alley behind. He exited the rear door warily, for if he was following someone himself, this is how he would ambush his man. He had done such things in many towns over the years, seeking a prey within the confines of alleys and dark streets. Flavio thought he was finished with this life, but as he fell all too easily back into it, the frisson of excitement at the hunt and danger returned, sending the blood coursing through his veins and sharpening his senses.

He trod lightly, knowing danger was near at every corner and in every shadow. He reached the piazza and turned left to face the imposing façade of the grand cathedral, adjacent to which was a soaring tower, striped in contrasting stone and marble. Its large, curved casements were mullioned and grand, offering unsurpassed views over the city, and a delicate tower surmounted the whole, giving it a regal appearance. No doubt some wealthy merchant's home, Flavio decided, seeing it as a useful point of reference when navigating the streets.

He looked left and right, seeing neither Bani nor anyone who may be following him. He found that he had lost the prickling at his neck that came when danger threatened borne of long journeys on dangerous roads, and he strode off past the infirmary down the via San Antonio, seeing once more the sign of a pestle and mortar. It was no doubt a productive position, with the apothecary shop so close to the infirmary. Pushing open the door he was again assailed with the same smells and sights as the day before when he had first set foot in Dezi's shop. Wooden shelves lined the walls, laden with tall glass bell jars, each marked with a label denoting the contents in Latin written in copperplate script.

A smiling man, younger than Signor Dezi, came forward to stand behind the counter. He was handsome and of honest countenance, Flavio decided, asking the question Dezi had told him.

The young man smiled benignly and replied with the lines of the formula Signor Dezi had given him in the correct order, finishing with charcoal as the final piece of the code. Satisfied, Flavio continued.

"Signor Dezi sends his felicitations and asks that you help me to acquire greater knowledge of any and all who may be disloyal to the virtue of the city. You should know that an attempt was made upon his life yester eve, though he is safe, praise be to God," Flavio intoned piously. He had wanted to test the reaction of his new acquaintance, whose name he learned was Stefano Ventolini.

"*Dio mio!*" He cried out in alarm. "And his daughter, is she safe too?" There was an edge of genuine concern to his words. For Flavio, this was the final test, and when he nodded, Stefano beckoned him into his chamber in the rear, leaving his assistant to watch the front shop while they talked in private.

They settled in a rear chamber, where Stefano offered all he knew. "The *Signoria* is still guided and overseen as *podesta* by Giovanni di Sciarra di Vico. His family's influence is manifest, and after being thwarted by the *Signoria* and the papacy in the past, it would suit him well if he could be reinstated as the puppet for Visconti, holding the city as the last impediment before Rome with an army of mercenaries at his back.

"And the merchants, for their part – well you know them of old, I am sure. They are weather vanes that spin to and fro as the wind blows, ever seeking greater profit and with that power; for the towers of babel they build represent the dominance of each, and are like small fortresses within any town. The mentality of the mercantile classes is as transparent as their methods."

"And what of the Papacy? Cardinal Pielo I hear is close to the Holy Father."

Stefano nodded with a Latin shrug, a downward turning of the mouth and his thick eyebrows raised. He tilted his well-formed head: "*Si,* as you say, they maintain power in their own right, and there is of course the papal palace here which acts as a governance in its own right, mostly benign unless forced to act. No outward force can be invoked without due reason – and upon such restraint does danger lie," he warned.

"So what do you advise?" Flavio asked, confused as to how he should proceed.

"My advice, for what it is worth, is to invest yourself in the company of di Vico. By trade or service, I know not. He is the power above all here, and it is he who must be courted if you are to discover anything of value. For if he falls, the whole city will come under the reign of tyranny, and following that the country may fall to the combined forces of Salimbeni, Visconti and di Vico. Have great care, Signor Sabatini, for many are the forces weighed against you," the handsome apothecary urged.

Flavio left the shop, promising to keep Stefano appraised of all he learnt, and as he did so he spotted Bani loitering opposite, talking with a man and asking for directions. Flavio dropped through the doorway of a local tavern, and once happy that they were not watched or followed, Bani joined him. They still conversed in Latin, although Bani's grasp of Italian was increasing daily with his total immersion in the language. They found a quiet table away from the midday clientele, the conversations of workers, artisans and a smattering of merchants masking anything they may say in lowered tones. Seated and with food ordered, Flavio told Bani all he had learned.

"You are on a fool's errand," Bani opined. "This city is vast. Why the walls alone must be some four leagues around, and there are no fewer than twelve gates set into the walls; this without those churches and other buildings that have wicket gates let into them. The whole city is a sieve, with many opportunities for a traitor in someone's pay to let in the enemy."

"I agree, and this is why Cardinal Vitelleschi set me upon this task. For such treachery needs to be stemmed afore it can be unleashed. And speaking of treachery, what manner of villain followed me this morning?"

"He was of nondescript appearance, neither peasant nor noble. I let him be as you ordered, though I could have caught and killed him many times, for he was careless and assumed he was unwatched himself."

"That is well, for he will be even more unwary from now on. Let us not be seen together in the street, the better to know who trails me."

"Of which, where do you plan to go next?"

"Why I go to appease my sins and visit the church," Flavio offered, smiling at the irony of his own witticism.

He left the tavern and walked up the steps of the cathedral, pushing open one of the massive solid doors as the bells chimed for Sext. He was there as had been arranged with Cardinal Vitelleschi, and he walked to the row of candles before an ornate chapel, where the smell of incense assailed him mixed with a slightly musty aroma. It was a blessed relief from the stench and humidity outside in the dusty streets. A small choir was chanting to one side of the huge altar, and here in the side chapel a fresco of the Madonna was illuminated in its innocence. He reached for a taper and proceeded to light a candle, murmuring a prayer while inserting a coin into the wooden box. A priest came to his side, flicking rosary beads along a string as he muttered incantations.

They smiled at each other and Flavio asked him to step back and sit with him upon a pew set aside for those who would contemplate the frescoes of the magnificent church. "I have just asked an apothecary for a cure for a headache, and now come to seek a cure for the deeper ache in my soul." Flavio repeated a coded wording provided by Vitelleschi. The correct response was forthcoming.

"You speak with the accent of Corneto, my son, and therefore you have travelled far."

"Thank you, father. Cardinal Vitelleschi offers his prayers for you and asks that you may be with God always."

The old face of the priest creased into the knowing lines of a smile: "If I know the cardinal – and I surely do – the thoughts of himself and the power he wields will always be secondary to passing on blessings to another of his calling," he replied cynically.

Flavio snorted, considering the priest's words as the best possible response he could have wished for, given his own view of the cardinal and his morals.

"And now that we have agreed upon such matters, how may I aid you in his name?" the priest asked.

"I am persuaded that I need to become acquainted with Giovanni di Sciarra di Vico, as he may be able to help me find who may be a traitor to Viterbo, or if not to his own faction."

The priest raised a hand, and a cleric clad in the robes of a bishop appeared from the nearby shadows and approached them, introducing himself as Bishop Ranieri. The priest repeated Flavio's words to him, before nodding and backing away.

"You aim high, my son, and I hope that like Icarus you are not brought down by the heat of the sun. Yet in this you are in luck," Bishop Ranieri stated, clearly pleased with himself. "In two days' time the town will celebrate the Ferragosto, and every year the di Vico family holds a vast *festa* to celebrate the occasion in their palazzo in town. I am of course invited and will ensure that you also obtain an invitation to the festivities.

"There I will facilitate an introduction to Giovanni di Sciarra di Vico himself, and you can see if there is some mutual ground upon which you can compromise. For who knows, he may even help you for reasons of his own. In any event, you will be able to assess him in your own way and decide if he is for or against your cause."

Flavio nodded and agreed to be at the papal palace in two days' time, where Bishop Ranieri would take him in his carriage.

Chapter Twelve

The carriage containing Flavio and the bishop made its stately way around the ornate fountain that was set in the centre of the piazza and pulled to a standstill in front of the grand entrance to the di Vico palazzo. The entrance was close to the Porta Fiorentina gate, and horse drawn traffic was still coming through the gate under the watchful eyes of the guards.

The evening air of the *Ferragosto* was fragranced by jasmine, lavender, hostas and stocks that wafted a heady perfume across a city that was otherwise in the doldrums of a fetid summer heat, rancid with the stench of clogged sewage channels as everything rotted so quickly within the walls of the city.

The gardens surrounding the grand palazzo on the Piazza della Rocca to the north of the metropolis were alive with the tinkling of water as fountains burbled forth, the droplets reflecting diamonds of light from the many brands and flaming torches lining the wide pathways to the palazzo beyond. The water seemed to lighten the heavy air, splashing and frothing in the high humidity that accompanied the summer heat.

Other carriages queued before and behind them, and the sticky smell of hot horses' sweat mingled with the natural scents of the plants as the horses pulled and fretted at their harnesses. The carriages were for the most part open to the weather, silk lined with crests and personal liveries that reflected the status of their occupants in Viterbese society. Bishop Ranieri was dressed in a light silk version of his usual robes and Flavio was decked out in a bright turquoise silk doublet, contrasting coloured hose of the finest wool and low-heeled kidskin boots. An ornate belted chain was buckled around his waist bearing his dagger, whilst his beloved arming sword lay nestled out of sight within the cushions of the carriage seats. A dagger was the most armament any were allowed to bear to such an event, and tonight Flavio's was lodged in a jewelled velvet scabbard, rather than its usual plain leather sheath.

The bishop pulled his heavy gold chain of office to his chest as he rose when the carriage stopped. A servant opened the door, producing a set of steps for the clergyman to step down, avoiding the effluent in the street. Flavio followed suit, thinking that it had been a long time since he had last been in such elevated company – the grand days of Hawkwood in Firenze, and before that in his family home at the splendid balls his parents had used to host in their own palazzo, many years ago now.

He nodded to Bani, who had ridden postillion behind the carriage. Earlier he had asked him to ride with him and await his return, and to keep a good look out for anything untoward. The Copt nodded his acknowledgement, and Flavio felt that in the short time of their acquaintance he had come to trust his warrior protector as much as any of his own men, with whom he had shared so much over the last few years. The feeling was strange to him, and he shook off the sixth sense that was telling him not to be complacent and remain ever watchful, trusting to no one but himself and his own abilities. He took his place by Bishop Ranieri's side and walked sedately, with seemingly not a care in the world, commenting on various aspects of the garden whilst all the while keeping his senses alert. He should after all not be here, he told himself, yet he had used the bishop's influence to obtain the necessary audience with Giovanni di Sciarra di Vico.

"Come, my son, we will have no trouble entering the lion's lair," the bishop reassured him.

"It is not the entering, your grace, it is the leaving that gives me more cause for concern," Flavio responded, half in jest. They passed through the archway to the well-kept gardens and climbed the flight of marble steps to the grand double doors, with two livered servants on guard and large brands in iron sconces flickering, their smutty flames giving life to shadows in their glow.

"I am his grace the Bishop Ranieri, and this is Signor Flavio Sabatini of my household," the bishop announced. The two servants recognised the bishop and at his command allowed Flavio to enter unchallenged. The major domo announced their presence into the main hall of the gathering, which was itself a glittering spectacle of light and movement beyond the receiving line, where stood the lord and his lady.

Di Vico was a handsome man, and generations of breeding had sculpted his well-formed features. He was dressed in a beautifully tailored silk doublet with puffed shoulders, and a bejewelled belt was cinched about his waist, accentuating his fine build. The dark, deep set eyes offered his guests an air of arrogance as he looked down his long aquiline nose, apparently disdainful of all he saw. Each made his bow to the other as Flavio was introduced, then he passed quickly onto the beautiful lady who stood at Di Vico's side. He flashed a genuine smile at di Vico's wife, and was favoured in return with a row of even white teeth and eyes that whilst hard, seemed softened by what she saw. Her beauty was enhanced by a net of pearls that adorned her hair, and teardrop diamond earrings hung from her lobes. Her scent was seductive in itself, and Flavio made a bow over her hand and gently kissed the beringed fingers with a brush of his lips. When he rose erect again, he made eye contact and lingered in her grasp a little longer than he should have, reluctant to break contact.

Accomplished in the art of flirtation and seduction, the smile etched upon his lips promised more than a thousand words, and she responded in kind with a delicate nod of her head.

He moved on, remaining at the bishop's side as they moved into a large salon full of people, ladies in elegant dresses displaying an amount of décolletage that bordered on the indiscreet, their hair piled high in intricate designs, flashing jewels in the candlelight that added to the intense heat, despite all the doors and windows having been thrown wide open to balconies beyond. A quintet was playing an enchanting light aria that fell easily upon the gathering, mixing with the laughter and gaiety of all there. More than one set of eyes fell upon Flavio, the men perhaps envious of the coquettish glances he received from the ladies. Flavio's devil-may-care looks and the spirit of danger that surrounded him had always been a magnet to the ladies, and in settings like these he enjoyed such sport. Husbands gripped harder upon their wives' arms as he approached, even in the company of a senior clergyman.

He found himself introduced to this merchant and that, each of them eminent in the city's hierarchy, defined by their wealth and power that they wore like a mantle to denote their position, many of them highly placed in the *Signoria* that governed here. Any one of them, he reflected, could be involved in a plot to overrun the city if it suited their needs or if they had been snubbed by others in the struggle for dominion within the governance of the state capital.

With her husband seemingly occupied in talk of business, a lady broke from her group of acquaintances and sidled over to them, ostensibly to speak with the bishop. She engaged Ranieri in conversation before fixing her attentions on Flavio, who remembered her as Tiziana, the wife of an elderly banker who was high in the guild of *Arte di Cambio* and fabulously wealthy. Her beautiful, slanted eyes outlined in kohl were downcast but challenging, and she fluttered her long lashes beneath the fan that she used as much for artifice as to cool the air.

"Tell me, Signor Sabatini, what do you do here with the

good bishop, or are you too a priest?" she asked. "If so that would be such a pity," she continued with a provocative smile.

The bishop raised his eyebrows, coughed discreetly and begged leave to fetch a goblet of wine as his throat was dry.

"Ah, my lady. I fear that you mistake me, for I should be as much use to the priesthood as wine to a drunkard. My morals I fear are much too lax," he replied, smiling into the beguiling eyes that were looking up at him now above the edge of the fan that she spread before her face.

"Oh, how fortunate. A scoundrel, for I would hate to encounter such piety in one so ... so inappropriate," she finished, pressing a hand gently upon his arm almost accidentally as she brushed the silk of his doublet. They continued to flirt, each becoming more suggestive as the conversation flowed between them, until Flavio saw a movement from Bishop Ranieri from the corner of his eye. "Ah, my lady, I am being pressed to another cause far less entertaining than this one. I think the bishop fears for my soul."

"Go then, let him shrive you. Mayhap we can talk more of your salvation at a later point. Where do you board here in Viterbo?"

"At an osteria, *La Locanda delle Capra.*"

"I know of this inn, and I shall send word to you there, for I shall be lonely when my husband ventures north to Firenze on matters of business and I know not what. I shall ride out to our mountain home to escape the sultry heat of the city, and perhaps you too would enjoy the cleaner air for a while?" she offered with considerably more meaning in her voice than her words admitted.

Ever one to grasp the moment, especially as her husband was attached to the bankers of Florence, Flavio acceded with alacrity. He may learn much from her circumstances that could aid him in his endeavours – and there were worse ways to spy upon someone. Outwardly he smiled and responded chivalrously. "My lady, you unman and favel me, I am ever your servant and shall await your command."

He bowed over her hand then moved away from her to answer the summons of the bishop *A coil, Flavio? Indeed, and you fall ever deeper into it!* he thought to himself.

The bishop was deep in conversation with di Vico himself, and the host's wife was in a party of women nearby, looking furtively over as the members of her coterie giggled and smiled with glances in his direction. Flavio was presented to the lord of the party, and lost no time in asking a favour,

"My lord di Vico, I would presume to ask that you may grant me the honour of a private audience with you, as I reside in Viterbo for but a sennight and feel that there might be matters to be discussed to our mutual benefit."

The level of scorn and arrogance in di Vico's expression as he looked at him was something that Flavio found hard to stomach, and his ire rose along with the blood that suffused his face.

"How so, Signor Sabatini?" he demanded.

"My lord di Vico, I would not blemish your *festa* with matters of commerce and more besides, yet will hint that for the benefits and the power of the city vested in you as *podesta*, you might consider its security. I have matters that may aid you in such a cause," Flavio answered obliquely, yet with enough of a suggestion that the lord of Viterbo may see through the thinly veiled threat to his city.

Di Vico studied him again and beckoned both him and the bishop to follow. "Attend me now," he demanded less sharply,. "We have a few moments afore we sit to dine, and I always reserve this time to answer any favours that may be brought forward to me in my house on the occasion of the *Ferragosto*. Added to which I am intrigued and not a little irked at your presence here tonight, and would wish to understand the reason for the bishop bringing you with his entourage." He looked hard at Bishop Ranieri.

The bishop presented a bland expression, saying nothing. He knew enough about the calibre of the man before him, and remaining silent was the best approach when he was in such an antagonistic frame of mind. They moved away from the main throng of the guests and stood next to a panelled wall.

"My lord di Vico, I begged an audience with you as I have reason to believe that forces are arrayed against this city that may cause its downfall," Flavio said, "and I wondered if you had heard similar rumours?" he halted here, awaiting the response from the man who stood before him.

Instead of dismissing the reports, as Flavio half-expected, di Vico moved away to a table and poured himself a goblet of wine, which he sipped carefully. "I am always interested in the safety of the *civitas*," he waved a hand, "Do tell me more."

Something warned Flavio that if di Vico was being this civil, it boded ill for him, so he proceeded cautiously. "You are gracious, my lord," he said, and began his rehearsed lie.

"In my travels – I am a trader in goods from Bolsena to the coast at Corneto – I meet many people. Traders, merchants and soldiers. In these meetings I have heard rumours abroad of a plot to conquer Viterbo by forces that would be against the best interests of the city." Di Vico nodded his understanding, giving nothing away. "I have heard that such forces will be aided by those within the city who wish for new governance once the city is conquered," Flavio finished.

"What are these forces? Do you refer to Comte Visconti, who I hear is even now barking at the doors of Firenze like a rabid dog, where all quake and send out brave Gascons of Bertrand de la Salleto to defend them as the master Hawkwood once did? For long is his shadow and none it seems is able to fill the void left by him, though Bernardon de Serres is an able sword and a good master of tactics. Yet I wonder if he has the steel to defeat Visconti? Or the Salimbeni family, for I know that Agnolino is covetous of our city, as it holds the key to Rome and the papacy as with the Colonna. Yes, I already know of all these threats that lurk without our walls. Yet look around you, do you see weak walls? I think not. We are a fortress town, stout in our hearts and staunch in our endeavours. No master of war shall defeat us, and in the time it takes to overcome us by force or siege, why the papal armies will aid us, will they not, good bishop?" Here he turned to acknowledge once more the presence of Bishop Ranieri.

"As you say, my lord," Ranieri responded.

"It is not from without that the threat lies, my lord. It is from within," Flavio continued. "From those who are treasonous to Viterbo and would benefit from a new authority.

Can you think of any who may be suspect in such cause? For strong gates and walls are of no use if they are opened in the face of an attack by those who seek to betray you from within." Flavio wanted to pierce the arrogance of the man – or the defiance that sought to stifle such an idea. Was he after all complicit? Would he be returned to full power if the church was crushed?

"Enough of such nonsense," di Vico scoffed. "We have explored what you came to ask, and I find it wanting. Take your fanciful imaginings elsewhere, Signor Sabatini. Viterbo will be safe under my control." He dismissed Flavio with a wave of his hand, bowed to the bishop and called for a servant to take them back into the main salon.

Once the door had closed, a look of dark anger etched itself upon di Vico's face. A hidden doorway within the delicate wainscoting in the corner of the room where they had been talking was pushed open as a secret catch was released. A man in his early thirties emerged, a courtier by his manner and well dressed for the *festa*, yet he was no fop. His face bore the marks of battles fought, and his musculature showed that he was used to arms.

"Well, Marius, did you hear all?"

"I did, my lord, and it bodes not well. What does this Signor Sabatini do that he should be so well informed, and how does it serve him to bring it to your attention?"

"I know not. He claims to be aiding the priest, who in turn will answer to the cardinal and the papal army if it should be invoked to aid defence," di Vico said. "Yet something is not right here. He is presented and presumes to tell me how I should run Viterbo. No, have him followed when he leaves, I will arrange for Bishop Ranieri to be delayed at the last moment. Waylay Sabatini if the opportunity presents itself and learn what you may from his lips – by any means necessary," he finished.

Marius nodded and made to leave, collecting a small group of men as he went.

Flavio left the room fuming, unable to bring himself to speak to the bishop at his side.

"I did warn you," Ranieri muttered quietly. "He is arrogant beyond belief and suffers not those whom he considers fools or beneath him."

"Aye, he is an arrogant buffoon, right enough," Flavio agreed, feeling as though he would rather run his sword through the man and have done with it. Such was the way he had dealt with similar men in the past, seeing conquered towns fall before him and Hawkwood and many a pompous fool vanquished. Then he paused for a moment. Was all this a ruse? Was the arrogance and disbelief an act to cover di Vico's real purpose, and was he in league with Visconti or Salimbeni, or even both? Either way, he would use whatever or whomever he could, and if the wives of the rich and influential sought his company he would use them as much as they would use him and learn what he could. Flavio sat with Bishop Ranieri and other guests for the formal dinner, mingling as much as he could with any who would engage with him. Some he recognised as recipients of his contraband. He began to form a broad opinion of who was potentially loyal to the security of Viterbo and who was not. Yet such was the size of the populace that it was a seemingly impossible task that Vitelleschi had set him. Despite his outward smiles and charm, Flavio was still angry at his treatment by di Vico, yet he mentioned not a word to Bishop Ranieri in hearing of anyone. Once the dinner was over, he made to leave.

With this resolve he bade the bishop a curt goodnight, saying he would make his own way home and gather Bani on the way. Yet before he could depart from the gathering, his path crossed that of Valentina, di Vico's wife, who, with her maid as escort by her side, laid a soft hand upon his forearm. "Signor Sabatini, do you depart our company so soon?" she said. "Are we too dull for your tastes that we bore you so?"

"My lady, you could never bore me," Flavio responded. "Yet I fear your husband does not share my view of your company and wishes me gone."

"How very tedious of him. He is all business and no pleasure, whereas I am quite the opposite. Mayhap we shall see each other again in different circumstances?" she offered, looking up at him and maintaining eye contact.

"My lady, I shall look forward to such a moment with great anticipation," Flavio responded with a smile.

"I do hope so," she replied archly, flashing her fan in a quick flick before her face, leaving her eyes bright with challenge above it. Flavio bowed over her hand, scandalising the lady-in-waiting as he kissed the ringed fingers. Her fingers squeezed his with a promise of more. Then she was gone in a cloud of heavy perfume that he would not forget in a hurry, her figure swathed in colourful silks that flashed the light from a thousand candles that lit the marble entrance hall. He shook his head from side to side, a slight wolfish smile playing upon his lips. He would have his revenge for the slight rendered upon him by di Vico and maybe gain information into the bargain, for he was sure that he would meet Valentina again.

Flavio looked up as he descended the steps of the grand entrance, noticing immediately that the air had become heavy and forbidding as it often did at this time year, preceding a downpour that rarely lasted more than half an hour. He knew that when the rain came it would be torrential, often causing flash floods and swamping the streets with gushing water, the central gutters unable to cope with the excessive flow. He went around to where the carriages were being kept in lines awaiting their retrieval. Bani was there at his ease, talking with another groom and practicing his Italian, as always learning quickly, picking up nuances here and there.

"Bani, I leave now and shall return home on foot, I cannot abide this sewer any longer." He waved his arm back towards the house, and Bani raised an eyebrow in a questioning manner along with the other groom, who was also surprised. "I favour more honest fare, where intentions are not hidden by walls of pretence and subterfuge," Flavio declared, suddenly tired of it all.

Bani nodded and made to go with him. "No, stay here and protect the bishop. I fear I may have stirred up a hornet's nest and would that he be safely delivered home despite my presence in his company."

Flavio reached into the carriage and picked up his sword and scabbard, buckling it to his belt and pulling free the blade as was his habit. He loved the balance of the sword, which had been made for his father in Milan along with his fitted plate that was a work of art, forged and cast by Milanese armourers who were masters of the art. He twirled the blade, rotating his wrist, pleased as always with the balance and natural grip of the hilt. Satisfied, he returned it to its scabbard, ensuring that it could still be freely drawn, and with a smile upon his face he advised Bani. "Raise the canopy, for if I'm not mistaken it will soon begin to pour with rain, and you will be too late to save his grace's cushions when it comes."

With that he sketched a wave and was gone, whistling as he went, a spring in his step to be free of the claustrophobic gathering, alive to the sounds of the night, aware that he was being followed even as he strode forth. That itch at the back of his neck was there, warning him that all was not well. He moved off down the wide street, knowing instinctively which way he was to go. As he went, lightning flashed, illuminating the walls that surrounded him, and the first crack of thunder boomed above his head, bringing a small smile. He would soon be in a deluge, where the hunted could so easily become the hunter, and he would show them – whoever they were – the true value of a *condottieri*.

They had seen Dolus, who now rested, hidden behind a mask of anger. While he slumbered let them now sample Ares in his wrath, Flavio thought. He walked along the cobbles, feeling more alive and alert than he had since he left Hawkwood's service. It was a life he thought he had left behind, yet here he was revelling in it once more, realising in that moment how he missed the danger and the testing of his martial skills against another. It was something that could not be replicated in any other way, and he thought back to his sparring and training with Galeazzo da Montova, one of the best and deadliest blades he had ever encountered apart from Fiori himself.

With his blood pulsing through his veins and his heart singing with the prospect of battle, he strode along the via Caroli, a wide street in which he was unlikely to be attacked, seemingly without a care in the world – a late reveller replete with food and wine, at his ease and looking forward to a soft, comfortable bed. He hummed a tune, one of the arias he had heard earlier that evening, the notes floating back to him. He ambled along, looking continually up at the sky. wondering when the first droplets of rain would fall. He could feel it approaching like a cool wall, driving the air before it before the sudden curtain of rain was upon him. He twisted and turned into smaller and narrower side streets, narrow and restricting where he would rather be confronted by an overpowering force. The moisture permeated the air, preventing the use of crossbows as the strings would stretch in the damp, losing much if not all of their power. This is how he wanted it, a test of steel against steel, no assassin's bolt to take his life or maim him. Let them come, he smiled to himself. He passed the Piazza San Plebiscito and made his way down the narrowest alley he could find, hearing the patter of footsteps above the sounds of the night. So they were in front and behind him, he thought. He took two quick steps almost at the run and darted left, drawing his sword in a soft hiss that sounded like two palms rubbing together, retrieving his dagger in his left hand. He was partially hidden in shadow behind an arched pillar, and he calmed his breathing, in and out, holding his breath for a few seconds as he had been taught by Firori, despite the energy that coursed through his blood. At that moment the sky released its load, and huge droplets of rain began to drop like volleys of arrow heads, pounding to the slate cobbles, at once slick with moisture as visibility was suddenly reduced.

Then in a moment that was almost comical, the two parties who had been hunting him found themselves facing each other, discomposed for a moment by the sight of each other, taking a few seconds to recognise their error as they emerged into the narrow street from either end. The leader of the following group cursed and asked where he his quarry had got to, realising that they would now be unlikely to take him alive. "For assuredly he will fight when we bring him to bay."

Flavio gave them no quarter. Dry and with his vision clear, he stepped into the storm, attacking as he did so without cry or warning, for to his mind if they wanted him they could have him, steel and all. The blade of his arming sword drove forward, piercing the lower ribs of the nearest man, then with a twist and a grate of steel upon bone the blade was free, sucking ominously from the wound that spurted blood through the gambeson.

The leader recovered first, slashing around, all thought of taking this demon prisoner and torturing him evaporating. He cried out in anger, driving the blade from the wrist with all his force, using his hips in the turn. Flavio held his own sword in the vertical guard, flipped upwards at the quillon to deflect the stroke. He stepped in and drove his dagger into the man's chest, pushing him into the oncoming relief party that had been approaching from the front. The tangle of limbs caused chaos on the rain-slicked surface of the cobbles, and cries of anger and anguish rang out in the ensuing melee. It was dirty street fighting, and Flavio excelled at it, as he had learned the craft in the tangled throughfares of the towns he had vanquished in his former days. His quillon smashed into the eye of the next man as he moved constantly, darting as Fiori had taught him: *'Never be still, always move when you can, seek angles that suit you, never your opponent'*. The words were embedded in his brain and muscle memory. Flavio twisted, still catching a dagger thrust that scored his shoulder. Heedless of the wound, he kicked the man between the legs, doubling him up in front of the next attacker, allowing him to reach over the man and thrust the point of his sword into the newcomer's face. Of the six original attackers, three remained. Better odds, he calculated, running two steps for the pillar once more. In their greed for revenge, two followed. He swung around, his sword leading straight into an oncoming stomach, that offered resistance at first, then none as the material and skin were punctured, releasing a gush of hot blood. He pivoted back out of sight and slashed around, catching the next man on the hand, severing a thumb. The man dropped his sword, howling in agony, clutching his damaged hand and running backwards.

The final man, seeing his comrades in arms so taken, backed up, turned and ran away from the devil before him. Flavio laughed wickedly. He felt good, better than he had on the parapet more than two weeks ago in Corneto, when he had been weakened by his spell in prison. The Devil was upon him, driving him as of old, no mercy offered, just slash and kill. He turned and ran himself, wanting no part of the

Watch or the hue and cry that would follow. Only a fool stayed to the end, where darkness could hide another foe in her folds. He was but one in a city of many who might wish him harm. The cobbles, now slick with blood and rain, were slippery and he took care padding away on the balls of his feet, aware of the change in the atmosphere and scents around him, his weapons still unsheathed ready to deal death once more.

Yet aware as he was, he did not see another figure emerge, a sodden crossbow by his side, a smaller assassin's weapon, useless in the sudden downpour. "So, Signor Sabatini, you are as good as ever, and I would not cross you with a blade, so this night you are lucky," the man muttered to himself before he too slipped away into the veils of rain.

Chapter Thirteen

Bani had returned to their lodgings the previous evening, and now upon a fresher morning Flavio was awake, oiling and sharpening his sword and dagger against the dampness and the action that they had seen the previous evening. With the oil, coarse cloth and sand, Flavio removed any flecks of rust that may have appeared as a result of the downpour.

Bani noticed the raw mark across his bare shoulder, that although not very deep was weeping and red with dried blood. "You were attacked, and knew that you would be," he said accusingly.

Flavio nodded and continued to tend to his blade. "I was also concerned that an attack would be made against the bishop as a reprisal for enabling my entrance to a *festa* where I should not have been. An attempt may have been made to punish him on my account, and I could not let that happen," he explained.

Bani agreed, yet he was still not satisfied. "Why do you think that they attacked you?" he asked

"I know not for certain, but I assume they wanted to question me, probably torture me to tell all I knew that lay behind the real reasons for my questions. They said something before I attacked them indicating such was their intent. Whether I was meant to live or die I know not, yet someone, probably di Vico, does not want me to continue asking questions or sowing dissent in Viterbo or amongst its citizens.

"For all that, I learned much yester eve, and if I am not much mistaken I shall learn more from certain ladies who may aid me."

Bani raised an eyebrow and Flavio wondered if he may not be some sort of monk, knowing little of the Coptic rules concerning women. It would not do, he decided, and he was not about to be taken to task by someone else over his morals, especially when there was much to learn and in a more pleasurable way than being attacked and having his life threatened. Yet what gave him more cause for concern was how he was to find the traitorous element within the city and prevent its betrayal, for di Vico himself could be the culprit.

He was surprised when a messenger appeared at the door of the inn bearing a note for Flavio as the bells tolled for Nones. It was scented, he realised, bringing the parchment to his nose as he received it and inhaling the perfume, which brought back more interesting memories of the previous evening. He broke the seal and read the words, a small smile playing at his lips.

"Tell my lady that I shall attend upon her as she requires," he ordered the messenger, who bowed and left to relay the message.

Two days after *ferragosto* he made his way to the quarter directed within the note as the early morning light fell upon the streets, casting long shadows. He had bidden Bani to stay behind, yet he sensed rather than saw a presence behind him and assumed that the faithful Copt had disobeyed his orders.

He arrived at a palazzo on the via de Cava, dismounting from Carbone. He found himself in the northeast quarter, where many of the bankers resided and carried out their commerce. The elegant building to which he had been summoned displayed the wealth and opulence of its owner, one of the leading figures in the *Arte di Cambio*, the bankers who ran Viterbo. Tiziana had invited Flavio to her palazzo, yet when he knocked upon the gates a servant appeared and told him to attend upon the head groom at the rear of the property. Perplexed and annoyed he strode around to the rear entrance through a large archway, leading Carbone by his reins. Passing through the arch, he saw a full livered carriage awaiting his arrival, a driver and postilion in place. He was addressed and with his identity confirmed, he was beckoned by a groom to enter the carriage. Ever suspicious and mindful of a trap, Flavio tied his horse to the rear and kept his hand upon his dagger, ready to draw and defend himself. Yet before his eyes alerted him to anything untoward he was aware of the heavy perfume that had drenched the note two days ago.

A vison of beauty was draped upon the silk cushions, her sweeping gown a riot of deep reds and yellows that favoured her colouring. On the opposite seat was a maid, decorous in comparison to her mistress, her hands demurely clasped in her lap, with an arched eyebrow the only concession to emotion, a ghost of a smile seemingly about to break upon her lips. "Tiziana, why you have me at a disadvantage – yet a most pleasant one," Flavio said suavely.

"I do hope so," she replied, her eyes flashing in predatory allure. "We have awaited you these few moments as we could not be seen to entertain you within. My husband would not be as understanding as he should be, and there are neighbours who would cast aspersions upon my virtue." With a downward cast of her eyes and a flick of her fan she continued. "We journey for the mountains and our summer home, to Monte Razzano. Do you wish to accompany us and offer your protection?"

"Indeed, my lady," Flavio acceded with alacrity, "I would be most upset to think of you travelling without protection from the predators of the road."

She smiled back, and they understood each other perfectly. "It is but five leagues or so to the north," she continued. "Yet the air is cooler, and the mountains are clean and pleasant."

Flavio nodded, yet still a part of his mind wondered if this was a trap or plot to remove him from the city whilst it was undermined. A robbery upon the road, an honourable death in the service of a lady, and the cardinal's plans would be thwarted. Had he exposed himself too much? he wondered.

Yet his face showed none of these thoughts, and upon Taziana's command the carriage set off upon its journey, the horses pulled at the traces, Carbone pulled against the indignity of being tied to the rear of a carriage, but soon accepted the inevitable. It was over an hour later that they came to their destination just beyond a small village. The air was cooler and the humidity gone, and the gently sloping fields were greener here or filled with lines of vines marching off across the slopes of cleared land, protected by small woods and bisected by bubbling streams. It was good land, Flavio noted; productive, fertile and peaceful. Not unlike his own parents' home many years ago near Montalto di Castro.

The carriage pulled in through a pillared gatehouse onto a gravelled driveway that seemed to progress ever onward, lined by mature cypresses reaching skywards, guarding their passing as sentinels.

The villa, when it finally came into sight, was an elegant, stuccoed terracotta building on multiple levels with gables and sloping roofs leading off from a central courtyard, creating a raft of layers that sloped this way and that in an attractive display of chaos. The gardens were formal, and fountains tinkled and gurgled in the late summer sun. The whole was a peaceful setting, and as he looked over the fields that fell gently away from the villa, Flavio hoped that it would remain so and that he as not being led into a trap brought on by his lust for this woman and the information he may gain from her.

He jumped down from the carriage, stretched his back which was stiff from the journey and offered a hand to Tiziana She accepted it gratefully, stepped down and beckoned for him to follow her into the villa. Inside, servants welcomed them into the cool space, which was filled with tasteful furniture and brightly coloured arrases lining the walls, interspersed with portraits of family members hanging in places of prominence. It was clearly her family home, and as though reading his thoughts she said: "It has been in my family for generations, and was part of my dowry to Massimo. I love being here, and feel liberated by the mountains without the stuffiness of the city. Massimo will return here on his journey back from Firenze, so we must be careful," she warned, whispering the last words. "Though it should be three days before he is due, so we have time to ... enjoy each other's company," she finished with a smile, dropping her eyelids to cover the full force of her alluring eyes.

The following morning Flavio woke with a start. For a moment he did not know where he was, then it came back to him. Too much wine, a heavy supper and an unusual brandy flavoured with a hint of almonds that was made on the slopes near Corneto. He looked across at the sprawled figure beside him, still fast asleep. She had been an energetic and voracious lover and had seduced him as much as the other way around. He raised his head and instantly regretted it, as a light pierced behind his eyes. He squinted away the pain, rose and went to the flagon of chilled water by the dresser. The liquid felt good as it ran down his throat. He moved quietly away, pulled on some clothes and went to sit on one of the many loggias in quiet contemplation of what he had learned.

Tiziana had first told him that hers was a marriage of convenience based upon a mutual progression of both families' wealth, and she had been dragged kicking and screaming to the nuptials. Finally resigned to her fate, she soon learned that her older husband placed little demands upon her physically and settled down to enjoy the fruits of her life.

Her husband's bank was in very close contact with those in Florence, and one in particular that funded the *Signoria* for the town that had strong links with the Colonna family in Rome and arranged loans to the Milanese court. If these banks tied in with the Duke Visconti, who all believed was set to conquer the city, then what better way to bankrupt it than by blocking the funding for arms and the men who fight to keep her safe. It was well known that *condottieri* were only loyal to money, and would flit from one master to another at the drop of a bag of coin. Hawkwood had been a prime example of a man who sold his sword and those of his men to the highest bidder, moving on and changing sides when the payments dried up. If nothing else, the city would collapse should funds be withdrawn by its external bankers, which would have the same results as storming the walls. The gates would be opened, and Visconti would be welcomed without the need to have the city sacked and raped. Bankers always flourished in such times, as even dukes needed to be funded.

Is that how they would take Viterbo? Flavio wondered. For if Florence fell then the Marema would be made impassible and Viterbo would be held to ransom, with Rome next. Upon its capitulation and with such forces arraigned against it, a new pope would be seated upon the throne of God, one who favoured new masters, Visconti and the Colonna family, and Milan would rule Italy.

Yet Flavio knew there was much more to this. To return to Vitelleschi and say that a banker was probably involved would make him a laughing stock, and even if that banker were to be arrested, little could be proved. No, he needed more, and looked forward to two more days and nights of satisfying Tiziana and her appetites. He hoped that he had the stamina to continue pleasing her, for she was a force of nature!

He woke exhausted in a tangle of sheets on the third day, his back bearing more scratches and scars than he had gained in the battle on Corneto's walls. He left her sleeping again, and now with a key that he had found in a small inlaid box he stole down to her husband's private solar, where within a locked drawer he found formal papers, details of loans and more importantly the names of those involved in each transaction. There were only six, it seemed, that were relevant, and aware that he had little time and could be disturbed at any moment he pulled a sheet of paper free from a drawer and in careful script began to write down the names on each agreement that corresponded with each transaction, forming in effect a master list.

Then as quickly as he could he pushed the bundles back into the drawer, but he found that they met resistance, and did not go as far as they should. He reached in with his fingers and found that the drawer was too shallow in comparison to the depth of the desk. Getting down on his hands and knees with his head once more protesting at the rush of blood to his hungover state, he probed and found a raised brass stud which he pulled then pushed and then pressed sideways. With a soft click, a secret drawer hinged at the rear dropped down, and here he struck gold, for within was an ornate leather bound ledger reinforced with brass, bound and locked in place with a thick leather strap and a brass lock.

He did not have a key to this, and was momentarily thwarted, for he did not dare cut the leather binding betraying his presence. With a sigh of frustration, he looked around, and finding a small paper knife he began to prise and twist the point into the simple locking mechanism, which soon yielded to his efforts with a reluctant click. He kept pausing, listening for any sign of life above stairs from Tiziana, yet all was silent save for the soft passage of servants in the passage without beginning their daily duties. Each time they passed by, he froze ready to dive for cover behind the large mahogany desk.

When he opened the ledger he could not believe his eyes. Here were columns listing all parties and the details of each transaction – some minor loans, some of far greater import. While some were plainly written, others were in a form of code that would have to be broken by Vitelleschi. He scribbled away as quickly as he could, and with his task completed locked the binding once more to secure the ledger and replaced it in exactly the same position he had found it. Satisfied, he waited until a maid walked by on soft soled felt poulaines that Tiziana insisted they wore to avoid the clacking on the terracotta and stole from the room, giving it a final glance to ensure all was as it should be.

He sighed heavily in relief and returned the key to the box from which he had taken it seemingly hours before. Slipping out onto the loggia he settled to enjoy the view across the fields, only to be disturbed moments later by a vexed Tiziana, "*Amore mio*, you must leave," she said. "For I have a missive from a messenger lately arrived informing me that Massimo arrives this day sometime after Nones, and you must not be here when he comes."

Flavio smiled, feigning sadness – although his primary

emotion was relief. He kissed her cheek, which is all that he dared to in front of her lady in waiting, and said: "Ah my lady that will bring me such sorrow, for I have enjoyed the delights of our sojourn here. Are you certain sure that he is soon to arrive?"

"My love, I dare not risk such consequences," she assured him. "For if he were to find you here we would be ruined. He is a vindictive man born of malice and would have assassins sent after you, ordered to take your life." Flavio had the impression that this had happened before to some other poor soul, so he muttered platitudes and begged leave to pack what meagre belongings he could and asked that his horse be saddled for him. She agreed, and said that sometimes Massimo made better time than expected, especially if he set off early to avoid the heat.

Flavio turned at this, and a thought occurred to him. He had a sudden desire to tweak her tail a little to see what response he would receive.

"My lady, do you not fear the servants repeating all to Massimo? For such could be calamitous."

"No *amore*, they are mine own, hand-picked, and have been with me since before my marriage. Fear not, for our secret shall be safe. Now please hurry for I would have you safely gone. I would receive but a beating, whereas you would forfeit your life," she pleaded.

Flavio bent to kiss her lips and made his way back to their recently shared bedchamber, whose bedclothes he noticed had already been stripped and made ready for her husband's arrival. He shook his head. He would have need to be careful when dealing with people as artful as these.

He was saddled and ready to depart but a half hour later, as tears filled Tiziana's eyes, a fan clasped in her shaking hand. With a guide to lead him to the correct road, Flavio departed with fond farewells, but once he had waved for the last time, Tiziana, now out of his hearing, turned to her lady in waiting, "Tell me, did he find and use the key?"

"Yes, my lady."

"And did he also find the ledger?" she asked anxiously.

"Indeed, my lady. I spied through the peephole and had placed the papers so that he would find it difficult to fit them back into the drawer. He is curious and not stupid. He finally found the catch and was surprised and pleased, and not at all bashful in his search. He seemed to know exactly what he was searching for."

A knowing smile played upon Tiziana's lips as she flicked her fan to and fro. "Now we shall wait to see what he does with the information. You did well, Marisa, I am most pleased. For Flavio Sabatini is no vagabond merchant of opportunity. No, his cause goes much deeper, aye and he has seen conflict and war by the scars on his body. I will wager that this shall have deep repercussions, so let us see where they lead.

The lady in waiting dropped a curtsey and moved away to her duties, secure in her faith in her mistress and pitying the poor lothario his seduction.

Chapter Fourteen

Flavio set Carbone off at a steady trot, wishing to make the *osteria* in Viterbo before the heat of the day became unbearable. Having bidden farewell to the groom who guided him onto the main route back to Viterbo, he turned his mind to all that he had learned from the briefest reading of the documents and the ledger. The burning question to his mind was not just the complicity of the parties named, many of whom were bankers or well positioned nobles in upper echelons of Viterbese society, but what each of them stood to gain if the balance of power changed within the city. That would be the hardest thing to gauge, for within the answer lay the resolution of the whole puzzle, or so it seemed to Flavio.

Carbone was uppity, prancing and fresh, having had no exercise for three days, grain fed and feeling his oats. He curbed and skittered at every sound and pretended to be frightened, and it was this that saved Flavio, for as he pushed the stallion into a trot to release some of his pent up energy, a pheasant suddenly took flight from roadside bracken, rising with a clatter of wings and a screech. The horse pivoted and sidled sideways, nearly unseating his rider just as the first twang of a crossbow cord rang out and the Flavio heard the ominous whistle of a quarrel in flight as a second missile was loosed. The first bolt grazed Carbone's whither as he span and took a quarrel that was meant for his neck, burning a red line along his skin. The animal reared in anger and fear, pitching Flavio backwards off the saddle. At the sound of the first quarrel Flavio was already making to bail out of the saddle, knowing that a horse was always the first target for an archer or crossbowman. As a result, the second bolt missed him completely, hissing through the air where his torso had been a fraction of a second earlier. He was already twisting in midair, knowing that he had but thirty seconds or so before the next bolt would be flying towards him to end his life. He rolled like any good horseman to avoid being winded, coming to his feet in a crouch, ready to dive away once he had located the rustling and straining that would define the position of the ambushers. They were closer than he realised, two of them, even now pulling back upon the prod, a foot each in the stirrup and using a goat's foot lever to draw and span their lethal weapons as three more men rushed forward from their position, seeking to finish Flavio off while he was supposedly winded on the ground.

Flavio carried his forward roll, ready to meet a new threat and face odds of three to one. The men were lightly armoured with thicker brigandines that would turn most blades, yet they wore no obvious mail or plate because of the heat, though each was helmed with an open faced barbute, offering some protection. It would be difficult, he knew, and speed would be everything once he was in motion. He ran for the tree line away from the road to gain a small advantage and prevent himself from being surrounded. He wished he was still mounted, for on Carbone as a war horse he would make them pay for their attack. As it was, the stallion stood off and backed into the trees as he had been trained to, avoiding the deadly quarrels that would quickly end his life if they found their mark.

Flavio settled with his back to the trees as the attackers ran towards him, shouting their cries of anger as their blood pumped, seeking to pounce and kill their prey now that he had been brought to bay. A calm came over Flavio as he drew his dagger and sword, knowing that if he fell to their attack, he would at least take many of their number with him. As was ever the case, some of the men were faster than others in their eagerness to strike and kill. Flavio moved with blinding speed borne of long practice, bring his dance of death to bear, stepping forward with a long stride and wielding his sword from the wrist as fast as he was able, crossing first one blade, from middle guard, flowing with the unleashed energy, driving a dagger forward, punching through a thick brigandine, slicing into the fabric skidding off an unseen plate and driving home between the layers. Then he span, and was through to the next man, sword slashing to beat the odds, his wrist rotating to deliver two cuts in less than a second. In that moment of battle, when subliminal thought comes unbidden, Flavio wondered why no more were already upon him, despite his flurry of blows and movement.

The cries of pain and anguish broke his trance of battle, as with the next man falling his throat slashed came the whistle of arrows – one, two, three in the space of a second, it seemed – and three of the men were still falling even as a fourth arrow found its mark to skewer a crossbowman at full span who was about to release a quarrel.

There upon his horse, riding like a centaur, was Bani, with three arrows between his fingers, a fourth nocked against the shaft, his thumb ring pulling back in a constant motion of draw release, draw release, almost faster than the eye could follow, as Flavio had seen demonstrated that first day back in his *enceinte* in Corneto.

"*Dio mio, he is fast,* Flavio thought as the final man-at-arms rushed him. He left the second crossbowman to Bani, confident in his ability to find his target.

The last man came on, closing the distance quickly, knowing his safety lay in being close to his prey where the lately arrived archer could not pick him off for fear of hitting his own man. He hopped left, putting Flavio between him and Bani. Flavio took the offensive, wanting it over with, slashing left, then right, then left again, his wrist flexing and bringing the blows to bear with terrible speed, each testing the attacker, giving him no time to take the offensive.

The man had a sword and buckler, and was well protected with mail under his brigandine. He took Flavio's final blow on the buckler, deflecting upwards, immediately countering with a fast slash high to low that pushed Flavio to defence, his dagger and sword straight out at half guard. Flavio deflected the next blow and thrust his own arming sword at the torso suddenly vulnerable through a gap. The point hit the plates of the man's brigandine, deflected and moved off the centre line. Flavio needed to close inside the buckler guard, so he followed his sword in, crossing with the pommel at his opponent's exposed face, and as the buckler came to guard he drove the dagger under the helmet at the exposed neck that was devoid of plate, into the soft flesh beneath just before the sideways slash of his attacker's sword blade came into contact. But he was inside the man's outer gate now, away from the long reach of the lethal blade. The man gulped and gasped like a gutted fish, and dark crimson blood erupted from the wound as Flavio withdrew the dagger, leaving him to sink to the sward in his death throes.

He span around to face the next attack, never still, always expecting more to come, yet all he saw was the dead or dying, skewered with arrows or cuts. Bani rode up, his bow with a nocked arrow at the cord ready to loose, the thumb ring glinting in the sunlight.

"Bani, *dio mio*, you are a sight for sore eyes. How come you to be here? For it seems I am once more in your debt."

"My lord, it is my duty to watch over you, so you are not in my debt. As to how, why I followed you and stayed at a small *osteria* in the village near the signora's villa. Your attackers stayed one night at the same inn. They thought me but a harmless traveller bound for Firenze and avoiding la Maremma, but I listened to them. I have watched the road daily since you arrived and followed a small track that runs parallel to here, scouting ahead. I was nearly too late to aid you and, I am glad I returned when I did, hearing noise of arms and knowing that you must be the cause," he explained simply, as though it was the most natural thing to expect.

Flavio shook his head in amazement, and for once was annoyed with himself for being so lost in thought, wondering for whom the assassins acted. Had he been set up by Tiziana, or even her husband, Massimo Collemi? Agents of di Vico who may have seen him leave, or the same unknown enemies that had struck at Signor Dezi? So many unknown factors, pieces of the puzzle that became more disparate as he was sucked further into the secrets of Viterbo and her politics.

"Then let us journey together, afore these *contidini* are missed by their masters and more are sent to deal with me," Flavio urged, gesturing around at the bodies lining the road. Two were still breathing and in the manner of a true *condottieri* he put them out of their misery with a swift stab of his dagger.

Flavio explained to Bani all that he had found in the desk at Signor Collemi's villa and the implications of the conspiracies that swirled around Viterbo and her populace.

"Do you think that whoever those assassins served knew of your journey here, and if so who informed them?" Bani asked. "And these attempts upon your life and the attack upon Signor Dezi, are they the actions of one person? For whoever it may be, signor or signora, they are connected in some way with the plots to capture Viterbo. It remains to be seen if one is pulling all the strings or there are unseen threads linking all by accident as much by design."

"A woman, you say? I had not considered such a ploy," Flavio admitted thoughtfully. "Though Catherine of Siena was one such stateswoman, moving to and fro as an agent of who knows whom. She went about forging treaties and brokering alliances in the names of many powerful influences within the land." Flavio explained about the woman born and raised in Siena, whom some had called a saint and some a whore of the devil's spawn. In either event she had been a powerful tour de force in Italian politics with a wide range of influence from the church to the worst *condottieri*, helping to bring about the downfall of the powerful and raising others up in their place.

On such matters their ruminations brought them to Viterbo's gates a short time later, after stopping briefly at an *osteria* to make a repast along the way.

"We shall remove to *La Capra,* refresh ourselves, and then I wish to visit Signor Dezi and see what news he may have for us," Flavio said after they had been passed through the gate, trotting their horses through the crowded streets and making headway against the pressing throng of people.

As the bells of the nearest church were striking for Vespers, they left the *osteria* and made their way the short distance to the apothecary's shop. It was closed up, with the glazed front door shuttered and sealed. The two men looked at each other, a feeling of unease coming over them.

"The rear entrance," Flavio motioned to Bani. They moved off to the side entrance and slipped into the rear courtyard and thence to the door that offered access to the rear office and rooms where he had first found Signor Dezi. The door was unlatched, and they moved inside. It was dark and lifeless as though all the soul had departed from the air. A noise distracted them as an object flew through the air, shiny in its flight, accompanied by a cry of anger and pain. Flavio ducked just in time as the vase smashed against the wall where his head had been a moment before. In the dim light a figure flashed towards him, and he grabbed at the upraised arm, stopping the downfall of the dagger.

"Ilaria!" he cried out, "it is me, Flavio. *Con calma*, we mean you no harm."

She broke down in sobs, beating her hands against his chest until she stopped and fell crying into his arms.

"Tell me what ails you?"

"My father was murdered yester eve. Stabbed and left to die in the street outside our shop," she said between sobs.

Flavio and Bani exchanged glances.

"Who did this foul deed, did they catch the *assassino*?" Flavio asked.

"No. I was alerted by men in the street who came to his aid after hearing a garboil outside my room. He was returning from supper with an old friend, Signor Tullio Cannas, a merchant. They met regularly at *La Torre in Pietra*, a taverna not far from here, and had done so for years."

Flavio comforted her and bade Bani fetch some brandy to calm her nerves. "Did you speak to him afore he died? Did he say anything about his attackers?"

Ilaria sobbed again at the thought: "*Si*, he held ... he held his crucifix tightly, pulling on the chain and said something like 'it is all to do with the church, seek the church', or words like that ... I do not know," she wailed.

The church again, Flavio thought. What does it mean? "Do you think that he will be there this evening, this merchant Signor Cannas?" he asked gently.

"I know not. Maybe, he sups there regularly, I think," she finished weakly.

"Bani, stay with Ilaria. I shall go to this taverna and seek out Signor Cannas and find out if he knows of ought of this terrible death."

With Ilaria settled, Flavio left the apothecary's shop and made his way to the taverna *Torre in Pietra*, which was as Ilaria had said was but a short walk away. He was careful as he went, yet nothing untoward happened. No one attacked him, and he checked more than once to see if he was followed. Satisfied in this regard, he pressed on. The taverna was set against the north west wall near one of the many stone towers guarding Viterbo, which had given it its name. He pushed open the door to find a typical taverna, half-filled with clientele, none of whom paid him much attention as he entered. He made his way to the stained wooden bar, seeing clean rushes upon the terracotta floor and a second door to the rear that no doubt led to the latrines and the rear entrance. He was always cautious in new places, and wanted to be aware of where trouble might come from and where he could escape should he need to.

The landlord was a jovial man who asked Flavio what he would like, and Flavio ordered a local wine. When it arrived, he sipped the cold, white nectar with appreciation. It was *Est! Est! Est!*, a wine from Montefiascone that had been named by a passing German bishop escorting the pope over a hundred years earlier in recognition of its excellence. He asked the landlord if he knew Signor Tullio Cannas, and if so whether he was in the taverna.

The landlord's attitude changed slightly, becoming more wary as he asked Flavio why he wished to become acquainted with the signor.

"I am a trader dealing in cloth, spices, wines and other goods. I understand that Signor Cannas may be interested in buying some fine cloth from Firenze," Flavio replied.

The landlord became more animated, and Flavio realised that he too might be interested in acquiring wine and brandy tax free from outside the area. He promised to inform the merchant of Flavio's interest should he appear this evening. Flavio ordered a local dish of minced pork flavoured with fennel in a tomato sauce and seated himself with his back to the wall at the rear of the room. He watched the comings and goings of customers as he ate, and as he was mopping up the last of the sauce with some fine white bread, he looked up to see a newcomer, a man who looked well set up in clothes of excellent quality, trimmed and edged in clear contravention of the sumptuary laws and wearing the well-crafted shoes of a townsman. This he assumed would be Signor Cannas, and so it proved. For as the newcomer gave a familiar wave to the landlord and made for what was clearly a favourite settle, the landlord himself came over rather than one of the serving girls. A hushed conversation ensued as the seated customer gave his order and glanced once then twice in Flavio's direction. With a final nod of his head, the newcomer finished, and the landlord made his way to Flavio's table.

"That is Signor Cannas, and he would be delighted to make your acquaintance." The landlord gestured over the to the table at Flavio's right hand side.

Flavio thanked him and rose, holding a flagon of wine and his goblet. Arriving at the merchant's table, he saw a man of around the same age as Signor Dezi had been, corpulent and well-padded with success, his sharp eyes bespeaking a shrewd mind and a head for business. Flavio introduced himself. "*Piacere, sono* Flavio Sabatini," he began, explaining how he was a trader and brought goods to sell down river from Bolsena and the north.

"Ah, Signor Sabatini, but I have heard your name mentioned by others of my guild, albeit in hooded terms. Though by repute the quality of your wares are beyond reproach – even if your methods are not," he said with an arched eyebrow and a twinkle in his eyes.

"Ah, signor, I fear I am much maligned," Flavio replied suavely with a shrug. "Alas, with competition being what it is, there are always those who would wish to discredit me."

"And those who would wish to tax you as well, no doubt," Cannas rejoined. Flavio knew these merchants well; it was always their way to banter and debase before settling down to business, as tenacious negotiators.

"I am certain sure that you are too clever to succumb to such scurrilous rumours, or have I misread my man," he flattered.

Cannas laughed. It was a rich sound and without malice or guile: "You will do, signor. Come join me and tell me how we may benefit each other, for I always have as big an appetite for business as I do for my supper," he joked.

Flavio smiled and began to explain how he smuggled goods down the river. Rich cloth from Florence woven from the best English wool, spices, wine and brandy. It was, he described, a cornucopia of goods to suit any respectable trader. Signor Cannas was intrigued and interested, and as they talked Flavio assessed him, wanting to know his man, who for all the world seemed to have no knowledge of his friend's recent demise. It was perhaps cruel, yet Flavio needed to be sure in this devious world of fickle alliances and loyalties before he exposed all to the merchant. At length he decided the time was right as they finished his flagon of wine.

"Signor Cannas, I also trade in spices as you know and I was bidden to speak with you by a daughter of an old acquittance, Signor Dezi," he halted for a moment to assess the response.

"Ah yes, Ceasar. Why I met with him but yester eve in this very taverna, how does the old rogue?" he responded jovially.

"There are tragic tidings that I must bring, for your *amico* died yester eve outside his home."

The man before him seemed to shrink. His face paled as he frowned, and he raised his hands in disbelief. "*Dio mio*, how? For he was right well and hearty when we left the Torre in Pietra last night. A little in his cups, yet nothing to disable him," he said, his voice sharp with genuine grief.

"Then sadly I must tell that you that he was killed. Murdered in the street and left for dead outside his home to be found by his daughter, who had been alerted by the garboil."

"Murdered, by all that's Holy, no. By the good Lord, no, not Ceasar. We have known each other since our youth. Did they catch the man who did it?" he asked angrily, and Flavio decided that his emotions were far too genuine for him to have been complicit in the crime.

"No, no one was seen, or at least not clearly enough to be recognised. They run free – yet fear not, for I shall seek them out and have vengeance. But tell me, did he seem ill at ease yester eve? Did he give any hint that he feared for his life or that he was followed? Any small matter that may aid me to find his killers." Flavio probed after Cannas gulped the last of his wine to ward off the shock.

The sharp eyes focused on the middle distance as though remembering all of their conversation and then snapped his fingers as though waking from a trance.

"He did. He was distracted, as though he was preoccupied with other matters, and he kept fingering his crucifix that was around his neck. When I teased him with a humorous comment about seeking God's help – which I now in hindsight regret most bitterly – he muttered something about it being all the fault of the church, not God. I asked him again, puzzled by such a comment and he said he had sought the answer and wished he had not, for what was perceived as pure was tainted by other means.

"I pressed him on this, and his reply was that it would be better that I did not know for my own safety. He would not give any more information, and I should have known then that he was in danger and accompanied him home."

"It is better that you did not. For he was clearly followed, and if those watchers had seen you converse in such an intimate manner they may have assumed that he told you all that he knew, and you too could now be lying cold upon a slab of marble."

The shocking thought hit home as quickly as a crossbow quarrel to strike Cannas's heart cold. He had not considered that aspect of what had occurred.

"*Mama mia!* I had not thought of such a thing. Do you

think that they will strike again, maybe at me or my family, or poor Ilaria?"

"I do not know. It seems that they are laying for those who know about possible traitors within Viterbo and those who may be colluding with whatever forces are mounting to try to take the city. Of which I must see someone else who is known to me here and is of the church, so maybe I will find out more of what has occurred there." Flavio answered, his mind elsewhere. "Yet I warn you to take great care, have a servant with you at all times and avoid dark alleys." Flavio said.

Signor Cannas looked at his food that had arrived with steam rising from the trencher, suddenly seeming to have lost his appetite. "Signor Sabatini, you look like an able man," he said timorously, nodding to Flavio's sword and dagger, "would you do me the favour of escorting me home once I have finished my supper? For I live close by, and such a favour would not take you much out of your way."

Flavio smiled in sympathy: "*Certo*, Signor Cannas, it will be my pleasure," he agreed, not just for the man's safety but also because he had found another willing customer from whom his trade would spread within the guild with Tullio Cannas as a friend and ally.

An hour later, as the bells of Compline were sounding, Flavio found himself standing outside the doors of the cathedral of San Lorenzo. Cannas had spoken the truth in that his home was not far from the taverna, and he was most grateful for Flavio escorting him safely to his door. He had invited Flavio in for a postprandial brandy, but Flavio had politely refused, saying that he had much to do. Definitely a new customer there, he thought to himself with a smile as he walked away into the late evening. He had been alert all the way, his hand upon his sword, ready to draw and fight, yet the sixth sense that warned him so often of impending danger was absent, and he felt a little more relaxed now.

Pushing open one of the heavy doors, Flavio was assailed by the sickly smell of incense and the pure voices of the choir singing in harmony at the main altar of the cathedral. He knew that he would find Bishop Ranieri here for the final service of the day. Flavio made a bow at the side chapel, lit a candle and waited, searching the congregation and the upper levels where the higher echelons of the clergy were seated. There he saw for the first time a senior clergyman with the distinctive scarlet galero, whom he assumed to be Cardinal Pielo who wielded such power here. He could see little of the man, but hoped to obtain an audience with him in due course. Finally, with the service at an end and the congregation and the clergy parading out, Flavio saw both di Vico and his beautiful wife Valentina, who gave him a sly smile, full of promise beneath her diaphanous veil.

Then he saw Bishop Ranieri and made to intercept him. He began without any preamble in tones that were hushed yet full of urgency: "Your grace, we need to talk, for much has happened and I needs must explain all."

The bishop seemed surprised to see him, but once he had recovered, he bade Flavio follow him to the side chapel.

"My son," he began when they could not be overheard, "I had not heard from you for a while and was worried for your health. Is all well with you, for you seem troubled?"

"Troubled? That I am, father, for much has happened

and not to the good. Signor Dezi the apothecary is dead, murdered outside his home. I pray that his daughter remains safe – and Stefano Ventolini too. For all it seems is adrift with someone pulling strings and controlling everything," Flavio said.

"My son, let us pretend to contemplate the wonders of this fine chapel as you explain all to me. For the news of Signor Dezi is terrible, and it appears you have poked a hornet's nest in some way," he replied calmly. Flavio explained all that had occurred, including finding the letters in Tiziana's country villa and setting out the implications they contained.

"I needs must speak with Cardinal Pielo, for all points seem to direct me to the church, and I wish to hear and understand his thoughts on Viterbo and if he may furnish me with any more information to unravel this coil," Flavio finished.

"My son, I can make arrangements to meet with the cardinal, or at least ask on your behalf, although I say that he can be a little ..." he paused as if trying to find the most appropriate words without causing offence, "difficult and aloof, shall we say."

At that moment the cardinal, who had been in conversation with two other members of the clergy, nodded to them, disengaged and with a deacon by his side made his way purposefully over to Flavio, approaching from behind Bishop Ranieri. Flavio's eyes must have wandered, as the bishop frowned and turned to see what was distracting him at such a moment.

"Ah, your eminence, buona *sera*. I was just saying how

busy you were with matters of state, and how you are hard pressed," Ranieri said.

"Just so. Are you going to introduce me to the signor?" the cardinal asked. Flavio eyed him, assessing the cleric. He saw a man of later years, hair the grey of dirty snow, a hooked nose and deep set eyes that missed nothing. Yet there was about him a strength of purpose and a sense of determination that would not be deflected lightly.

"Ah yes, quite. So this is Signor Flavio Sabatini, who is here in Viterbo on matters of trade," he said diffidently.

Flavio made a bow, kissed the ring upon the proffered hand and despite a slight negative shake of the head from Bishop Ranieri jumped straight in. "Your eminence, I was about to beg a favour of the good bishop, and I wondered if you would do me the honour of a private audience on matters of church and state which I feel may be to our mutual benefit."

The face was impassive for a few moments, then broke into a tight-lipped smile. "Of course, my son. Attend upon me on the morrow at the papal palace at the hour of Terce, and I will arrange for you to be admitted."

He bade both men goodnight turned and left with an abruptness that was almost rude.

"You are very fortunate, Signor Sabatini," Ranieri said, "for he is not usually so accommodating." The bishop appeared somewhat disappointed at the turn of events.

Flavio nodded and made his apologies, saying that he had to return to ensure Ilaria's safety.

Chapter Fifteen

Despite the revelations of the evening and the fact that his mind was in turmoil, Flavio was determined not to be surprised again, and remained alert all the way back to the inn where he and Bani were staying. He had checked upon Bani and Ilaria and found that Bani had escorted her to the house of an aunt nearby, leaving him at liberty. The two men walked the short distance back to *La Capra*, where they found a carriage of a greater quality than normal waiting outside. The crest that would usually be seen upon the side was covered by a cloth, deepening the mystery. There were two grooms, one upon the wooden box seat and another holding the bridles of two fine horses, murmuring to them quietly. When he saw Flavio, the groom with the horses beckoned him forward, saying that his mistress was within and begging his attendance upon her.

Flavio went to the carriage door, from which a head had emerged on hearing the sound of voices. Flavio recognised Valentina di Vico immediately. Her face lit up in a beatific smile, framed in gold silk, and the flash of her white teeth sparkled in the iridescent light.

"My lady, *buona sera*," Flavio said. "What brings you to such a disreputable part of the city? Not that it is not a pleasure to see you."

She put a finger to her lips as she withdrew, then her other hand beckoned him inside. He spoke a few words of Latin to Bani, bidding him to go inside and telling him he would join him soon before stepping up into the carriage. There was another figure curled up in the corner of the softly upholstered seat, which proved to be Valentina's maid.

"Ah, my lord of the night," Valentina whispered. "I have missed you, having now sent a man to your inn twice to see if you were at home. He returned each time saying that you were abroad, so I left no message. Seeing you in church this evening, I knew I had to grasp the moment."

Recalling Bani's words of warning, he wondered if this was a trap. "Valentina, is this wise with your husband–"

"Who is even now at a banquet with other nobles," she cut him off. "And will return late tonight – if he does return before the morning, which I doubt. And you intrigue me, for I surmise you are not who you seem for all the intelligence I have managed to glean of your circumstances."

Flavio made to protest, but she knocked sharply upon the wooden panel above her head and the carriage moved gently into motion.

Flavio had a sense of déjà vu. What was it with these Viterbese women? Were none loyal to their husbands?

She seemed to sense his disquiet. "Be not alarmed, for I am not leading you to be ensnared. My aim is of a much more intimate purpose," she said in a voice that was full of allure. "For the pleasures of Viterbo pall after so many years, and my husband strays. I will tell you more later."

"May I know where we are travelling?" he asked, still half suspecting a trap, his hand close to his rondel dagger and his senses ever alert.

"We go to our palazzo. My husband and I have our own chambers, and once within the private piazza none will be the wiser of your presence, for you shall wear my livery ere we disembark."

The rest of the journey was spent in silence, with just the flutter of Valentina's fan cooling the air in front of her face. They stopped a few minutes later, and Flavio heard the sound of gates opening as he slipped on a large doublet bearing her crest of arms upon its tabard at her urging. The carriage halted and Flavio stepped out, helping Valentina down, followed by her maid in waiting. Flavio bowed in a semblance of servitude and followed the maid to allay suspicions of any watching servants in the evening dusk that was dimly lit by smoking sconces. The small piazza was fragrant with jasmine and stocks planted in vast terracotta pots in regimented lines on each side of the gravel. Lining each side was an array of ornately carved pillared cloisters, flagged with marble that echoed to the clack of her slippers. They fell into deep shadow before entering through a solid wooden door that moved inwards on silent hinges and closed softly behind them. She said not a word, but bade him follow her up a spiral staircase lighted with cresset lamps in alcoves that barely gave enough light to see the marble steps.

They ascended two flights to a cool landing that was

fanned by a gentle breeze as the shutters were thrown open with only the lady-in-waiting for company.

Valentina dismissed the maid, who bobbed a curtsey and disappeared through a side door, where another chamber lay, Flavio decided, still worried about any plot that might trap him. Valentina then beckoned him to follow through the doorway to her own chamber, closing the door behind him and bolting it.

"There now, are you more reassured? For you have been on tenterhooks since you stepped into my carriage. There are two more doors – one to Maria's rooms adjacent and one leading off to the connecting chamber and the rest of the apartment. You may search and reassure yourself of our privacy, for you are like a caged wild animal, uncertain and expectant, and I would sooner have you relaxed," she said gently but with a slight edge of irritation in her voice. "This night is for pleasure, not wariness. I have little enough to give me pleasure," she purred, "so I take it when and where I can."

Flavio looked around at the beautiful, sumptuous chamber with its looking glasses, red and blue glass ornaments from Venice and finely woven arrases upon the walls mingling with beautiful frescoes and decorous furnishings. He decided that if this provided little pleasure the lady was indeed spoiled. She may be beautiful and desperately alluring, yet she was wilful and indulged.

"And do you always get want you want?" Flavio responded with a smile, knowing there was no artifice here, just an animal lust and a mind to conquer everything she could.

"What do you think? Ere my enforced marriage to my husband, a merging of the powerful families, I was a Sacchetti of Firenze," she said with pride and arrogance.

Now it all started to make more sense to Flavio. He had of course heard of the noble Sacchetti family, for they were ancient in their rule of Florence and their high nobility, and if Valentina was of that line she would indeed be spoiled and indulged beyond belief.

"My lady, with such charms as you possess I have no doubt of it, and rightly so, for such beauty as yours deserves to be celebrated," he flattered, going from cynic to lover in one smooth step. "And your husband is a most fortunate man who is foolish to leave unattended that which all other men must covet."

She smiled like a cat that stretched, preened and purred with stroking and attention, flattered easily by the adoration like so many beautiful women.

"You are a most wicked man to favel me so, yet you are not without your own charm. Rumours have spread about a mysterious pirate, a *vagabondo* and former *condottieri*. Your name is well known in Firenze, and I hear it linked to exploits with the great John Hawkwood."

She poured two goblets of wine with her back to him, and ever suspicious when she brought them forward he made to sip, yet did not drink. Poison was ever present, a powerful enemy and the preferred weapon of a woman, and she could, he realised, have easily slipped something into his goblet. She placed her own upon a side table, apparently reading his mind, gently prised Flavio's grip from his before sipping the wine from it.

She canted her head to one side, apparently appraising the taste of the wine. "No, it is not poisoned," she said after a few seconds. "Yet I blame you not, for such a means of death is common in Firenze, so why not in Viterbo?" The smile she wore cast no blame as she took his hand and guided him to a wide padded couch that stood with pride of place near an empty fireplace. He settled beside her as she began, immediately taking control.

"Now what may I do to allay your fears?" She asked gently, taking his hand and planting a chaste kiss upon it.

"I am interested in the woman behind the beauty. Tell me more about yourself," he encouraged.

"Ah, where to start? Well my family is a supporter of the Guelphs, and with this in mind an alliance with the di Vico family was of paramount importance, for they should be united to combat those who might destroy us. You may know that my husband is supported by Ladislaus, King of Napoli, and has no love for the Holy Father, whom he seeks to resist. To our marriage, though my husband be handsome, he brought baggage – as did I, and the two are not always easy bedfellows."

Flavio kept his face impassive, yet this could be the reason for selling out the city to an invading army if it meant holding out against the church. So many strands to tie together.

"Ladislaus, the self-styled King of Napoli," he snorted. "He seeks the unity of the Papal States under his control, I'll warrant, with the Holy Father as his puppet."

"He does, and brings much to offer in that regard. So my husband seeks to ride his power and command Viterbo as he did before his family was ousted years ago. He hopes that all will fall his way, for he bears much bitterness as to how his ancestors were treated and wishes to rule supreme in Viterbo as they once did."

"Yet whomsoever he aids would surely control him in their turn?" Flavio asked.

"You are naïve. Since when did states rule Roma? No, they seek to unify the States away from Roma, then to rule from there under a unified Italy. A small pawn such as Viterbo, though important, would pall compared to the might of Firenze or Siena. They are the jewels that control all. Now fie on you, for this was not how I envisaged the evening unfolding, yet I seem to have been led down a reluctant path," she said, her mouth pouting in displeasure.

"Then I am at fault," Flavio declared, not wishing to lose her interest. "There are much more important matters to discuss about you than your family's politics. For example, your adorable eyes. From where did you inherit them? Your mother perhaps?"

This brought a smile, and now that he was on much more favourable ground he began the art of seduction of a most willing prey. It was in the middle of the night, as they lay entwined together in bed, that his thoughts turned to matters of state as the jigsaw of Viterbese politics began to fall into place. Yet, if di Vico were the villain, who aided him? For Ladislau was in Naples far away, and how would he control the victors – if indeed they won? The Salimbeni or Visconti families? So much still made little sense. Who had set the assassins upon on the road from Collemi's villa and why? Who knew of Dezi's involvement and why should he be killed?

With his mind reeling, he slipped out of bed, leaving Valentina's still form in her slumbers, her face beautiful even in repose. She had been an ardent and skilful lover, full of yearning and desire and as keen to please as she was to be pleased. Yet still he was not comfortable here, nor was he able to relax with a potential enemy so near. With that in mind he dressed quietly, carrying his boots and sword belt, letting himself out softly. Once upon the landing he looked out over the open casement. He was two stories up, and he hoped there were no guards on the stairway, or looking out over the street. He could not risk leaving the way he had entered, so he undid the braided ties from the curtains that framed the casement. Knotting them together he produced a length of cord of some ten feet. Long enough to reach the sturdier trunk of a mature *gilicine* that had attached itself to the wall and spread upwards. Tying one end to the shutter hinge he belayed the cord and slid down to find that the trunk where the lead ended was some nine inches thick and easily able to bear his weight. He let go, praying the lower branches would hold as he rustled his way down to the street below.

Pleased with himself, Flavio offered an ironic salute to the window of Valentina's apartment above, brushed himself down and made his way surreptitiously back to *La Capra*, always aware that the Watch may be abroad, keeping to shadows and taking his time.

He woke the next morning with a smile upon his face, and decided that he very much liked his way of obtaining information, even if it was not how Cardinal Vitelleschi would have envisaged it, and wondered how Valentina would feel this morning, with a thick head no doubt (if his was anything by which to judge) and waking to an empty bed.

Having informed Bani of all that he had learned, Flavio bade him come part of the way to the cardinal's palace, and to go from there to look in upon the young apothecary Stefano Ventolini.

Chapter Sixteen

An hour later, as the bells rang out for Terce, Flavio found himself in an ante-chamber of the papal Palace. It had been built more than a hundred and fifty years ago for the popes who were being persecuted in Rome and who had fled the Eternal City in fear for their lives. It was the first time he had been in the palace, and he had time to marvel at the frescoes upon the walls before he was led into the elegant Conclave Hall devoted to the Guelfs. He went on into the heart of the palace, to the magnificent Gualtiero Hall, with marble floors and upper walls lined with beautiful frescoes, murals and a carved vaulted wooden ceiling that was in itself a work of art.

There were numerous doorways leading off the main hall, and he watched a flurry of servants and clerics going to and fro, swift and almost silent in their movements, offering benign nods and sombre expressions in passing as Flavio awaited his audience with the cardinal.

Finally the doors at the end of the hall were opened and

the cardinal entered as two guards parted to allow him through, followed by a clerk and servant.

Flavio bowed and extended a leg before kissing the cardinal's ringed finger. He was, as Flavio remembered from their meeting the previous evening, a man of great inner strength, yet he could not detect any godly presence as he had with more lowly priests, especially those who had accompanied Hawkwood and had provided great solace to the scared and the dying within his armies. It seemed to Flavio, as he had reflected on many occasions, that the higher in rank one rose in the church the further removed a man seemed to become from his real purpose in being there, and the cardinal was no exception. He would bear watching, even if he was not in quite the same league as Cardinal Vitelleschi.

"Your eminence, it is most gracious of you to grant me an audience when you are so pressed for time with matters of state," Flavio began.

The cardinal sat, turned his head slightly and nodded, accepting the compliment with due grace. "My son, as you say, time is pressing. What do you have to discuss with me? For I would aid you and this city however I may to ensure its safety."

"Your eminence," Flavio said liking the fact that the cleric was not going to stand on ceremony, and he could cut to the chase directly. Churchmen of this elevated rank made him nervous, as much by the power they wrought, as by their direct presence. The sooner he could sow the seeds of concern, assess the reaction and be away, the better. "I have intelligence that there are plans to surrender the city to outside forces who would wish to conquer and govern, with a view to ultimately taking control of Roma and the whole of Italy, enforcing dominion over all."

The cardinal gave no outward sign of having heard this and remained silent, unlike di Vico, so Flavio continued. "There are agents – men who were devoted and loyal servants to the city – who have been murdered, and forces are already undermining the safety of Viterbo. One such man, before he succumbed to his wounds, told me I should look to the church, for there lay the answer, and I wondered therefore if you had any information that may aid me in my quest to root out this evil."

"May I ask whose authority you act upon, to take on such an onerous and, if I may say so, altruistic task? For as I understand it, you are not of Viterbo, but rather Corneto. Why should you care what occurs in this city and concern yourself in such matters?" Pielo responded calmly.

"Because, your eminence, I was tasked to do so by one of your brothers in the church, Cardinal Vitelleschi. For he had…" here Flavio hesitated, not wishing to call them agents, "… friends within the city, men of repute who had heard rumours within their business dealings and had advised the cardinal accordingly."

"Then why did they not come to me as God's servant within the *civitas*?"

It was a loaded question, and Flavio realised that he had been trapped, yet he had had enough of games with churchmen. He was trying to help and to carry out the mission that had been imposed upon him by Vitelleschi, and was now being held to account by yet another high ranking cleric.

"I know not, your eminence, for I do not read men's

minds. I merely try to help where I may," he replied tartly, caring little for the offence given.

There was a tightening around the cardinal's eyes as he clearly took umbrage at Flavio's sarcastic response. "Take care, my son. My patience is like my time, and neither are limitless," he threatened. "And what have you learned from your endeavours, pray tell me?"

Flavio kept an impassive face, neither taking offence nor showing judgement. He placed his faith in feats of arms and the Devil take the hindmost, and so let it be with this feat of words. He offered the cardinal an expedited version of what he had learned, giving no names, save that of Bishop Ranieri and poor Signor Dezi, though he did mention the banking connections linking Florence with Viterbo and di Vico that he had discovered, and the ledger itemising all.

He achieved the first real sign of emotion from the cardinal with this evidence: "A ledger?" he exclaimed. "From where did you obtain this document?"

"I do not recall, and it matters not," Flavio replied. "What is important is that it links, by virtue of finance and agreements of usury, Firenze and certain citizens of Viterbo, who may by virtue of their connexions be open to pressure or blackmail and succumb to betraying the city."

"May I see this list?"

"Unfortunately, your eminence, I do not have it about my person. I have dispatched it to be examined by those more skilled in such matters than am I," he replied, enjoying the ploy, for he had been ready for such a request.

The cardinal raised an enquiring eyebrow, half in disbelief, half in frustration it seemed to Flavio, in response to his deliberate obfuscation. "Then have it fetched or recall as many of those names upon the list that could be indicted and I will see that they are questioned or at least watched," he ordered.

"I needs must give it some thought, your eminence, and I will be sure to provide such information in due course. Given my concern for the *civitas*, may I ask what numbers of papal troops are available for the protection of the city?"

"Such things are none of your concern, but we have sufficient to aid and protect the church as is necessary when called upon," the cardinal replied with a sardonic smile of his own.

Of such evasions are statesmen made, Flavio thought. He had expected an answer of this nature, and he knew of course that large private armies were forbidden within the city as a threat to order and the possibility of insurrection. Which meant that the defence fell to the local militia and what private force the church could bring to muster – a poor showing if he was any judge.

Questions followed to and fro in the manner of an interrogation, and then as if by some unseen signal the audience seemed to be at an end. The cardinal, a master of diplomacy and tact, gave off an unseen aura to that effect. A servant hovered and indicated that Flavio should leave. He made to go, offering his parting salutations and the cardinal rose from his seat and finished with one last barbed order. "Forget not your promise to furnish me with the information, for I shall not forget – even if you do."

Flavio nodded, bowed and turned to leave. At the top of the steps he looked up to the blue morning sky and breathed deeply of cleaner air away from the stultifying atmosphere of the palace. He shook his head and made his way down. Matters were becoming clearer to him, and he knew above all else that he must ensure that the ledger and papers were stored securely away from his own rooms, which were sure to be searched. He made his way back to the La Capra, thinking about what he should do.

Inside the palace, Cardinal Pielo called a servant to him. The man looked innocuous enough, yet a feral intelligence was reflected in his face.

"What say you, Danielo? You heard all?"

"As you say, your eminence. I wonder who it was that provided Signor Sabatini with his information – and indeed if it all came from one source. I suspect there is more at play here than meets the eye. For a mere sword for hire, he has done well in a short period of time. I wonder where he will next seek answers?"

"That is of no matter, for we shall put him on a path that will aid our own ends. Have my clerk attend upon me, for I wish to write a missive to be delivered this day without fail, within the hour if possible," he ordered.

Flavio reached the inn to find Bani already returned with the good news that Signor Ventolini was alive and well.

"Bani, I want you to take my notes revealing all those who borrow money from Signor Collemi and the copies I made of the ledger and take them to Il Grappolo upon the river, for Maurizio will now have returned, or will do so very soon. Ask him to send a messenger downstream and have them delivered to Cardinal Vitelleschi, who will know what actions to take," he ordered.

Bani nodded and asked: "My lord, what are you to do?" his voice was full of concern, feeling that the net was closing in and that his master was at its centre, ready to be caught.

"Me? Why I shall go to beard the dog in his den and attend upon Signor di Vico with my news to test his reaction, the better to know who to trust. But first I shall see Bishop Ranieri and tell him of my meeting with the good cardinal," he said with a wolfish smile.

Bani admonished him, saying that it was foolish to provoke one as powerful as di Vico, particularly as he had been intimate with his wife the evening before.

Flavio brushed it off: "Bah, she is as guilty as me and has more to lose. Nothing will signify in that regard."

Not to be dissuaded, Flavio handed over the papers and saw Bani off as he rode for the western gate to ride down to the river they had left, what seemed an age ago. Flavio sighed and first walked to the house of Ilaria's aunt, where he hoped Ilaria was still secreted safe from harm's way. He found her there, sad but coping with her life. Her aunt, a widow without children of her own, had been most solicitous, and was engaged in helping her run the business of clerking and providing written documents for those who could neither read nor write. It was a good occupation as it kept her from direct contact with anyone who might report her presence there to any who could use it for ill intent. He decided that he would introduce her to Signor Ventolini in due course, as there may be some mutual profit to be made between them with her father's demise.

With his conscience clear, he strode purposefully along to the cathedral, considering what he would say to di Vico and how to impart his knowledge of circumstances without betraying Bishop Ranieri, Tiziana or di Vico's own wife. He met with the cleric in one of the chapels of the cathedral.

"Where were you, my son? I feared for you," Ranieri asked suspiciously.

"Fear not, your grace. I am much harder to kill than you imagine."

"I think that you are not telling me all of your conversation with his eminence, Cardinal Pielo. I also begin to think that I myself am being watched and followed, for twice now I have seen an unfamiliar figure – the same man, mind you – at my heels, and pretending to have some innocuous occupation when I turned. So if they fear not the church, have a care my son, for they would be even less well disposed towards a mere agent of Vitelleschi."

"Father," Flavio assured him, with a devil may care smile. "I have much better protection than purple robes or crucifix. I have a strong right arm and the skill to use this." He patted the sword hilt at his belt.

"By God's grace you may need more, and I say with my blessing, go with God my son," Ranieri said piously, making the sign of the cross in the air before Flavio. "And upon your return tell me all, for I have only half the story I am bound," he said, and with a flourish of his hand was gone.

Flavio was, he had to admit, enjoying himself immensely – despite, or because of the danger. His blood sang and he felt alive with the alertness of combat that he usually only experienced upon the battlefield or just before action. But for all that, he took precautions, twisting and turning, walking into shops and carefully scanning about as he left.

He could detect no undue presence, and with this in mind he finally made his way to di Vico's palazzo, which he had only left but a few hours before – though in happier circumstances, he thought to himself, a rueful smile upon his face. He begged an audience with the great man at his door, and the major domo, for some reason, seemed better disposed towards him than the last time he had called. He was shown through to an ante-chamber where he was kept waiting for a long period. The bells were chiming for Vespers when he was finally admitted, at the beckoning of a liveried servant.

He followed the flunkey and schooled his temper along with his features. It would do his cause no good if he was visibly irascible at the man before he had attempted to gain any information and watch his response to his questions.

Di Vico looked careworn and tired, as though he had overindulged the night before, as his wife had hinted would be the case during their brief liaison the previous evening. With such thoughts in mind, Flavio smiled inwardly at the realisation that he had cuckolded this arrogant lord before him and was now serving him in his turn. Then he brought his thoughts to focus and constructed around himself a different personality.

"My lord, you are most gracious to entertain a meeting with no appointment."

"I have but a few moments, for many matters of government occupy me at this juncture. How may I be of service?" di Vico responded brusquely.

"My lord, it is I who shall be able to offer service I believe, to return if I may to the safety of this beloved *civitas*."

"*Dio Mio,* you wish to bore me with such matters once again? I will offer you but moments," di Vico said, obviously irritated. He flicked his hand dismissively and called upon his major domo to fetch a servant with some watered wine.

Flavio began to explain that he had come by information relating to loans made to those in power supplied by Florence.

"Who?" di Vico demanded. "Who is named on this list that you so carelessly acquired?" he demanded, his anger driven by more than a little fear that was noticeable to Flavio's eyes. *Ah so you are guilty, my lord,* he thought.

"I know not, my lord. A messenger was received who provided me with a package – a missive unsigned, I know not from whom. As to the names, why it is all in code and I have not yet been able to decipher it, though a key will soon arrive that will explain all," he lied.

"So there is no definite proof of this imagined deception?" di Vico said, a flicker of relief passing over his face.

"Not as yet my lord, but I felt honour bound to enlighten you as to the presence of some potential grand treason, for with names and loans bound upon duty and the usury involved, those at risk may succumb to bribery or blackmail and be forced to surrender the *civitas*," he offered gently.

"I should still like to know exactly how you came by your information, for I feel that you deceive me, Sabatini," di Vico growled..

"My lord, you do me wrong. I am innocent of such a charge and will endeavour to find the answer. Now my lord,

I should not wish to presume upon your generous hospitality any longer and would be gone."

Before di Vico could argue, Flavio offered a flourish of a bow and turned to leave, gaining the door before he could be halted.

As soon as he had gone, di Vico called his major domo and said: "As we planned, have it done now."

The servant bowed in acknowledgment and left silently.

Outside, Flavio squinted at the low sun as the stifling heat left the day and smiled to himself. *Now let us see what occurs*, he thought. He had stirred the hornet's nest and waited to see who left the palazzo urgently, and upon what business.

He paused to see where he may secure a goblet of wine, that would also give him a vantage point where he could see who came and went from the palazzo, for he was sure that new movement would soon be forthcoming. Securing a seat by an open shutter at a nearby *osteria*, he had but sipped at the cold liquid twice before he saw a messenger leave, intent upon delivering his missive, making for the papal palace. Having already paid for his wine, Flavio took a final mouthful and made to follow him out into the street.

He moved off, following the man at a distance, pushing through the early evening foot traffic. As he went to cross after his quarry, he heard cries of alarm from pedestrians in the street. A carriage rushed down the narrow thoroughfare travelling much too fast, the driver struggling to contain the two lumbering beasts who were clearly upset and agitated for some reason – bitten by a horse fly perhaps, for they were prevalent and vicious insects at this time year.

Two men, rough in their garb, made to halt the horses, clearly knowing what they were doing by their actions and prepared to dash away if they failed in their attempts, raising hands to distract and stop the runaways. Flavio was unable to pass and made to help them, grabbing the running reins and bringing the carriage slowly to a halt. It was the last thing he knew; a cudgel crashed sideways to the side of his head and blackness enveloped him. As he sank downwards, strong arms grabbed him, no *contadino* this, but a well set up stranger of good clothes and respectable demeanour.

"Poor fellow, he has fainted in the excitement," the man called to any who could hear. "And bravely done too, for the carriage and pedestrians are saved."

The carriage door opened, and a lady beckoned to her coachman, saying that she would take the poor fellow to a surgeon to have him remedied. The two rougher men sprang to her aid, and with their help Flavio was bundled into the carriage, which set off at a spritely pace, all seemingly now under control. The incident was soon forgotten, and peace returned to the street, as water in a pail when a hand is removed. The whole thing was no more than another minor incident in a busy city.

Chapter Seventeen

Flavio woke some half an hour later lying on the ground and feeling groggy, in that state of semi-awareness that arrived just before waking completely from being knocked out. But he knew from past experience, even in this state to keep still and say nothing, and to make no sound. He heard faint voices from far off. He tried to hear as his ears rang, as he performed the minute checks that every soldier and horseman does after a bad fall or fight before attempting to move properly – checking each limb by contracting and releasing the muscles and flexing each joint very carefully. There was nothing broken, he decided, he was just bruised and battered. No belt was cinched at his waist, so he had been disarmed, and he saw or heard at least five men around him. The odds in his half-conscious state were not good, and he decided it was better to wait it out and see what the fates brought.

"Do we throw him down the well?" one gruff voice

asked. Flavio recognised it as that of one of the men who had attempted to flag down the carriage.

"No, *idiota*." This was a more cultured voice, clearly the leader. "We lower him down, for we want him alive. The fall may kill him, and he would no longer be able to answer the questions our lord wishes answered. Two days in the well and he will be begging for water and to be let out at any cost." He sneered down at the recumbent figure before him.

With Flavio still feigning unconsciousness, a rough cord was slipped under his armpits and around his chest and he was pulled over the edge of an old well. His legs were manhandled over the raised stone wall, and he was unceremoniously heaved over, to hang like a rag doll from the rope, dropping gradually as the hemp slid over the old wooden winding bar that creaked and squealed as he was lowered. In his befuddled state he wondered why he would need water if it was a well, and why he should not drown. His answer came quickly as he was dropped the final few feet. The bottom was damp but there was no obvious sign of water. The rope slid from around his torso under the weight of his body, and he managed to flex his knees at the last moment to cushion his fall, to end an ungainly heap upon the muddy bottom of the old well.

He recoiled, for in the light that came from the hole above him, he saw rotting clothes and the flensed bones of skeletons who had once been living men. A tomb for the dead and dying, holding foul miasmas in the damp and fetid air. He caught himself, for he was not afraid of the dead. They were old companions, he and death, tolerant of each other as easy bedfellows. These skeletons were way past decomposition, and all ills would have leached from their bones long ago. Yet he knew enough about wounds not to let any raw cuts come within contact with these bodies, for that could be the death of him. Flavio touched his head where it throbbed, finding a lump that was pronounced and swollen, yet the skin had not been broken. Saved by his hat, he reasoned. He looked up as he heard more laughter.

"A companion for you, Signor Sabatini, to hear your sins afore you die," came a shout from above.

He heard querulous cries of fear and alarm as another figure blocked the light and as a fully conscious man was lowered over the spindle above. As he dropped closer, Flavio saw a priest's robes and recognised Bishop Ranieri.

"Father!" he called, reaching out to aid the descending priest's landing as best he could.

"Enjoy your time together. We will return to see how you fare," came the scathing call from above. The voices disappeared as the laughter faded.

"Bishop Ranieri, how came you to be caught in this spider's web of deceit?" Flavio asked in anguish.

"They must have followed you my son and seen us...seen us together. Now we are caught and shall die here, may God have mercy on our souls," Ranieri whispered.

"No, for they will not kill you. You are here to be punished alone, I'm bound, and for aiding me in my charge to find all I could about the plot to sell Viterbo," he said seeing the strategy. "Did they hurt you? How were you taken?" he asked in concern, for the bishop was older than him by some years and not hardened to the ways of war and violence as was he.

"A side chapel, as I was leaving confession. My robes were pulled over my head and foolish did I feel, like it was a child's prank. I was then bustled out, I assume by a side door, for I lost consciousness due to lack of air, and I could not breathe," he replied, clearly upset and exasperated.

"And you my son?" he asked now settled, seated on the damp ground.

"I was taken in a stupid trap, with my own plans turned against me. They lured me into thinking that I was the predator, not the prey. Oh and how they turned that against me, and I fell for it like a green *ragazzo*. And here you find me, with no one knowing where I am, save that I met with the cardinal and then di Vico – and it was he who plotted this so well, I am sure, for I baited him. He may have had some word aforehand of my intentions to be so well organised, yet he kept me waiting a considerable time, well long enough to arrange my capture." Flavio said thoughtfully, trying to blot out the ache that thumped within his head and continued to befuddle his thoughts.

"You met with his eminence first. Did that augur well?" Ranieri asked gently, " for I feel guilty at being the architect of such a meeting that led you to di Vico."

"Ah, bishop, the fault was not yours, and still there are missing pieces that need to be put in place. I have been led a merry dance, it seems. Yet I know not who, if indeed there is only one person, pulls the strings to make me dance as a mawmet upon their command."

"Then tell me, my son, for we have nothing but time, as upon our last meeting you were in haste and mayhap I might be able to help you solve the riddle."

Flavio decided, with a sense of resignation, that he had better tell the priest so that he could get a message of some sort to Vitelleschi if he should die. He told the bishop much of what had occurred – leaving out the sordid details of his *mésalliance* with both of the married women he had seduced. Or had it been the other way around? He knew not the details, and were the bare bones enough? He wondered as he paced the bottom of their impromptu cell, touching the walls of rough stone that were held in place by crumbling mortar.

He looked up to the fading daylight above as he finished his tale, through which the priest in the manner of his kind used to hearing confessions, had nodded and occasionally asked a question, not wishing to interrupt Flavio's train of thought.

"That, your grace, is my sad tale, to end in such ignominious defeat," he finished. "For soon we shall be thirsty upon the rule of threes. After three days without water a man's spirit will break, and he will do anything for release. For though the lip of the well be only thirty feet or so above," he said, looking up again at the frustratingly close top of the shaft, "it may as well be a league without a rope or steps to ascend."

He looked about him and mentally spanned the diameter of the shaft, realising that it was too wide to 'walk' up by bracing hands and feet. He tested the mortar again with his fingers. It crumbled, yet offered insufficient purchase to provide foot or hand holds, and without his dagger to prise such deep and strong enough slits to hold him, it was futile.

"Fear not, my son, we shall pray to God and in his mercy

and mayhap we shall be released. For I think not that they will kill me, a man of God, and the bare bones as you say," he nodded pointedly at the skeletal remains on the earth, "shall be enough to see justice done."

Flavio followed his gesture, pleased that he was keeping a strong spirit, for he could not abide to aid another who fell short of his own indomitable will.

Then a thought occurred: "By the good Lord, father, you have the right of it. God has indeed provided with the bare bones."

The bishop looked on in puzzlement as Flavio bent to rip the rotting cloth from one of the dead bodies. With a sickening crack, he pulled free and cleaned what would once have been a rib, hooked and curved to a vague point. "Come father, aid me, for has the good Lord not provided?" he said, a smile upon his face. The bishop pushed himself to his feet, unsure if Flavio had already turned to madness.

"Your grace, I hesitate to ask, but please tear a strip of your robe and untie your cincture, for I have need of it." Still puzzled, Ranieri obeyed, untying the cord from around his waist which proved to be some eight feet long. Flavio knelt again to pull more ribs from the broken skeleton, and with cloth binding the bone he started to scrape out the first line of mortar with his makeshift chisel. The first line was about three feet from the ground and here, damp and rotten as it was, the mortar came away easily, so that a whole stone was soon released.

With this foothold opened, Flavio reached as high as he could and started again, this time seeking just an opening, as wide as the three-inch mortar joint. This also crumbled out, and he tested the handhold with fingers that were strong from use of arms and handling horses. His grip held and he grinned, his teeth flashing in the dim light. "Father, we may yet be saved," he said. He tore out more ribs, pushing them into the tops of his boots so that they flared out, greyish-white in the last of the light. Taking the bishop's cincture he made three loops, tying them off, one at each end and one in the middle, resting the cord about his neck for easy access.

Then with his foot secured in the first open cavity and Ranieri pushing, he reached upwards, driving his fingers into the opening. With one foot upon the priest's shoulders he could now balance some eight feet above the ground, and using his free right hand he gouged another hold as high as he could reach, his arms aching with the effort and his head throbbing.

"I am tiring, my son," came the feeble voice from below.

"Just a little longer father, I am nearly done," Flavio begged.

Then, just as he felt the priest began to falter, the sharp rib went into a cavity, protruding some four inches. It was enough. He hauled upon the bone, pulling himself upwards, his shoulders hunching with effort as he did so. He wedged his foot into the hole below and he was up. With his right hand now gripping the rib, he began again to gouge at the mortar, sweat pouring off his brow, his shirt and doublet soaked in moisture at the exertion. He scraped and gouged, finally securing enough space to force in the next rib, testing its security. It wobbled and he almost fell, losing his footing. He scrabbled and scraped against the wall, finally getting his booted foot back into the slot beneath, breathing hard.

He slipped the top loop of Bishop Ranieri's cincture over the lower rib and twisted it around his wrist, giving him more security and relieving his tired fingers. He scraped above once more to contrive a deeper and more secure hole. Satisfied, he drove in the bone again, and this time it held. He gouged a lower hold until he had two footholds and one handhold. He stepped up and heaved again. He was, he estimated, over half way up now, and he slipped off the cord to repeat the process. Twice more he made hand and footholds, gradually climbing the wall.

Near the top he dropped a rib as he pulled it out of his boot, cursing as it fell below. The rim of the well was tantalisingly close now, but his arms were tired and the mortar here was harder, baked by the sun to a firm crust. He decided to gamble. He took the looped cord and with one arm flung it out and up over the spindle. It went over, but the looped end was still too far up for him to reach. He cried out in frustration, wiggled the cord and gradually it lowered, inch by inch, with the weight of the looped end finally dangling just above his head.

Flavio reached up, praying the rib below would hold, and slipped his fingers through the loop. He was now held, suspended by the cord, with one foot on a rib. With a final prayer he swung his feet upwards to the beckoning lip of the well, all weight upon his arms and the spindle, which creaked and groaned under the strain. Flavio's heels found the top of the wall, and he puffed and panted, trying desperately to gain purchase and 'walk' his feet across the parapet to take the strain off his arms. At last he managed to hook them over, pulling himself closer, willing himself to overcome the sharp pain in his calves and the back of his knees as the rough stone cut into his legs. Finally, on the point of balance, he felt the spindle give, and just in time he gripped the upright to save himself from toppling over backwards. He shouted a warning to Ranieri below as the heavy spindle fell into the well. It struck with a soft thud that worried him as he sat on the parapet, his chest heaving.

"Father?"

"I am all right, my son, it missed me. God looks after his own," the bishop called back, seemingly in good spirits.

"Thank the Lord for that. Father, I have no way to release you, yet I shall return with a rope, food and water as soon as I am able."

"I shall await your return and console myself in prayer, thanking Him for our deliverance," the bishop replied piously. Flavio laughed. He was free, and had defeated death once again. He looked about him, flexing his arms and legs to ease the strain from them. The well was hidden from view by a small grove of trees, yet through them he saw the mighty walls of Viterbo some distance away, showing under flares and brands upon the battlements in the dusk now. He was still high up, and looking round he saw the river. *Ah to have been so close, yet not near enough*, he lamented. For there in the distance he spotted smaller lights twinkling downstream and judged it to be Il Grappolo. He hoped that his men had arrived and had been met by Bani.

"Father, all is well. We are not far from aid. I shall return *subito*!" he shouted encouragingly down the well. The older man affirmed that he would wait for him, still apparently in good spirits despite his now lonely captivity.

Chapter Eighteen

Taking his bearings by the twinkling of lights and the lighter hue shown by the moonlight on the ribbon of water, Flavio readied himself to set off in the dark, hoping to come across a path or track that would make his journey easier. The anxious feeling of being watched prickled at his neck. He had no weapons, and if there was an armed guard left to keep watch over the well he would have been hard pressed in his tired state. Seeing a stout branch lying under one of the trees surrounding the well, he picked it up, pulled off the top twigs and found that it was about three feet long. It would do, he decided, and would aid him in his travails through the countryside. He proceeded down the hill, stopping to listen from time to time. He went through a hedge, where he came upon a small steading nestling into the lee of the bank. Banging upon the door, he was met by a fearful farmer who opened it tentatively, armed with a long sheaving knife in his hand to a chorus of two barking dogs. It was a time of distrust when none should be abroad after dark if they had good intent, Flavio reflected.

"*Scusi, signor*," he began gently. "I am sorry to trouble you this night, yet I have need of your help. Do you know the old well yonder on top of the hill?" Flavio pointed back up from where he had walked.

"Si signor, my *padre* had a farm there many years ago. The well is all that is now left, and it is dry and no good," the man replied.

"I know, for I was trapped inside it, and one remains still there, a bishop from Viterbo. Ask no more questions, yet fetch a rope and haul him out, for he will be most grateful. Here is a florin for your trouble." Breaking two stitches, Flavio took a coin from inside the lining of his doublet, an old soldier's trick to hide coins, and passed it across to the astounded old man.

He begged a drink of water and a bite of bread, wolfed this down and saluted the farmer, then went on his way, trusting the man to fulfil his promise. For two more hours he struggled, then he came to a track that led down to the river. It was only a farm track, yet it served better to him than the rough undulating countryside, and he made better time as a result.

It was after midnight when he reached the river banks, and following a narrow trail he swung inland up river to find the glowing lights of Il Grappolo still burning, for many wished to trade here in secret, and cargoes often arrived after dark, the smugglers knocking quietly to raise the landlord and owner who was available at any hour for the right price. Flavio found a rowing boat tied to the bank, he did not want to use the swing bridge that was at this moment back on the other side of the river to aid security and to avoid collision with late travelling craft.

He slipped the knot, settled himself and began to pull steadily on the oars, finding a stiffness in his arms from his recent climb out of the well.

Reaching the far bank, he tied the boat and made his way to the door of Il Grappolo that still bore lights shining from inside as well as brands fluttering in the dark, highlighting the stout wooden door. Upon his knock a small hatch was opened, he was identified and permitted entry with bolts being slid smoothly back from within.

A tall man of huge girth permitted him entry, a long knife at the ready in case of deceit. Once in the full light, the custodian relaxed, recognising Flavio from the many occasions that he had visited the warehouse and trading post as a smuggler. "Signor Sabatini, you are welcome at this late hour," he growled in a deep voice that matched his stature.

"*Grazie*, Marco," Flavio replied, then turning he saw a welcome sight, for Maurizio, Bani and more of his crew were awake and drinking at a quiet table towards the back of the tap room.

"Flavio!" Maurizio called as he and Bani rose as one, the latter surprised to see his master arriving so late. "What becomes you to be so transported here at this hour?" he questioned, concern in his voice, seeing Flavio's dishevelled appearance and lack of weapons.

Bani was less vocal but equally disturbed at the sight before him; "What befell you, master, for all is clearly not well?" he said, moving aside and offering a chair and a goblet of wine. Flavio raised a tired hand and gratefully grasped the proffered cup, draining it in one long gulp.

"Ah, that slides down exceedingly well," he said, dropping exhaustedly into a waiting settle, tearing at the remains of a cob of bread that was sitting on the table before him.

"Marco, some more food, *subito,* for Flavio has worked up an appetite," joked Will, Flavio's archer captain, amused at his master's sudden hunger.

With more food brought, including a platter of hot pork stew, and Flavio finally sated, he began upon his companions' urging to impart all that had occurred, ensuring that none, not even Marco, heard his full story. For there were names that he did not want spread about, and secrets that he wished to keep until the right moment.

In his newly acquired halting Italian Bani asked: "With all that you now impart and your adventures in the well, do you think you are any closer to solving the riddle of who is to betray Viterbo and who would look for your death?" he asked carefully.

"I have ideas as to who may be behind such matters, yet for even that I must have care, for if it be di Vico – or at least his hand in part – then we have a powerful enemy that even with all of you at my back I wouldst fail to defeat. For he has his own company of arms at his beck and call. No, I must be subtler than that, and with such knowledge as I have, trap him, as he sought to trap me. For he thinks me languishing in a well – though I suspect that with the rise of morning he will be informed otherwise – and I hope that the good bishop is too released from his gaol. Upon the morrow we shall enter Viterbo by one of the smaller gates, quietly and unannounced."

With this final decision, a room and pallet were found for Flavio and he fell soundly into an exhausted sleep, watched over by Bani to ensure that no harm came to his master.

* * *

With a deal done on the goods to be stored with Marco Gubbio the landlord, and all stowed safely away, Flavio and his men set out on hired horses for Viterbo the next morning. Flavio sent one of his men to check with the farmer to see if he was all right and if he had been successful in releasing the bishop. With a force at his back, however small – for they numbered but six, of which two were English archers that he always valued – Flavio felt better able to cope with the seemingly overwhelming forces arrayed against him.

They rode around the city and entered by the southern gate of Porta del Carmine.

It was a gate little used by main traffic, and was for merchants or farmers in from the countryside, and the guards were accordingly more relaxed, knowing many by sight.

They had a borrowed a farm waggon, covered with borel sacking and roped in place and pulled by two mules that came up behind the riders. Neither guard paid any attention as it was driven by one of Gubbio's men who they knew, and bribes were paid accordingly to turn a blind eye. Passing under the gate, Flavio and his men waited until the waggon caught up and made for the house of Signor Dezi, the apothecary. The southern gate was close by, and it was but a short distance.

Flavio arrived at the shop expecting to see it closed and shuttered. Instead he found it open and ready for business. Jumping down from his horse, he pushed open the door to the ringing of the bell, his borrowed dagger ready to be drawn.

"Signor Sabatini!" came a voice from inside, as Ilaria came into view. "We were worried about you, for we had heard nothing for two days."

"Never mind me," he soothed her qualms. "What are you doing here in the open?" he demanded.

"I could no longer remain cooped up. My aunt is kind, but it does not suit me to remain inside. They will not come for me, and I want to do something. My father was killed, murdered here, and I sulk around hiding. I have nothing if not to live for his revenge. If that means my life then so be it, but I shall go proudly with a thirst for revenge and a dagger at the ready," she said haughtily, bringing a lethal looking stiletto from beneath her apron in a flash of defiance.

"Where did you get that?" he asked.

"I have it here," she motioned, "a small scabbard fashioned to my own design. It is good, no?" she said almost innocently, deliberately mistaking his meaning with a smile and a tilt of her head.

Flavio threw his hands up again in exasperation: "If you defy me I can do nothing for you!" he said.

She did not even blench: "I do not wish you to do anything for me, I wish to be of use. For its seems that you are struggling in this city of deep secrets, and I can help. I know many people. I can ask questions and all pity me since my father was killed. They will help me and in that way, I will help you," she pleaded with both anger and pity in her voice.

Flavio turned away to find his men grinning at his shoulder, impressed with the spirit of this young woman. Bani was more concerned for her welfare as he emerged from the back of the shop having taken a more circuitous route to ensure all was well within. He liked the spirit of the lovely young woman and did not wish to see her harmed.

The horses and waggon were stabled and stored in the rear yard and the men settled in as Ilaria prepared a hasty and simple meal. Flavio explained in detail all that had happened since they were last together, and she asked: "So you do not know who attacked you? What they looked like? How it happened, nothing?" she asked.

"No, how could I? One moment I was helping to stop a runaway carriage, the next I was shoved down a well," he responded.

"Then this is how I shall help. I know the street that you describe well and many of the shopkeepers there are friends – or were friends of my father. Someone will have seen something that may aid us," she said defiantly. Before any could stop her, she pulled on a light silk head shawl and stepped quickly out of the shop and through the door into the street.

"Bani, go after her. You know these streets as well as any now. Ensure that she is safe from harm. No mercy, kill anyone who tries to hurt or follow her," Flavio ordered, shocked at the wilfulness of the girl, yet showing respect at her pride and fortitude.

Bani caught up with the girl easily, seeing her brightly coloured scarf in the distance. Being taller than most of Viterbo's inhabitants he did not need to follow too closely, and was able to keep an eye out for any possible attackers. Using the backstreets, she quickly made her way to the street where Flavio had been taken and began ducking in and out of various stalls and shops, seeking answers to her questions. She soon learned the exact spot where the kidnapping had taken place and that it had caused some small curiosity, nothing more. A few merchants remembered the incident – more so their boys, who stood outside hawking for business. It was these youths who Ilaria targeted, flirting and engaging with them with the promise of a smile or a future fraternisation that would have shocked and shamed her departed father. Yet, the end was the means to her mind, and she could cope easily enough with their overzealous youthful advances, she reasoned. At one shop, a cloth merchant, she spoke with an apprentice who had seen it all on the day as he had been stacking bundles out on the open decking of the shop when it had happened.

"I saw it all, fair one," he told her with a shy smile. "The carriage was caught and the man who fell I think was hit from behind, but it all happened so quickly. Yet now you ask me, there were two things that were very strange," he said, rubbing his youthful beard, squinting his eyes.

"*Sì* Manrico, tell me?" she urged with a gentle encouraging voice.

"Well, the carriage was occupied by a signora, a lady, well-bred and of high quality, well dressed in fine clothes, for I notice such things working here," He jerked his finger over his shoulder at the shop behind him.

"Anything else? For if she was a lady she would have had a crest upon her carriage?"

"Yes, but it was covered by her trailing cloak, deliberately I feel. I do remember that she was very beautiful. Like you, signorina." The boy smiled, showing white even teeth.

She gave him a smile and a dismissive shake of her head and waved her hand to mock his shameless flattery. "Pah! You are like all the rest, a few gentle words and you think you can make love to me," she replied, but her voice was soft and forgiving.

The boy offered Ilaria a look of mock hurt, and from his vantage on the other side of the street Bani smiled at the byplay of love, the timeless dance between the young. "But Signorina Ilaria, there is more. If I could but see you again I will tell you," the boy said.

"Mayhap," she replied coquettishly with a toss of her head.

He accepted this as invitation enough, and continued. "The two men who made to stop the carriage, after they helped the well-dressed stranger lift the injured man into the carriage, they too mounted up onto the front and back and all drove away, save for the stranger who merely shrugged, smiled, and waved them away as if nothing was the matter. I looked about and saw him mount a tethered horse nearby. He rode off to follow the carriage." Here he nodded his head as if to say, so what do you think of that?

"You are certain of this, and would you not recognise the lady again?"

"She was well-bred, as I say, with a net of pearls dressed in her hair, dark blonde hair and eyes that slanted like a cat."

"You seem to notice women a lot, Manrico. Is each so beautifully adorned in your eyes?" she scorned him playfully.

He was completely unabashed. "No, signorina, none compared to you."

"Pah! Yet I thank you for your information."

"And may I call upon you?" Manrico asked.

"I am still in mourning for my father – yet maybe soon, sometime in the future. We shall see."

And with a swish of her skirts she turned and made to leave the major thoroughfare to return via a side street. As she did so the young Romeo offered her a bow, a smile on his face. Turning away, she had gone but two steps when she bumped into a large figure in front of her.

"Ho now, watch where you go, signorina. Why are you in such a hurry?"

The man before her was tall and strong, and he gripped her shoulders as if to steady both her and himself, the fingers gripping harder, his breath sour as he spoke, causing her nose to wrinkle in distaste. She sought to shake her shoulders free from his hands, at which he span her around to place her back against the recessed wall of a house, now in shadow and away from view of the main street. Ilaria opened her mouth and filled her lungs with air to scream. Sensing this, the man reached out a powerful hand for her throat, cutting off the sound before she could utter it, and he came closer, his stinking breath as much a threat as his physical presence.

"Now, my pretty, why do you go around asking questions? Who wants to know about what happened here days before, eh? Tell me, or you will be sorry. That pretty face shall not be so lovely to tempt the boys if it is cut. Or would you like to lie in the gutter as your father did, gutted like a fish?" he snarled.

Her eyes widened at this reference, anger in them as she tried to knee him between the legs. The blow hit his thigh as he twisted to avoid it. He came from the street, and knew all the tactics of a brawl. "Feisty eh? Well now we shall see."

He began to close his hand around her throat, pinning her right arm so she was unable to draw her dagger as a guttural croak emitted from her lips. "Tell me all, or you will wake to regret it afore you leave this world," he threatened, releasing the pressure by a small amount as her throat wheezed and contracted. Her hand came up to rake his eyes, her sharp nails finding soft tissue. His head recoiled in shock, but he kept his grip and made to bite her wrist with his rotting teeth. Then the pressure was relieved as suddenly as it had been applied. The assailant's back arched in agony as his greasy hair was gripped hard, pulling his head back to prevent any cry from his stretched throat. Ilaria sucked in huge breaths of air, grasping her sore neck as she backed away, seeing Bani's fierce image in front her as he smashed the man's nose to pulp against the wall and whispered closely in his ear.

"You may still live; the wound is not yet fatal. Speak! Who sent you upon this errand? Tell me and I will not geld you to go to the afterlife like a eunuch, squealing as you die."

The man croaked as he sought breath, his lower back in

agony as he realised he had been stabbed. Through his rotting teeth he begged, "Mercy!"

"Tell me," Bani snarled.

"I know nothing...I was paid to question the signorina or anyone who asked questions. We all are," he rasped, the pain in his lower back growing now.

Bani was starting to lose patience, knowing anyone could come along the alley at any moment.

"Who pays you? Where are the others?" he demanded, releasing his hold, allowing the man to lean against the wall as he breathed hard. It was a mistake, for in his mercy, the would-be interrogator drew his own dagger and made to stab Bani. Yet no sooner had the move been made that Bani punched once, twice, thrice with the point of his own rondel deep into the heart and stomach. The attacker wheezed and sank to the ground, his life ebbing away.

"Come, we need to move fast," Bani urged, grabbing Ilaria by the arm as she stood rock solid, shocked by the sudden violence. Bani pulled her none too gently to get her going, breaking the spell. She said not a word until they arrived at the apothecary shop and Bani explained the events to Flavio.

"Well done, Bani. You saved her from a terrible fate, for he would have taken her or killed her," Flavio said. He turned to Ilaria. "Now you see why I worry for you?" he said to her. "So, we have a mystery lady, and I think I know who she may be – yet I still do not believe it," he said shaking his head.

Chapter Nineteen

Flavio waited until dark, then choosing Will, Maurizio and Bani he made his way through the night-time streets. He had wanted Will along as an archer. His war bow was left unstrung, and in the dim light it seemed nothing more than a wooden staff. Bani's recurved bow was strapped to his waist and Maurizio, with his buckler and side sword, was as dangerous as any. They would be good men to have at his back, and Flavio would wish for no others as he watched the comings and goings outside the wall of di Vico's palazzo.

The guard moved inside the double gates and locked them, leaving just two flickering brands illuminating the entrance. But it was not through the gates that Flavio sought to enter, for the wisteria was as strong and solid as it had been when he had descended but a few days ago. With one final look along the empty street he padded across and began to climb it, and reaching the first casement he hauled himself inside and stood silently, listening for any evidence of human presence. Nothing. He levered off his boots and moved up the flight of stairs and across the landing, the hard polished tiles making no sound beneath his feet. Pulling his dagger free, he prised at the door until the lock clicked and the catch was raised.

Once inside he placed the boots carefully upon the floor so that anyone coming in would knock against them. He moved from memory and found himself watching Valentina's sleeping form, her chest rising a falling in the steady rhythm of sleep. She was naked but for a light sheet, and despite his mission of revenge he felt a pulse of lust at the sight of her and the memory of her perfume and their lovemaking days before. He shook such thoughts from his head and was at her bedside in seconds, a hand across her mouth and a dagger to her throat. Her eyes flew open, at which he bounded up onto the bed, pinning her arms with his knees.

"Shh," he ordered in a menacing whisper. "Now, my lady, you may live to see this night out if you are good, to whore for your pimp of a husband again in the future. I care not; one more life in a litany of lives taken is nothing to me. And you deserve to die as much as any other I have sent to the underworld. Dante will be there to guide you on your journey, I am sure," he said with a wicked and mirthless smile. "Now I want answers to questions – of which I have legion.

"Do you agree to tell me, or do I just slit your throat and move on to my next quarry? Blink twice if you agree. But think on't, you may cry out, however I will probably leave unscathed, for this dagger's point shall not leave your throat, one slip and it will bleed you out so that no surgeon can aid you."

Valentina blinked her eyelids twice and Flavio moved his hand slowly. He saw anger as well as fear in her expression and he was wary. This was a woman of spirit – deadly, amoral and completely without scruples.

Her lips clamped shut as she mastered her emotions. "*Bene*," Flavio said. "Now tell me. I know it was you in the carriage the day I was taken, and I know that you aided my abduction. Why?"

"No it was not...I don't know–" Flavio's hand clamped over her mouth again.

"Valentina, I care little for you or your whoremaster husband. Tell me what I need to know, or you will end your usefulness and my revenge will be complete. I was left to die in an old well outside the city, put there by the men who drove your carriage and one other whom I did not see. Tell me who that man was, or I will string you up from these bed posts as a seeming suicide. No one will know but you, me and God, whom I will pray to for forgiveness at my next confession. Your husband won't care and will move to his next mistress. I ask you, is this worth dying for? Now once more, why?"

He lifted his hand ready for a scream that did not come. She cursed him fluently, then as the tirade finished and she had vented her spleen, she sighed deeply. "It was Giovanni, he wanted you silenced. You knew too much, he said, after we pieced together what you told me and what you had implied to him. He was waiting for you as you left the audience and knew that you had been to see Cardinal Pielo. He believed more was to come of debts and indebtedness to others connected to Firenze, and he feared the worst." She shrugged as though that was the whole. Flavio knew it was not all. "He wanted to know your sources and where you had kept your copies of the financial transactions. We searched your rooms to no avail."

"So he sent you to seduce me? It was prettily done, I grant you."

She shook her head, sneering at him. "No, he is not that low or that callous. He sent me to charm you and seduce your mind, and I chose to seduce your body for my own ends."

"Yet you learned little, and I more. For I am free and still you and your husband are tethered to your ambition and wealth. What drives you to such extremes? Seeking so much power from so much sacrifice, and seemingly unhappy enough to seek solace with another man."

"Don't favel yourself. You were not solace but a sport, a whim of chance, no more. As to ambition, what would you know? I am of Firenze, from one of the noble families, and my husband and his family ruled Viterbo for generations. Now we are held at bay, yet soon we shall rise with the power about us, and no force will be able to stop us."

Flavio was disgusted at the sight of the scornful woman before him. He gripped her hair, threw her over onto her front, bound her struggling arms and her legs and gagged her with a silken scarf. She struggled in vain, tightening the well knotted bonds further, muttering unintelligible curses within the gag.

"*Buona notte,* Signora, sleep well," he said as he made a mocking bow. He picked up his boots and left the room in darkness, the candle extinguished. He was sick of this, he decided, and the depths it had brought him to. Would he have killed her, he wondered, his own conscience such as it was? No. Yet he had been tempted, seeing the sneer on her face, and her plotting to have him killed in turn. He had not sunk that low, yet worse had befallen those of her sex on the roads of the *condottieri* which he had travelled in the past, and that too sickened him.

He made his silent way to back to his men and then to the apothecary shop, rather than La Capra, as it would attract attention that he did not want.

His men were alert, yet did not question him, knowing he preferred silence at such times. The morning came and the light pushed the darkness away, flitting through the slatted shutters and bringing with it, Sergio, who had checked upon the farmer and his release of Bishop Ranieri.

"Is the bishop all right?" Flavio asked.

"We know not for certain, as he was not there when the farmer arrived to free him from the well."

"Not there?" Flavio exclaimed "There is no way on God's earth that Ranieri could have escaped the well as I did. Someone must have aided him – and to that end I must go to the cathedral this day and see Cardinal Pielo, to ensure the safety of the bishop."

Later, washed and fed, Flavio found himself waiting once more in the cathedral. He was hoping to see Bishop Ranieri before he attended upon the cardinal, to see how he fared and solve the mystery of his miraculous escape. He found him at prayer, seemingly none the worse for wear, and was greeted as an old friend by one who was pleased to see this errant adventurer once more.

"My son, I am right pleased to see you, by God's grace and praise him for your safe return," Ranieri exclaimed in joy.

"Yet, your grace, it is of more concern to find out how you come to be so safely delivered from the jaws of death or worse."

"That was indeed a miracle. For after you had escaped, another came to check upon the well opening, I know not from where. Calling down he realised it was but me remaining and that you had escaped. He freed me by means of a rope tied to his horse and pulled me up, begging forgiveness and saying he was only doing as was bidden by his master."

Flavio was incredulous. "He set you free? And what of his master? Did you learn aught?"

"No," he shook his head, "for he was tight lipped and surly, and after setting me upon my way to within sight of the city walls, he left me with hardly a word. I sought sanctuary for the night at the church of Santa Maria della Verita – which as you may know is outside the city walls, and where I am well known to the bishop."

Flavio nodded, suddenly seeing all and recalling the grand church, which was close to the city walls yet not inside them. And with that thought, much became clear to him. He asked one final question about the old priest who had first introduced them.

"'Tis most odd, for I have not seen father Stoica for a few days," Ranieri said vaguely. Flavio nodded, thanked the bishop, rejoiced in his deliverance and once clear bade Bani come close.

"Bani, the bishop. Follow him now, for if I am right he moves right soon. Let yourself not be seen, for he is a cautelous one and more wily than he looks."

The Copt raised an eyebrow, yet said nothing and faded away into the crowded streets, secreting himself in a shaded alleyway opposite the cathedral, where he could see the main entrances.

Cardinal Pielo on this occasion was more than ready to see Flavio, and his reception was warmer and more convivial. He was seated and offered watered wine for this private audience with the high ranking cleric.

"My son, what have you discovered?" he asked.

Flavio decided that the time for games was over. He needed this man's help for better or worse, and nothing could put him in a worse predicament than he was already in at the moment.

He explained about his abduction and declared openly now where he had found the information about the borrowings, and best he could the details of them. The cardinal's eyes lowered, he nodded and raised them again to study Flavio.

"My son, you must forgive me for not knowing your true allegiance. I sent a message to di Vico after you left me on the occasion of our last meeting." Here he paused, seeing Flavio's expression change and falter.

"You betrayed me? You informed di Vico of all that I had passed to you in confidence?"

"No, not all, but sufficient to alert him to your intent. I wished to see what happened as a result. Forgive me, yet I knew not how far I could trust you or what your true motives were."

"My true motives? I am Vitelleschi's agent, what more is there to know?" Flavio snapped.

"Many are not who they seem to be in this city, and I trust God, but no one else."

Flavio made to rise. "No, stay," The cardinal held up a hand. "For there is much I would say and that you should hear."

Flavio fought to control his anger and sense of betrayal, yet prudence, and to a certain degree curiosity, got the better of him and he sat and listened. The cold mask of anger upon his face softened as he learned more, until finally the anger was replaced by incredulity.

"You say that you informed di Vico of my meeting with you and intended that I be known to him as an *insidiore*? He should then know of my intent, so I become the prey not the predator. On whose authority and to what end would you do such an act?" Flavio demanded, aghast.

In the manner of his kind, the cardinal did not answer Flavio directly, but responded with a question of his own. "Are you aware of the obligations of the church, and that in such obligations the powers vested in the papal see are restricted? I refer of course," he went on before Flavio had any time to answer, "to the fact that the Holy Father must be seen as a benign force whose mission is to protect his flock. It this case, that flock represents not only those who are gathered in Viterbo, but also those elsewhere who come under his protection. In this way you may see that we suspected di Vico – whose family have long been one of the foremost, if not the most powerful family in Viterbo – of undermining the power of the *civitas*. With his strong private army of servants and men-at-arms, none could stand against him. If such a force were to be used in a less than benign way, why the city would be at his mercy."

"I fail to see how this affects my position, bearing in mind that I was sent by a member of your church to find out who may be betraying your city. I found duplicity, doubled dealing and indeed murder, with one of Vitelleschi's agents stabbed outside his own home; a harmless old man who did nothing other than aid me and pass on information.

"I in turn have been attacked three times: once inside the city and once upon the road returning with information from the country house of the banker Collemi. Then upon my return I was run over, beaten, kidnapped and left to die or rot in a disused well outside the city without aid or help to my rescue. With, I wish to add, one of your own brothers of the church, Bishop Ranieri."

Here Flavio's flow was halted as the cardinal suddenly became very interested, and his face took on an expression of anxiety and concern. "You say that you were put in the well with the bishop? Then if so, did you speak with him in a frank and open manner, telling all that you have imparted to me?" he asked quietly, a new edge to his voice.

"Of course, we were there alone, and I was not sure that I would survive at that point. He on the other hand was convinced that he would not be killed and would intercede on my behalf or at worst pass on all that I told him to the powers that be, hopefully ensuring the city's safety."

"Yet he did not do so, and that in itself confirms our worst fears," muttered Pielo.

"Ranieri, your own man, is in fact in the pay of di Vico and was there to dupe me and pass on all that he knew."

"You knew this?" cried Pielo in surprise.

"Not until I returned and met with him these moments past, for then I realised all. He gave himself and his true intent away, in more than one sense. I was completely taken in until that moment, and I have set one of my men to follow him. He will be caught as a rat in trap – though to kill a priest shall be beyond me," he finished piously, thinking all the while how he could achieve such an end without being caught.

"Leave him be, I order you upon the mercy of your mortal soul if nothing else. For we shall see to our own in a manner that befits his deserts," the cardinal ordered.

"You have not yet explained in full the nature of your deceit and how it now may benefit the cause of Viterbo," Flavio said. "For if di Vico is the main culprit, how is it that we or you – or indeed the church – may counter such a threat?"

"My son, for one so brave and clever you lack the niceties of diplomacy in this regard."

"Ah, so you mean to take such intelligence as I provided to di Vico and blackmail the rogue upon his own actions. Yet how will this strengthen your cause? For if he is forewarned, will he not prevaricate until he can bring his own forces to bear, seize the town and carry on with none to answer to save the victors who rush to Rome. Then, with the aid of the

King of Napoli, he will surely claim all," Flavio replied in dismay.

"Ah, you were not listening and caught not my inference. As you say, we cannot defy him openly, yet if upon threat of such fear of subjugation and with him bribed so as to not object – and indeed in fact approve – we shall upon being asked, use the papal troops as a shield, not a sword."

"You would do such a thing? By the good Lord I see you would, and 'tis a clever stratagem. Fill the town with papal troops based upon evidence of an impending attack, and with di Vico compelled to side with you none would object, for he holds sway with all of his class," Flavio marvelled, then a thought occurred to him. "Yet what of those who are even now preparing to attack? What if the timing is not right or he gets word to them? They could swarm the city ere papal troops arrive."

The cardinal offered Flavio a smug grin. "'Tis all in hand, my son. For an army lies just a few leagues to the south of Viterbo, ready to march in and save us all upon my word."

"What? How came you to be so well prepared so soon?" Flavio asked, surprised at the strategy.

"Ah, all is God's will my son, all is God's will." Pielo clenched his hands together and looked skyward.

They talked a little more and Flavio then asked. "A father, Franciso Stoica, met with me and led me to Ranieri in the cathedral near here, yet I have seen nothing of him recently. Have you seen him at the cathedral or elsewhere?"

The cardinal looked puzzled at this question, trying to recollect who the priest was and whether he had seen him. He could not. The great rise higher, Flavio thought, ignoring all below as stepping stones. For him the meeting was over, so he excused himself, kissed the cardinal's ring and made to leave.

"Remember, my son, I wish to have Bishop Ranieri remain unharmed," were the cardinal's parting words. Flavio merely nodded, turned and left. He was worried for the old priest and for the events that were about to befall the city. He hated not to be in control of his own destiny – and worse, unable to protect those about whom he cared.

Chapter Twenty

Flavio found Bani waiting for him outside at the bottom of the steps, and asked him where the bishop had gone.

"To a church outside the walls, Santa Maria della Verita–" he began, but Flavio cut him off.

"Of course he has! I should have foreseen all this earlier, for I have been a fool," he upbraided himself. "Now, Bani, make best time and fetch the others. Ensure all are armed for war, because I have a feeling that we may need our arms more than ever," Flavio ordered, and turning on his heel he headed west to the Porta della Verita, striding out and pushing those roughly out of his way who incurred his wrath. *I am in no mood for churls,* he thought angrily, realising that the cardinal in all his plotting had missed a trick that was essential to all wars and battles – timing!

Once through the gate he moved away to the north, finding a small cluster of houses like many small communities outside the walls, and a tiny *osteria* where he ordered wine and sat outside on a wooden bench that was shaded by an extensive sloping loggia. The city had grown so much with its wealth that it could no longer contain the bustling metropolis, and new dwellings, inns and shops had sprung up outside the walls, close enough to seek protection inside in times of war yet allowing them space to multiply in their own grounds.

Flavio sat with his face in shadow, able to see everything that moved from the church and cloisters of the della Verita. It was in effect a large monastery constructed around a central internal piazza, with outbuildings, a large dormitory, refectory, gardens and extensive stabling. The whole was very private and the bishop who presided over all was secretive, allowing the general populus into the church only for communal prayer.

It was perfect, Flavio saw, for any clandestine activity and for the collection of illegal troops to launch a fast attack, secret and unseen until the last moment. If a bulkhead could be forged here at the Porta della Verita, the whole city would be opened like an oyster, the pearl to be stolen at will.

His men arrived on horseback a few minutes later, and all settled with the horses loosely tethered, their girths still tight as Flavio suspected that they would soon be riding out along the northern road. He was annoyed, for they had permitted Ilaria to accompany them, claiming that they could not prevent it, save by tying her up and taking her horse, a small and well-made palfrey that Flavio doubted would keep up if they had to ride hard. He shrugged it off; he had more important things to concern him than the spirit of a wilful girl.

It was not long before Bishop Ranieri appeared, his two

servants with him, passing some two hundred yards away, yet close enough to identify the man. He looked every bit as pious as he pretended to be. Flavio shook his head in disgust, but then he was rewarded as the gates of the stables swung open to allow four riders to leave. The front rider was well dressed in colours denoting his rank, and Flavio noted that he carried his own sword at his belt. It was distinctive, with an emerald set into the pommel, and there was no mistaking it.

The two men with him were men-at-arms, their crossbows hooked to their saddles, and the fourth was clearly a groom or body servant. Initially they walked their horses at a crisp pace from the stables, and as soon as they appeared, Flavio finished his wine and made a surreptitious motion with his hand for his men to move, wanting half to be ahead of them, gambling on their route. Once the party had passed the *osteria*, the second half of Flavio's men followed, led by Maurizio. The group looked hard at the inn as they trotted past, but no recognition showed as Flavio was in shadow. As he suspected, once the horses were warmed up they broke into a steady canter, but were now trapped between the two halves of Flavio's men as they let them ride on for a few leagues after leaving the small settlement.

The four rode along the fairly straight road, once Roman, now a wide throughfare to the north west. Only one place offered the chance for ambush, and that was at the river crossing. There were trees in which to hide and the group would be slow to cross either by bridge or ferry lower down.

They crossed by ferry, pulled up and made ready to mount. Flavio's men had crossed by the bridge and set off at a good pace out of sight to arrive just to their rear after the crossing. The men regrouped, and Will and the other archers had their bows strung. They had dismounted and waited for Flavio to make his move.

He and the men with him moved out of their hiding place in the trees to stand before the oncoming horsemen. Flavio held up his hand ordering them to halt as they appeared.

"Do you know with whom you treat?" the leader of the group said. "I am Signor Garibaldi, in the service of Giovanni di Sciarra di Vico, lord of Viterbo. Move or die!" At a wave of his hand the two crossbowmen, seeing no threat of archers and with the ambushers mounted and no crossbows in sight, raised their already spanned weapons, loaded quarrels and made to fire. Bani moved fast. Bringing up his bow arm, an arrow nocked, he drew and loosed in the blink of an eye with no hesitation, then repeated the procedure rapidly. The whistle of flight ended with the two men skewered and down, one still alive, mewling in his pain.

Flavio removed the cowl from around his neck and Garibaldi recognised him: "You! You will regret this," he stormed as the groom looked on in horror, expecting his death at any moment.

"Leave us, boy, go back to Viterbo. You need not die here," Flavio ordered. The groom needed no second bidding, wheeling his horse and riding off as fast as he could. "You, Garibaldi, will hang for treason and murder."

"Ha! You think you can hold me? Come then, I shall return happily beside you as your prisoner. Di Vico will clear me, and no one will dare defy him," he said with a smirk upon his face.

Flavio realised the man was right. He knew well the ways of these provincial cities; money ruled all and the power of the overlords was omniscient. He was angry beyond reason and an old devil played upon his shoulders, putting thoughts of revenge and retribution into his mind. Garibaldi had insulted him and taken his sword, and he needed to die so that Flavio could have his honour returned. As Garibaldi turned to ride away, the rest of Flavio's men made their presence known.

"Dismount or die!" Flavio demanded. Garibaldi saw Bani's drawn bow, shrugged in assumed nonchalance and dismounted, raising his arms and shrugging.

"Now, what do you wish?"

Flavio too dismounted and drew his borrowed sword. "Unbuckle your sword belt and lay it on the ground, then walk two paces backwards."

Puzzled, Garibaldi did as he was bidden. Flavio walked forward, picked up his own dagger and sword and threw the borrowed sword at Garibaldi, who caught it in the air and struck immediately with a downward slash from left to right. It was an unexpected and evil blow, difficult to block or parry in the circumstances. Flavio saw the flash of sunlight on steel, yet he had little time. He rolled backwards, completing the action landing upright, his knees flexed, his own sword familiar in his hand once more, ready now as the next cut came low, his opponent following on, fast and deadly.

Flavio stepped back seemingly at odds, yet stood in the *stabile*, the 'boar's middle tooth', as Fiore had taught him, gripping the long hilt of his sword with both hands, his left leg back and his right leg forward in a broad stance, knee bent. It looked awkward yet it was deadly, allowing the user to defend and attack in quick succession.

Garibaldi came in fast, closing the distance, changing slash to thrust at the last moment, aiming for Flavio's chest to pierce his gambeson and taking advantage of Flavio's apparently awkward stance. Flavio brought his point upwards, flexing on the back leg, bringing his sword around and down to parry the strike as Garibaldi, sensing the change in energy, stepped out from the centre line, not to be caught in the trap so easily. Flavio turned with him, pivoting on the right leg, sword now low behind in the *stabile* 'long tail' position. Garibaldi stood in a high two horned *posta*, ready now and wary. He had thought Flavio a vagabond with some skill and a great deal of braggadocio, but now he learned differently. No one used the long tail who did not know what they were doing.

The swords came together in a clash of steel, the impact vibrating down the blades. They crossed and bound, each breaking free, and the dance of the swords began again. Both men realised that they were facing a strong opponent, and Flavio used his footwork, always moving, light on his feet. The centre line was everything, he knew, and he used it to his advantage, keeping Garibaldi at bay, as the man had great reach and was fast and strong in the wrist.

He sliced in from a middle guard, and Flavio met the stroke as they crossed, each testing the other's blade and strength. Garibaldi relaxed and slid down the blade, punching Flavio in the face as he did so.

Flavio's head rang with the blow as he pivoted away, using his feet to keep himself safe. Garibaldi came to the high guard, took his own blade in hand, came in half-swording and smashed the hilt forward like a poleaxe, seeking to drive the end of the quillon into Flavio's head. Flavio retreated two paces, his sword now in the archer's position, where it could be used like a bayonet. Yet with the greater gap he chose a risky strategy taught to him by Firori, who used this trick against many other masters' views. Flavio threw his sword.

Like an archer loosing an arrow, Flavio knew it was on target as soon as it left his hands, even before the lethal tip skewered Garibaldi's neck. Garibaldi had expected a thrust, and came back to mid guard to counter it, never expecting such a radical move. The blade of Flavio's sword quivered up and down as it stuck in Garibaldi's neck, and the man choked and retched, trying fruitlessly to pull the blade free as his life's blood poured down onto his chest. He sank to his knees and fell forward in a macabre parody of a bow, and in so doing, drove the blade more deeply into his neck, leaving his body balanced lifeless upon the sword.

Flavio came forward, kicked the body over and with both hands pulled the bloody blade free. Ilaria looked on with a hand to her mouth, seeing the lethal swordsman and *condottieri* revealed before her in all his anger. Flavio slit open Garibaldi's jacket, and using the blade he pushed aside the doublet and reached in to search for the missive that he knew would be hidden there. He was rewarded with a script sealed with red wax. It was addressed to a name he did not know at a bank in Florence. He broke the seal and read the traitorous words.

The others looked on, crowding closer and ignoring the dead. Bani asked what it said. Flavio was silent for a moment longer as he re-read the words.

"It is to a banker in Firenze, agreeing the release of funds to pay for troops and an army to come to Viterbo led by the Salimbeni. The letter says that the time is ripe to render the city unto di Vico. This is enough to hang him as a traitor, yet I suspect that Cardinal Pielo will not do so; instead he will use this missive to blackmail him into submission.

"Come, we must return to Viterbo and warn the good cardinal."

"What of these men? Do we bury them?" Bani asked.

Flavio snorted in disgust: "You are ever a good Christian, Bani, but no. They sought to take my honour and my life, and I have regained both by taking theirs and retrieving my sword. Yet we should pull them off the road so it will take longer before they are found," he responded, toeing Garibaldi's body to make sure that he was dead.

Chapter Twenty-One

They collected their horses and rode back to Viterbo, choosing another gate that did not by pass by the chiesa della Verita. Ilaria had been quiet on the return journey, saying not a word. Even though Garibaldi had likely been the architect of her father's murder, she could not shake off the bloody sight she had witnessed and the ferocity of Flavio in his battle madness. They lived in violent times, and violent death was a common enough occurrence, yet to see so brutal a scene played out before her eyes had shocked her to her core.

Flavio escorted her home and left the men at the inn and walked to the papal palace to pass on the missive he had taken from Garibaldi. He had to wait in the antechamber as the cardinal was engaged on state business, he was told. He turned and waited outside, preferring to sit on the steps in the fresh air until he was called to an audience. It was there that he was accosted by Laura, maid to Tiziana, wife of the banker Collemi, who had latterly returned from Florence. She was hurrying across the piazza, her face cast in worry, and upon seeing Flavio sat in contemplation at his ease, she ran across to him, out of breath.

"Signor Sabatini, *Dio mio*, all is ill," she burst out.

"Why, what ails you?" he asked, concern in his voice.

"Not I, signor, my mistress. She is dying, we think poisoned, and she needs medicine or at least the help of one who may know what ails her," she gasped.

"Poisoned? How? Why?" he asked, surprised and angry. He knew that poison was a common weapon to remove a rival, deadly and largely untraceable to the instigator. "Take me to her. No, wait, come with me – but we must hurry, for time may be of the essence." Flavio strode off so fast that Laura had to jog and trot to keep up. He found Stefano Ventolini out, and his apprentice unable to aid him. Then he had an idea.

They arrived at Ilaria's shop with Laura puffing and panting, such was his pace. Flavio found her there and explained briefly what Laura had told him as the maid regained her breath.

Ilaria listened intently, concentrating hard and thinking, her brow furrowed as she turned to the maid. "What signs does she have that she is not well?"

"She has vomiting, diarrhoea..."

"Does she have stomach pains, any skin irritation, headaches?"

"Yes, headaches and maybe a rash. She sweats at times."

Ilaria turned to Flavio: "I am not qualified. My father did not finish bringing me into the guild. I have another year of studying before they let me in – and then a woman, pah!" She threw her hands up in exasperation.

"It does not matter. What do you think of her condition?" Flavio responded, no lover of the secretive guilds and all their rules and regulations. It often took years to comply with their demands and enter their hallowed ranks due to the protectionist nature of their leaders – old men, he knew, who so often wanted to monopolise and control everything for their own ends and financial benefit.

"It sounds like two possible things, but I need to know more and when it started?" Ilaria said.

"A week ago, just after Signor Collemi returned from Firenze and they came back to Viterbo," Laura told her.

Flavio looked hard at her and then at Ilaria, his mind taking an alarming turn of thought. It was not difficult to see that if di Vico had calculated where the leaks of information had come from concerning money lending and bankers and who owed what to whom, then he would have put pressure upon anyone concerned. If Collemi, as a leading banker, was heavily involved, then di Vico would have blamed him, and he in turn would have become suspicious of who had provided the information that he kept most secretly. All it would take would be threats to servants, bribed or tortured, and the truth of Flavio's stay at the country house would become general knowledge and with that the identity of the person who had betrayed Collemi – none other than his wife!

"Could poison be administered in such a way as to build up gradually to kill the victim?" Flavio asked.

"It could, and there are a few possibilities," Ilaria replied.

"Though from what my father taught me, it is likely that two poisons could be employed: cantarell powders, which are a difficult compound containing arsenic, or digitalis purpurea."

Flavio and Laura looked puzzled: "Foxglove, the deadly pretty flower," Ilaria explained.

Ilaria was on the move, fetching down jars and making preparations in small bottles that she carefully measured and collected into a small wooden box with a firm lid. In minutes she was ready, and procuring horses, the three set off at a pace, pushing through the streets of Viterbo to the annoyance of pedestrians. Bani followed them, ensuring none came to any harm. They reached the Collemi palazzo and were passed through the gates to attend upon Tiziana, whom they found stricken in her bed. Flavio assumed the role of servant carrying the box and a basket, his head low and his manner subservient.

Ilaria came to the woman and examined her, looking at the pupils of her eyes and checking her skin carefully. While they watched, Tiziana raised herself up, her face pale and ghostly, to spew into a bowl by her bed, coughing up blood and phlegm.

"Flavio, you must leave us now, for there is much to be done, none of which can be achieved with a man present."

He obeyed, only too willing to leave the room. The sickness of a woman worried him greatly and disturbed him more than any battlefield gore. Just as he turned to go, Ilaria came to him and said: "She is well into her final throes of poisoning. If she receives one more dose she will be dead. Find a way to take her from this place so that she may be safe.

Her husband is gone for the day, she says, but we have little time. I will do what I can, but then she needs food that is safe from poison."

Flavio nodded and went down the staircase to make plans.

He made for the stables and ordered, in Tiziana's name, a carriage to be made ready at her behest. He went back up the staircase to the second floor, knocked and was told to go away. Ilaria would call through the open casement to the piazza below when they were ready for him. He went to the first landing and told Bani to fetch Will and two others and meet him at the gates ready for his signal. The rest he ordered to leave the inn, taking everything including Flavio's gear with them, pay the bill and leave no trace of their presence. He tossed a bag of coin to him for payment, then continued, "make the skiff ready at the river and be ready to sail as soon as they arrive."

An age seemed to pass before he was summoned and then bidden to lift Tiziana carefully and carry her downstairs wrapped in blankets. She seemed to weigh very little, and he accomplished the task easily, bringing her to the waiting carriage. Laura ordered the gates opened, and although the guards were discomfited at the order, they did as they were told. Bani entered with Will and the two other men.

Flavio ordered Bani to remain on guard at the gate with his horse, Will and the others he told to ensure that Tiziana and the two other women rode for the river and complete their safe arrival. It would be their choice from that point onwards.

He sat upon his horse, watching the carriage disappear

through the throng, and having told the guards that none would be allowed to leave on pain of death by a well-placed arrow, he sat with Bani for a while.

"Viterbo, I feel, has lost its appeal," he said calmly with a wry smile upon his face. "And we in turn have outstayed our welcome for the present. As such I have one more deed to accomplish, then I shall join you forthwith." At this he rode off at a fast pace in the direction of the papal palace.

He tethered his horse to the front of the imposing building and raced up the steps. This time he was admitted almost immediately and given an audience with Cardinal Pielo.

He passed over the bloodied missive, and the cardinal received it with some misgiving, holding it gingerly between finger and thumb. "What does this convey?"

"It is a letter written to a man whom I assume is a banker in Firenze. I am not familiar with his name, yet the message is clear. He is to provide funds from a certain account that is in multiple names, of which two are Signor Collemi and Signor di Vico. These funds are to be lodged against collection by the Salimbeni family and Visconti, Duke of Milano, upon his entry into Firenze." The words struck home as the cardinal's eyes shot back to Flavio.

"Yes, you would have been too late. The troops are now within striking distance of Viterbo, and I suspect some are already lodged within the walls of the monastery at the chiesa Santa Maria della Verita outside the city walls, awaiting a signal from di Vico that the time is right."

"I hear your explanation, yet I suspect that I only have half the story," the cardinal raised an eyebrow.

"Yet you have sufficient unto the day. For now you can arrest di Vico, or bribe and blackmail him into submission. If you move swiftly – more swiftly, I might add, than you have done to date – you will have papal troops installed and ready. If not, then the conquest of Viterbo lies upon your head. I have done all that I can and have but one more task to perform before I leave."

"You leave us? So soon? There is much to be done. A good captain is needed, a ruthless one who will accomplish all."

I like not the air here. It is...poisonous," Flavio said with snort of humour.

"There is still much I would know, and you are not being completely honest with me," the cardinal admonished him.

"Nor you with me, your grace. So we shall keep our own secrets, and I wish you well in your endeavours. Now I beg your leave to retire." With a swift bow, Flavio turned and went to the door, ignoring Pielo's calls to return and explain.

Flavio stepped quickly from the palace, returned to his horse and made for Stefano Ventolini's apothecary shop, where this time he found the owner. After answering his many questions as briefly as he could, Flavio broke into the discourse, for he was aware of time passing.

"Stefano, *scusi*. Forgive me, yet time is short, and I have two questions: Would you be interested in improving your interest and running and possibly acquiring a second shop, say in the Pellegrino quarter? And secondly, do you have a poison that could be administered by a narrow blade, a fine, very thin stiletto?"

Stefano gave him a look of suspicion, his eyes narrowing.

"Let me answer your first question. Certainly, though I lack the capital to buy another property. You are referring I presume to the late Signor Dezi's premises?"

"Yes, of course. Yet worry not about the funds." Flavio waved away the obstruction. "For such a purchase you could rent the shop initially, and I, as your landlord, would offer acceptable terms, I am sure. I should then have a ready customer for certain of my wares in Viterbo. Now as to the second point?"

Stefano inclined his head as one who understood yet was reluctant to comment. "Apothecaries are secretive beyond even the level of the usual guildsmen, and as well as helping to cure all we can with potions, herbs and poultices, we are also taught what may kill and what is dangerous. In this we have terrible knowledge that we treat with great care."

Flavio was impatient and knew that he had little time: "*Sì, sì*, but is it possible?" he asked.

Stefano sighed, shaking his head: "Yes, I could prepare a paste that would, if in contact with bare skin – or more importantly entered deeply into the body – cause death within a short period of time. Initially the victim would feel nothing, then nausea, loss of breath and finally his heart would stop as he gasped and died. Such a death would not be an easy one." He shuddered.

"This person deserves it, for he has betrayed Viterbo and his own wife. I shall buy a stiletto, and you shall cover it with the poison," Flavio said, and made to depart.

"Ensure that the blade has a sheath, you would not wish any to even land upon your bare skin," Stefano advised him.

Just as the bells for Vespers were ringing, Flavio found

himself in the street near the entrance to the guildhall where a meeting was taking place. He was at the front where the pedestrian traffic entered. He had lingered in a nearby *osteria* over a cool glass of wine, taking small sips, secure in the knowledge from a hesitant Laura and murmurings from Tiziana of when her husband usually returned on days such as these. The guild meeting was due to break up very soon, and Flavio had hurried to be in the exact position he wanted. Now as the doors were pushed back, a chorus of voices were heard, arguing and bantering. In the general hubbub, Flavio moved in from the side, merging and spotting his quarry, noticing the servant at the side of his target. His movements were gentle and yet he managed to insinuate himself slightly behind his quarry. The fine blade of the stiletto was so slim as to look more like a broad needle, yet its tip was as lethally sharp as a surgeon's scalpel. It would slide in easily, puncturing cloth and skin, and Flavio drew it carefully from its slim sheath that he had purchased from an armourer earlier that day. The man had been surprised until Flavio told him that it was for his wife, to keep her safe upon the dangerous streets.

Massimo Collemi felt no more than a prick like a wasp's sting, and he swiped his hand to the point of entry as if swatting an insect. No blood emerged as the blade was withdrawn as the skin closed quickly back upon the tiny puncture.

Flavio lost himself in the throng, disappearing down a side alley, where he watched as Collemi rubbed the spot, still walking and talking to another banker. For a hundred yards or more Flavio watched, thinking he had failed, then it began. The lethal paste started its deadly work as Collemi tugged at the collar of his houppelande. His servant came to his aid, and the man he was talking to held his other arm to support him. Collemi made to move on, pushing them away and coughing once. Seemingly better, he rubbed again at the puncture in his side.

"That is it, signor, walk on and pump your blood, the better to take the poison to your treacherous and murdering heart," Flavio muttered quietly to himself. He followed at a distance and saw the banker falter once more. Flavio realised that he would just about make it to his own palazzo, and perhaps fall outside it, as had Ilaria's father. He nodded and moved away into the centre to the *osteria* where he had tethered his horse. It was time to be away from this city, he thought, with its stench of deceit, murder and villainy. Viterbo could stand or fall, it was now in Cardinal Pielo's hands. Flavio had done all he could, and Vitelleschi could not complain. But as he turned his mind to the evil cardinal from Corneto, his thoughts took a terrible turn as the scales fell from his eyes.

Part Three

The Maremma

Chapter Twenty-Two

Corneto

Autumn had arrived, and the heat had dissipated to a certain extent, yet Flavio was still glad of the cool shade within the palazzo as he awaited an audience with Cardinal Vitelleschi. The lazy breeze drifting off the Tyrrhenian Sea carried with it the tang of salt and fish. It was good to be back home, he thought, and away from the stifling heat and intrigue of Viterbo. For all that, trade had been good; he had made two new customers with Tullio Cannas and Stefano Ventolini, and more would follow, of that he was certain.

They had smuggled Ilaria, Laura and a very poorly Tiziana down the river to rest at Flavio's palazzo, far enough away from any more poison. Bani was becoming ever more solicitous towards Ilaria, who was not rebuffing his advances, Flavio noticed. He wondered if perhaps Bani thought of his lost family, and hoped that Ilaria would fill the hole in his soul. For there was definitely a connexion between them for all to see, and Flavio looked on indulgently with the eye almost of a parent as he felt a responsibility for both of them in his own way.

Rumours had spread through Corneto, the way they do in a small town, that Flavio was entertaining no less than three women within his walls. It was not long before Federica heard the stories, and upon his first visit to Casa Cornucopia he was given a very frosty reception.

"I hear that you have been busy in your absence, and have a harem now, so you will have little use for me," she declared with a haughty look and an arched eyebrow.

Flavio did the only thing he could: he laughed. "Why Feddie, are you jealous? No, *non credo.*"

Federica clenched her fists and went for him, and Flavio had to bat off her attack. Falling backwards onto the bed, his laughter finally subsided as she pinned him with her knees. He took his time to explain that Ilaria was but a young girl and Laura was a lady-in-waiting to Tiziana, who would return to her family in Florence when she recovered fully from being poisoned to the point of death.

Still Federica was sceptical, and with no other course open to him and despite the late hour, he swept her up and took her screeching in protest to his palazzo. Here she saw a raven haired young beauty and the more mature blonde Tiziana, who was still very pale and hardly at her best, and was being waited on by her maid. Federica finally relented. Flavio took her back to Casa Cornucopia and a night of passionate lovemaking, and in the morning all was forgiven.

He sat now on the edge of her bed, contemplating all and for the thousandth time trying to understand women and what exactly his relationship was with Federica.

He was coming to a conclusion, which he was not altogether sure that he liked, when a servant came forward and beckoned him into the cardinal's private salon.

He gave a slight bow and reluctantly kissed Vitelleschi's proffered ring. "Your eminence, I come with news of Viterbo and news of an end to the danger there I hope, for your agent – or should I say agents? – are now in full control and aware of all, and the traitors exposed and largely brought to book."

The cardinal gave nothing away, and did not show so much as a flicker of emotion as he registered the barb in Flavio's words.

"Ah, yes. I heard the sad news of Signor Dezi, who lost his life in my cause, may God rest his soul." He crossed himself piously. "And of others, you refer to father Stoica?"

"No, my lord. He also I fear is dead, murdered by those who wish you harm and seek a change of government within the town – to wit di Vico and other bankers and high officials of the *Signoria*. I saw troops massing along the banks of the nearest river and the town will by now be under the control of your main agent there, Cardinal Pielo."

"Ah yes, a good man of God and a pious servant of the church," Vitelleschi offered, deliberately misinterpreting Flavio's meaning.

"Pielo is your servant above God's, and I will go further, for I do not have the patience to fence with you any longer. You knew, or suspected all that I found out, and you were merely using me as a catalyst to force those whom you suspected of treason to expose themselves upon my investigation," Flavio said, his voice icy cold, his anger rising with each sentence he spoke. "Father Stoica and poor Signor Dezi are dead, Dezi's daughter orphaned, and that *bastardo* Ranieri free as a bird because I kept my word to your agent Pielo," he finished, his voice rising in anger.

Vitelleschi was calm in his response to Flavio's outburst. "You are correct on nearly all counts," he said. "I suspected di Vico and others and now govern them under Pielo's good offices. Papal troops are indeed ensconced within the city, which is now under their control, and all is well.

"Of Ranieri you are wrong on two counts: I knew not of his complicity, but I am reliably informed that he is now no longer with us."

"How so?" Flavio asked puzzled.

"It appears that something he ate disagreed with him. A surfeit of lampreys perhaps? That seems to be the common cause for such ailments," Vitelleschi said offhandedly, with a small smile playing upon his lips. "Although I hear the climate in Viterbo is also none too healthy for bankers, who seem to suffer from fits of bad humours in the street, resulting in a lethal seizure and a grieving widow seeking succour within your walls."

Flavio looked at him and smiled without humour. "Succour? You mean she is recovering from a near deadly dose of poison administered upon her husband's orders because she risked all by aiding me in my endeavours to discover the plans for the betrayal of Viterbo? Then you have the right of it. Once she is fully recovered, she intends to leave my palazzo, accompanied by her maid, who is with her constantly as a chaperone, and return to her family home in Firenze. There she will hopefully be safe from the tentacles of revenge that are no doubt spreading even as we speak to find her and end her life," he said.

Vitelleschi arched an eyebrow: "How very noble of you, my son. And what will you receive in return?"

"Nothing. For she aided me in *your* quest, and I intend to pay my debts in that regard. Without her help I should never have uncovered the plot that you knew existed and merely needed me to unravel so that you could assume power."

Vitelleschi shrugged as though it was of no matter. "You aided the church, and with that the state, and the Holy Father shall be most pleased. And speaking of debts, I once more need your help, for I assume that you will travel on the main road north through la Maremma?" Flavio nodded, an awful sinking feeling creeping up his spine. "Then I have a fiat which I should very much like you to accept," he finished sternly. It was of course an order, rather than a request.

* * *

Porrona, la Maremma, Tuscany

Giovanni d'Agnolino Salimbeni held a goblet of wine in his hand, sipping at it occasionally but barely tasting the liquid. He was awaiting the congregation of his war leaders, who were even now moving up the staircase to join Remigio Lanfredini and others in the upper salon of the castle.

Once all five captains were assembled and seated, Salimbeni began to explain what he had planned.

"We have news that Flavio Sabatini was responsible for thwarting our plans to take Viterbo in the name of Duke

Visconti. Di Vico is now hamstrung and is at the mercy of Cardinal Pielo, so our spies tell us. The news was late in coming, and we must now plan in haste, for I hear that Sabatini will soon be travelling north to take the recently widowed Tiziana Pacchelli, wife of the late Massimo Collemi, a banker to our cause, to Firenze. Signor Collemi is sorely missed and his offices within the city were very important as an agent between bankers in Firenze and Viterbo. That is all you need to know.

"However, what is important is that Sabatini is now our target. He may have been cast adrift by Vitelleschi, we know not, and it matters little. Yet he thwarted our plans for Viterbo, killed Signor Garibaldi, one of our most able lieutenants, and caused the death of Bishop Ranieri. He must be taken and brought here to be tortured until he tells all of what he knows – or at the very least slaughtered and his body hung by the roadside as warning to others. He will no doubt travel by river to Bolsena and thence by road to Firenze, passing north of Acquapendente, and that is where you will ambush him, afore he reaches Bagni San Felippo to the north.

"How many men will he have with him?" the ever practical Lanfredini asked, picturing in his mind the terrain south of Montepulciano that he knew so well, having raided there on many occasions.

"Exactly? I know not. Yet he will be travelling by river – unless he seeks the longer road by Orbetello and Grosseto – and he will pass to the west of us, and we shall know aforehand which route he takes and how many travel with him. Moving inland will mean travelling by boat, and his numbers will be limited, for he must take horse and supplies to look after the women."

"I know the place where we shall meet and kill him." Lanfredini offered an evil grin. "There is a broad pasture of rough grassland through which the road passes. Often there are Maremma cattle grazing there. Stunted oaks line the road close by and about half a mile to the north the road narrows to pass through a gorge. We will wait until he passes and drive him forward into the narrow section of the road to complete the ambush. We shall need men, say fifty or so, well-armed and well armoured, for if Sabatini expects trouble, as I am sure he will, then he will be in full harness or at least maille. He will have his English archers that he values so highly, and they are deadly with greater speed than crossbowmen," he finished.

Salimbeni nodded, seeing the wisdom in his stratagem.

"But what if they should go by ship up the sea route or across via Grossetto?" Lanfredini asked.

"We shall know in advance. I have agents in place who will keep me informed and messengers who will bring the news here. All will be well, fear not. We shall have him as a rat in a trap," Salimbeni assured him. "Now we must prepare, for he shall commence the journey as soon as Signora Tiziana is well enough to travel."

The group of captains finally dispersed save for Lanfredini and Salimbeni: "Who is it that feeds us such valuable information on Sabatini? They must be deep within his coterie, or firmly ensconced in Corneto society itself," Lanfredini asked curiously.

Salimbeni looked at him with suspicion, refusing to

comment either way. "See to the men and have them prepared and ready, for as soon as we hear we shall move out and prepare the ambush," he ordered curtly.

* * *

Corneto

Three days after Flavio's audience with Vitelleschi, he wandered slowly up to the top ramparts of the town walls overlooking the valley, seeing his palazzo in the distance. The town's walls had been built higher since the summer when the Saracen attack had been foiled, and were now much more secure to the eastern side of the city. The city had already begun building to repair and refurbish the fire-damaged buildings, one of which Flavio had himself purchased, a small shop on the via Roma, just off the Piazza Cavour. Here he was going to enable Ilaria to set up and trade as an apothecary. With only one other old man in the town plying that trade, he was sure she would prevail and become a success. Bani and the young girl had become nearly inseparable, and he knew it would be a wrench for the Copt to accompany him north to Florence, yet he was adamant and would not shirk his duty, despite Flavio offering him the opportunity to do so. Flavio was pleased that Bani and Ilaria had found some solace to their sad situations.

All was looking well, with the only cloud on the horizon being Vitelleschi's fiat, which he was obligated to perform.

He turned away from the view that was fading into the dusk and sauntered along the walls to enter the Casa Cornucopia from the rear entrance through which Maria had escaped when the Saracens invaded on that terrible night. A single guard was on duty as only a very few were permitted to enter by the secret way. Flavio rang the bell, and a small hatch was slid back. He was recognised and permitted entry, and minutes later he was with Federica, eating at a private table as she acknowledged the regular members of her exclusive club with a wave and a smile.

"Are Signor Rossi and Signor Dragone in the club this evening?" Flavio asked innocently.

"Why yes, I believe I saw them come in but moments before you arrived. Why do you ask?"

"Just a whim of curiosity," he answered with a gentle smile and a reassuring squeeze of her hand. She arched an eyebrow, knowing that Flavio never did anything for such a reason, yet she pressed him no more. Hours later Flavio stretched, watched Federica's gently sleeping form as her chest rose and fell in sleep. Yet with the rising of his body she woke, and squeezed his hand. "Take great care, *amore*, wherever your road takes you, and return to me soon."

Flavio dressed quickly and slipped out through the back door to find Bani and Maurizio waiting for him.

"Well, what did you learn?"

"Bani and I followed our prey, and it was in me to slit their throats myself. For they left together, and then upon returning Dragone sent a messenger from his house to secretly navigate the streets, avoid the watch and leave the city by bribing the guard by the *cancello di Profello*," Maurizio said meaningfully.

"*Dio mio,* I am a fool. I had forgotten all about that postern gateway down to the *fontanils* without the city."

Flavio slapped his head in a dramatic gesture, recalling the secret external stairway that led down to the wells at the foot of the cliffs and the walls on the north side of the city. They were arched and walled in stone, yet hidden from view by deep foliage. Only Cornetani knew of their existence, and it was a secret they never shared, for in times of siege the city could gain fresh water for its inhabitants via a perilous secret external staircase to the fresh water below. With the city perched so high upon a steep escarpment, wells were deep and difficult to dig, and a supply of fresh water was essential to withstand a prolonged siege. The gate was narrow and guarded night and day. Yet with a bribe, Dragone's servant had slipped away – no doubt to a waiting horse below.

"So we know not where he went?" Flavio asked, disappointed at his own lack of foresight.

"Not quite," said Maurizio with a smile, clearly pleased at having outthought his master.

Flavio looked on in frustration. "How so?" he said, hoping against hope for a solution.

"Well, we seek to go north, so it stands to reason that any who wished to ambush us would travel that way. With but two roads to choose and gates upon that side, we had Will and Tom stand down, awaiting a branded signal from above. With any luck Will shall have seen the flame and made ready to follow the messenger as far as he may. We told him not to kill him, though he wanted to sure enough, so we merely await his return to find out in which direction the traitor rode," Maurizio finished, clearly pleased with himself and his ingenuity.

"Bravo!" Flavio clapped him on the shoulder. "That was

well thought out. Clearly though, to send a messenger, our readying of the boat has been noticed and upon such actions we are to be intercepted upon the north road to Firenze. Exactly where, we shall see. I must send a message to Captain Perina and have his troops make their move," Flavio said out loud, almost to himself.

Chapter Twenty-Three

They sailed up the Marta River towards lake Bolsena. Tiziana had responded well to rest, recuperation and Ilaria's tender ministrations, and now sported a much healthier pallor after returning from the jaws of death. She was currently sitting happily in the bows of Flavio's skiff, though she had shuddered as they passed Viterbo up river, along with a newly acquired second maid whom Flavio had not yet met, taken from the ranks of one of the Cornetani families who sat by her, hooded against the dawn chill. The boat was crowded as Flavio had taken all the men he dared from his palazzo. A second boat followed them closely, loaded to the gunnels with horses and supplies for their journey. He had planned to expand his trade for some time, and the second craft had been a timely purchase – though no doubt one that had been noticed by the spies of Dragone and Rossi. They had left Ilaria behind to stock and open her apothecary shop despite Bani's sadness at leaving her.

A few days later they dropped anchor and left the boats.

Settling the horses, they rode north towards Acquapendente. The ancient Roman town was bustling and formed one of the major trading routes that Flavio exploited for his transport of goods.

"How far now to Bagni San Filippo?" Tiziana asked Flavio.

She had been brave and borne up well, yet the hard riding had taken its toll. He did not dare provide her with a carriage, for they would have to ride hard and fast if the need became pressing, for which a carriage would not suffice. She had gone without complaint, in contrast to the spoiled countenance of her earlier disposition, Flavio thought, realising that she was clearly glad to be alive.

"It is some twenty leagues, my lady, though it will be hard riding through rough roads and countryside. With luck we shall make the walls of San Filippo this evening," he assured her with a gentle smile.

Tiziana returned the smile and composed herself to keep going without complaint. From now on Flavio was on his mettle, for his days as a *condottieri* told him that this countryside would be the ideal place to launch an ambush, and he was convinced that forces weighed against him were aware of his movements and that they would attack before he could deliver Tiziana to her family. The bankers would be delighted to have his plans thwarted, and with it the security of Florence.

They pushed on through the milder late Autumn sunshine, and Flavio and others of his band were pleased, for all were clad in maille and he himself wore some plate on his torso. It had been a while since he had last worn it, and he had practised for days before leaving his palazzo, accustoming himself once more to the feel of the armour and the idea of fighting in it. Bani had been interested, and saw how little effect his razor sharp scimitar had upon the hardened Milan steel that was so sought after by all. The armour had been made for Flavio during his time at Fiori's school, and fitted him like a second skin. At first it had been hard, yet he quickly reacclimatised himself to the minor restrictions of the weight, adapting and fighting in the metal. Bani had been surprised as to how flexible it was, as Flavio rolled, jumped and vaulted upon his horse despite the armour.

They left the grey green coarse grass of the plains that had been burned by the summer sun and started towards the wooded hillsides that were bordered by stunted Italian oaks and ashes, now canopies of orange, yellows and browns in their seasonal hues. A faint breeze rustled, and clouds above began gathering with the promise of a rain shower later. Flavio in his harness was glad of the perceptible drop in temperature.

He passed the word amongst his small band of followers, as Will and the other twenty English archers already had their bows strung and ready. "We are being watched, of that I am certain," he said. "The narrowing of the road before the gorge ahead will funnel us inwards. If we are to be attacked, it will be from there that they will come. Remember what we agreed and heed my orders to the letter. Upon my raised hand all will move to a canter."

Flavio watched the nods of his men and saw them crowd around the three women, each of whom wore a cowl up over her head to disguise their identity. He raised his hand and brought it down quickly, and as one the whole party pushed up into a canter with the apparent safety of the gorge in sight. They had gone but half a league, and the gorge was getting closer where they could hold off an army with twenty archers, when Flavio caught a movement behind him from the corner of his eye. Keeping his pace, he turned in the saddle and saw a stream of men-at-arms coming from the trees to their rear.

"Behind us! Make for the gorge." He called all to a greater pace, yet held back from a gallop, wanting to keep some of the horses' strength in reserve. War cries now came from behind, along with the sound of galloping horses, yet still Flavio allowed the pursuers to gain upon them as he gambled all on his hunch. The gorge and safety for archers drew closer – then his worst fears were realised. He heard a trumpet call, and from either side of the rocky escarpment rode a force to their front, emerging from the trees that formed a natural funnel to the gorge entrance and trapping them from the road ahead.

"Wheel right!" he shouted, signalling with his hand for the group to gallop. The band turned as one, each horse taking a flying lead change as the riders pushed them from canter to gallop, giving them their heads.

"Flavio, what do you wish us to do?" Will shouted from the side.

"As we did in *condottieri*, Will. Remember Hawkwood and how he fought? He would fight, run and drop. You and the other archers drop as soon as we get to the tree line, the women go in, dismount and hold the horses ready. Cross-bows ready, we'll keep them off your flanks until aid arrives."

"Aid? From where shall that come?" Will called in alarm and disbelief.

"Have faith, Will," Flavio said, feeling brave and praying for the miracle he hoped would come. Yet as they skidded to a halt, handing the horses panting and flecked with white foam and sweat to the three women, their hoods fell down and the second maid was, he saw to his horror, none other than Ilaria. The men must have known – no doubt she was in league with Bani! In the brief moment before battle took him, he was angry and dismayed. "*Porca miseria*, Ilaria, have you lost your senses? I left you in safety. Will you never heed my words? What is it with you Viterbese women? Do you disobey all orders?" He shook his head in disgust with no time to consider the matter now.

All thoughts of the women were forgotten as the twenty archers formed a loose semi-circle, Flavio and the others stood to the side, crossbows ready, spanned and with quarrels in the tillers. They had the trees to the front for cover as best they could, though the archers would be hampered if they could not find enough pace to draw and loose their arrows. The two charging forces now merged to form a wall of steel, outnumbering Flavio and his men by at least three to one.

"Will, the archers are yours, and are as ever upon your command," Flavio said. Will nodded, fingering his nocked arrow and looking down again at the row of arrows pushed into the hard earth before him, the quicker to pluck each and put it to the bow cord. He was a veteran of many such charges, and each time the blood never failed to sing in his veins, knowing the rain of death that he and his fellow

Englishmen were about to unleash upon these untutored Italians.

Judging the distance, he called: "Draw and loose at will!" Just when it seemed to be too late.

The archers needed no second bidding, and each man pulled and changed from chest to back muscles, bending into the strange, torsional S-shape so particular to the archers of England. The shafts flew, each man picking his target. With none of the enemy in full plate, the twenty shafts plucked their targets from the saddles. Then the rhythm of killing began: pluck, nock, draw, loose.

Yet they all knew that they were too few to end the battle here, as the enemy horsemen thundered closer, looking to kill and gain revenge for their fallen comrades who lay skewered on the dusty road. Closer they came, seeing victory in sight, their horses lathered with white spume, teeth bared for battle. Some now dropped their lances ready to strike hard into the thin defensive line that Flavio had arranged. At some thirty yards the last of the arrows flew straight, emptying more saddles, and he ordered: "Pull back deeper, into the woods."

He had gambled and lost, he knew. He would not be rescued, and he had failed in his last mission. Turning, he shouted to the women: "Mount and ride hard. Get away!" he called, yet they refused to leave, staying with the horses of the men. Ilaria looped her charges' reins over branches and with one hand drew her dagger, prepared to sell her virtue at great cost. "Let them come, and I'll geld a few ere they take me!" she cried bravely.

Bani turned briefly, yet dared not leave the fray or lose

concentration. He had been devastating in his archery, and his arrows so swiftly loosed had pierced their mail or leather brigandines easily. Yet he was, even now, down to his last two arrows, nocking and choosing his targets trying to bring down the leaders, before drawing his scimitar ready to fight with sword and buckler.

Flavio stood braced just within the tree line, with his kite shield and sword ready to deflect lance and sword, vowing to take the heavy-set leader who raced at the front of the attacker's ranks. Flavio dropped the visor of his pig faced bascinet helmet at the last moment, and standing in a line as he had so many times before, he waited to sell his life.

Then he heard it; the high pitched two tone notes fluting out across the land. Emerging from the gorge, flowing like a mountain stream, came two lines of knights, well armoured and with heralds proclaiming them as papist troops. As they came forward, they swung outwards in well-ordered precision to form a horned curve some hundred yards long. At the centre, Flavio recognised the banner of the captain, Signor Perina, a squire at his side ready for battle. He saw in the Italian style that they represented some hundred and fifty lances of roughly four hundred and fifty men, the tabards proclaiming their papal rank.

Upon hearing the trumpet's clarion call, many of the Salimbeni force made to curb their horses and face the new threat at their rear. Yet some, either unhearing or buoyed by the lust for battle, pressed home to try to fight the despised archers and Flavio's small *conroi* of men.

They crashed into the bracken, their force broken by the low lying branches pointing outwards to create a small thicket of defence, dividing them by degrees and forcing the huge horses to swerve and lose some momentum.

There was a clash of arms as some broke through to find the hated enemy and with that seek a way out of the trap through the trees and away to be lost in the forest. Flavio thought of nothing else save selling his life dearly, for with the arrival of the papist forces he had hope at least that the ladies would survive and be rescued.

The first man to reach him held his lance couched to pierce through the obstacle of the tree line. Flavio timed it to bat the point away, holding his sword in the long position of *instabile,* engaging the lance tip from a long distance. It was easier to deflect the lance from this position, and as the horse closed, breaking thin branches, he drove the shield to its vulnerable nose. The animal screamed in pain, shied and reared to avoid any further strikes. Its rider fought for control, his only defence now his shield. Flavio turned his wrist from the deflection to slash down at the exposed thigh that was clad only in a mail hauberk. The links snapped and the leg was cut to the bone. Flavio sawed the blade back and stabbed up under the lowered guard of the shield, driving the point home and twisted, knowing he must keep moving to survive. He felt the concussion of a blade striking his shoulder pauldron, yet the brilliant Milanese plate held firm as the edge slid off. This man was fully armoured too, and he realised in the brief moment of battle that he must be the leader.

Lanfredini for his part was frustrated. He could not use his war horse to good effect, hemmed in by the trees as he was, so he brought his shield down to cover his exposed leg.

Flavio responded, driving his own shield up to meet it, punching upwards as he did so. At such close quarters, he drove upwards with the point towards the unarmoured groin, sliding the point up the *cuisse* where there was no ridged stop to drive into the more vulnerable skirt of *tasses*, where Lanfredini's legs were splayed by his saddle. Flavio thrust hard even as the next blow fell upon his helm, rattling his head inside it. His point pierced through the mail links into the softer flesh below, yet he felt the resistance lessen as his prey, wily to the ways of war, deliberately fell sideways from the saddle to avoid the full penetration of the point. He rose again as the horse shielded him from Flavio, his leg paining him as he saw that it was already stained red with blood. With both men on foot now, Flavio advanced, knowing that he had already caused a grievous wound and that this was no chivalrous knightly combat where one could yield. It was a brutal battle between two *condottieri* out for blood and seeking nothing more than the other's death.

Lanfredini braced himself for the expected rush to unbalance him, aware always of the clash of battle all around and the pressing of the papal troops behind and hearing cries for mercy as his men fell prey to the overwhelming force of the rescuing army. Flavio came in with mid guard, shield raised, then created an opening with a seemingly novice mistake, bringing back his shield to drive for an upper slash, turning his torso as his blade flashed forward. Lanfredini thrust through the open gap, seeking the line of the gorget, hoping to drive under the plated protection. With his ruse complete, Flavio dropped quickly, the opponent's blade glancing off the top of his bascinet.

Twisting his wrist, he now drove downward to slash at Lanfredini's extended undamaged leg, cutting through to break the bone as the leg flew upwards and Lanfredini fell back with a cry. With no mercy, Flavio drove his sword tip up under the visor into the exposed flesh there, knowing not what he skewered, sawing the blade back and forth to a final death cry from his opponent. He stamped upon his chest as the next man came forward, who upon seeing his dead leader fell to his knees, all thoughts of battle gone and pleading for mercy.

Arms were dropped as men surrendered, hoping for the leniency of the papal see and praying that they would not be hung outright for their misdeeds. Their hopes were short-lived. After disarming them, Captain Perina had them herded up and bound their arms behind their backs. Then he gave the order for them to be hanged from the stout oak trees that lined the forest road. The screams and pleas for mercy all went unheeded. Some tried to fight and break their bonds or run, only to be brought down by crossbow bolts, saving themselves an ignominious death by hanging.

As the last man to be strung up kicked and writhed his way to death, Captain Perina turned to Flavio. "Where now do you go, Signor Sabatini?"

"We journey on to Firenze, where I shall deliver Signora Tiziana to her family," he explained. "Yet afore we depart I must thank you for your timely arrival. I was, I must confess, worried that you would not arrive in time."

"Ah, for that I must apologise. We received your intelligence late in the day and only just managed to catch the tide from the harbour. We were then delayed when we came ashore at Grosseto as you suggested, where we encountered a small number of Salimbeni's troops who had been ordered to put a blockade upon the port. One of the men we captured told me that they were expecting a small force such as your own. Salimbeni did not fully trust his intelligence that you came by boat and horse from Lago di Bolsena."

"As to that, it was a good ruse, and I thank the good Lord that you arrived here in time," Flavio replied. "'Tis only a shame that we did not capture Salimbeni himself this day, yet he is too cautelous for that, leaving others to be caught and killed in his stead. One day I shall find and kill him, that I swear. And will you journey on with us to Firenze?"

"No, sadly not, for we should like to give you safe escort. The city is not *simpatico* to the Holy Father as yet, and seeks its own path. Yet his grace Cardinal Vitelleschi is ever hopeful of converting them to our cause – particularly as I hear that Comte Visconti even now marches south to subjugate all before him in his quest to place all of Italy under his thrall. Padua and now Bologna have fallen, and Firenze shall be next unless it is robust in its defence – though I hear that they are spending fortunes, and the bankers there are profiting greatly from the re-arming and hiring of *condottieri* to establish a new army to repel his advances. Do you think that you shall join them?" he asked cautiously, seeking, Flavio felt, to read his mind.

Flavio grimaced. "No, my days of fighting and hiring my sword to the highest bidder are gone. I now serve only the master of my purse, which I like to see full of florins at little danger to myself."

"Yet here you are, fighting a just cause and aiding a papal

army," Perina said cynically. "I shall inform the cardinal that you were true to your word and completed your mission of scapegoat."

"Ha, yes, yet through chivalry and *noblesse oblige*, not through choice, for I serve my lady Signora Tiziana and aid her return to the bosom of her family. Following the death of her husband, she now finds Viterbo unsafe."

"Ah yes of course," Captain Perina said, slapping his gauntlets into his left hand a small smile upon his face. "I recall now, her husband died in...unfortunate circumstances, I believe. A seizure, very sad. 'Tis good of you to look after her so."

Then, without time for a riposte from Flavio, Perina saluted flamboyantly with a wave of his hand and made for his horse. "I pray that the next time we meet we shall still be on the same side."

"As do I *Captinao* Perina, as do I," Flavio responded.

He then turned to face his men. Maurizio came forward to meet him.

"We lost three men, Flavio. One archer and two men-at-arms. We were lucky. *Dio mio,* when I saw them charge us, I said my prayers and hoped to die and not be taken by that *bastardo* Lanfredini from the stories I have heard."

Flavio agreed with him and the turned to the three ladies who now were unburdened of their equine charges. He fixed his stern gaze upon Ilaria: "What in God's creation are you doing here? I left you safely ensconced in Corneto, with a shop to run, secure in a new business. Yet here you appear, in the thick of danger, to what aim, I ask?"

Ilaria raised her chin, cocked her head to the side and declared: "Because I wished to."

With that she gave a sly wink to Bani who had been collecting arrows that he may reuse, and looked on aghast at her impertinence.

"Dear God, heaven preserve me from Viterbese women. And you, Signora Pacchelli," he said, giving Tiziana her maiden name as all Italian women kept their own surname even when married, "you are just as guilty. *Porca miseria!*" he shook his head in disgust, realising the futility of his ranting. "Come, let us to Firenze, afore the ground shall swallow us up and we be a feast for the carrion."

Tiziana smiled at this retort, saying nothing. With a boost up into the saddle from Will, she caught Laura's complicit smile, turned her back on Flavio and rode off sedately towards Florence. He looked at her departing figure in frustration, mounted and made to follow her, once more entwining his destiny and hers in the fight for Florence that was to come.

Historical Notes

General background

As ever I do not wish to bombard with dry facts, so this is a quick overview, but I am always delighted to answer more detailed questions and can be reached at: **simonfairfax author@gmail.com**

The story takes place in what is now modern day Tarquinia, Viterbo and north in the Maremma country.

At the time and until the 1800s Tarquinia was called Corneto and was pretty much as I describe it. A fabulous local guide who helped me tremendously, Claudia Moroni, filled in a lot of the gaps.

On the timeline late 14thC I have kept it a little vague to encompass all that I wanted and have compressed the influence of Vitelleschi (a really 'good' baddy!) but he was pretty much as I portray him and he did fight in the wars with Hawkwood.

The terrible scandals and corruption were rampant at the time and the priests were as bad as anyone else. It was a time of terrible upheaval and strife within what we now call a unified Italy, state against state, tyrant against tyrant and little help from a corrupt and disputed papacy.

The influence of Viterbo is also accurate and the same for Corneto which was a major port and they still produce (to this day) the best wheat in Italy. The river Marta is still there, but not as fast flowing or as easily navigable as it was some 600 year ago.

The Saracen invasions were regular occurrences and what better time than when the 'new' walls had not been completed. If you ever visit Tarquinia (and I would recommend it) you will see that the only real place that you could have any hope of success would be from the south. The term *Saracen* is generic and even now they still say in Tarquinia that anyone from Civitavecchia is a 'Saracen' and encompasses Moors, Saracens in fact any invader from the east.

As with my AKAS series the events portrayed did all

happen in one way or another, or at least in a very similar fashion, with intrigue, scandal and power plays the order of the day.

The buildings and streets that I describe are, by and large still there today and have not really changed since this period. Viterbo has a real feeling of the period and is still described as having the 'most medieval centre' of any city in Italy.

If you have read AKAS 1412, you will understand how the guilds, sindaco, etc., acted with all their rules and regulations and every bit as corrupt as you would expect.

I have not been as faithful to the language of the time as with AKAS (it would have been impossible given the settings) but there are no 'modernisms' as far as I am aware, and I hope that this does not spoil the enjoyment or period feel. Maybe it flows better for it for some readers?

Characters

Many of the characters both in Corneto/Tarquinia & Viterbo are real people that existed in that period, especially Vitelleschi, di Vico, Cardinal Pielo etc. Obviously, all my added bit players, wives etc., are added on in my imagination.

The Salimbeni were real and acted much as I portray them. They ruled the roads north to Florence etc., and were a terrible force to be reckoned with, as evil and ruthless as I describe.

The political allegiances between these characters, moved and shifted like sand, although many were of two factions: those for and those against the papacy, with many blurred lines in between.

Count di Visconti was a very real character and he will feature much more heavily in book 2, The Fight for

Florence, taking on the next events in the tumultuous period.

Firori del Liberi is of course real and he will feature later along with Galeazzo da Mantua who is an amazing character from the period and of whom we shall see a lot more. I have leaned heavily upon his fantastic treatise for the fight scenes – see below.

Weapons and warfare

I have tried to be as accurate as possible with my fight scenes and the descriptions of the weapons. There were a good deal of English archers around in Italy, having come as mercenaries from France, after being discarded by the English king and they did serve Hawkwood and so why not continue with Flavio?

Bucklers and arming swords were very much the regular armament and full plate was rare although obviously it did exist.

Bani's recurve bow is exactly as I describe and they do or did, loose arrows on 'the other side' compared to western long bows. They also held arrows between their fingers as I describe and I have researched the power and penetrability of such weapons to keep it all realistic.

Bucklers, were very much the order of the day especially with the condottieri who like to travel and fight as light as possible. The fight scenes depict their use which was very prevalent at the time as the method of fighting was often very different to the all-out set piece battles seen deeper into France.

Chapter One

A message from Simon

I know that you have a million choices of books to read and I can't tell you how much it means to me that you chose time to read one of my books. I really hope that you enjoyed it and found it entertaining.

If you did I would appreciate a few more minutes of your time, if I may humbly ask you to leave a review for other readers who may be trying to select their next reading material.

If for any reason you were not satisfied with this book please do let me know by emailing me at simon@simonfairfaxauthor.com

The satisfaction of my readers and feedback are important to me.

Best wishes,

Simon

About

Simon Fairfax writes in three different genres: International financial thrillers, medieval fiction and classic westerns.

He is a former Chartered Surveyor, Editor of an online polo magazine (having played polo for a number of years) and has practiced martial arts, fencing and shooting. He now restores old classic sports cars for fun.

As a lover of crime thrillers and espionage, Simon turned what is seen by others as a dull 9 – 5 job into something that is exciting, and as close to real life as possible, with Rupert Brett, his unwilling hero.

His latest medieval series now has now 6 books released in the 6 book series. The first, A Knight and a Spy 1410, is set in a tumultuous time at the English court. It tells the story of Jamie de Grispere, squire in training and his two companions as they fight the French to save Calais, Welsh treason and Scottish revolts. The fourth in the series, A Knight and a Spy 1413 will be published on the 31st August 2022.

The new western Plainsman series has been published, with the third book to be released in July 2024.

Details of all his books can be found at www.simonfairfax.com or email him at simonfairfaxauthor@gmail.com

A Knight and a Spy 141

Subterfuge or sword, which save the kingdom?

Sir James de Grispere, squire in training, is thrown into a world of treachery, the Hundred Years' War, revolts, battles, the wool trade, piracy and pivotal events. Medieval history is brought to life in this story of fifteenth century England and the fight for the crown.

Then put the link in here as *Click here to read*

Please do write to me with any questions or comments as I do like to hear from my readers:

simon@simonfairfaxauthor.com

To obtain two free short stories of the backgrounds to Jamie- A Squire in Training & Contessa Alessandria-Florence 1401 go to my website www.simonfairfax.com

And sign up to my mailing list for news, competitions and new releases.

A Deadly Deal

The trading floor should be counted in deals not bodies, yet they are mounting in number. Can a dealer trade on his wits and manage to stay alive?

Set in the 80s flowing from London to Italy it features Rupert Brett, a new kind of hero, an ordinary man thrown into extraordinary situations.

Buy A *Deadly Deal* today to see if Rupert can leverage his only commodity and survive the brutal game of winner takes all?

Click here to start reading instantly

Law of the Gun: A Classic Western adventure (Plainsman series book 1)

In a lawless land, one man begins forging his future with a gun.

Nate Carlton wants peace and to take up the life he left behind. Instead, returning home to South Carolina from the Civil War, he finds under the Reconstruction, death and destruction of all that he held dear.

Homeless and cast adrift, he saves a stranger's life from an Indian attack, an act that will change his life forever.

In a lawless and Wild West, having lost everything, he must make his way with the only tool he has-a gun. But will he learn and master the deadly skill before he is killed by Carpetbaggers, and outlaws?

Buy Law of the Gun today to enjoy an exciting and classic tale of the Old West.

Acknowledgments

First of all my great thanks to my team who again helped so much in putting this all together: editor Perry Iles for smoothing out and making my book come alive; my proof reader Clare Donoghue and my trusty BETA readers: Patricia, Kate & Sam. A special mention to my cover designers More Visual Ltd who again did an excellent job on the new cover. And my map designer, Jorges, for his excellent work. Finally to Claudia Moroni for all her time and effort and my Medieval guide around Tarquinia.

As always research has been the key to my work and it again surprises all that happened in this turbulent time in Italy's history

To this end and in an effort to fully understand the events and people of the period I again researched and read extensively, including

Hawkwood -F Stonor Saunders

Mercenaries and their Masters – Michael Mallett

Of course all these accounts differ to a greater or lesser degree on dates, timing, who said what and where and it was up to me to decide which account or facts that I wished to use. So any errors are all my own and I apologise if I veer off the accepted path.

On sword fighting, I also delved deeply into *The knightly*

art of battle by Ken Mondeschien who explains the art as propounded by the brilliant Fiore dei Liberi. Also, Hans Talhoffer's *Medieval combat in colour* and *Armourers* by Matthias Pfaffenbichler.

A big thank you to Mark Berryman for his excellent HEMA EXILES videos, on dagger fighting and poleaxe work and for allowing me to attend his weekend workshop in Cheltenham. You can see some of these links on my FB page and website.

www.simonfairfax.com

Printed in Dunstable, United Kingdom

73367136R00172